DAWN OF THE CLANS

WARRIORS

PATH OF STARS

WARRIORS

Warriors: Cats of the Clans
Warriors: Code of the Clans
Warriors: Battles of the Clans
Warriors: Enter the Clans
Warriors: The Ultimate Guide
Warriors: The Untold Stories
Warriors: Tales from the Clans

MANGA

The Lost Warrior
Warrior's Refuge
Warrior's Return
The Rise of Scourge
Tigerstar and Sasha #1: Into the Woods
Tigerstar and Sasha #2: Escape from the Forest
Tigerstar and Sasha #3: Return to the Clans
Ravenpaw's Path #1: Shattered Peace
Ravenpaw's Path #2: A Clan in Need
Ravenpaw's Path #3: The Heart of a Warrior
SkyClan and the Stranger #1: The Rescue
SkyClan and the Stranger #2: Beyond the Code
SkyClan and the Stranger #3: After the Flood

NOVELLAS

Hollyleaf's Story
Mistystar's Omen
Cloudstar's Journey
Tigerclaw's Fury
Leafpool's Wish
Dovewing's Silence
Mapleshade's Vengeance
Goosefeather's Curse

Also by Erin Hunter

SEEKERS

SURVIVORS

DAWN OF THE CLANS

WARRIORS

PATH OF STARS

ERIN
HUNTER

HARPER

An Imprint of HarperCollinsPublishers

Special thanks to Kate Cary

Library of Congress catalog card number: 2015933522
ISBN 978-0-06-206366-3 (trade bdg.)
ISBN 978-0-06-206367-0 (lib. bdg.)

Typography by Hilary Zarycky
15 16 17 18 19   CG/RRDH   10 9 8 7 6 5 4 3 2 1
❖
First Edition

ALLEGIANCES

CLEAR SKY'S CAMP

LEADER

CLEAR SKY—light gray tom with blue eyes

STAR FLOWER—golden she-cat with green eyes

ACORN FUR—chestnut brown she-cat

THORN—mangy tom with splotchy brown fur

SPARROW FUR—tortoiseshell she-cat with amber eyes

QUICK WATER—gray-and-white she-cat

NETTLE—gray tom

BIRCH—ginger tom

ALDER—gray-and-white she-cat

BLOSSOM—tortoiseshell-and-white she-cat

THUNDER'S CAMP

LEADER

THUNDER—orange tom with white paws

LIGHTNING TAIL—black tom

OWL EYES—gray tom with amber eyes

CLOUD SPOTS—long-furred black tom with white ears, white chest, and two white paws

PINK EYES—old white tom with pink eyes

LEAF—black-and-white tom with amber eyes

MILKWEED—splotchy ginger-and-black she-cat

KITS

CLOVER—ginger-and-white she-kit

THISTLE—ginger tom-kit

RIVER RIPPLE'S CAMP

LEADER

RIVER RIPPLE—long-furred silver tom

DAPPLED PELT—delicate tortoiseshell she-cat with golden eyes

SHATTERED ICE—gray-and-white tom with green eyes

NIGHT—black she-cat

DEW—gray she-cat

TALL SHADOW'S CAMP

LEADER

TALL SHADOW—black, thick-furred she-cat with green eyes

PEBBLE HEART—dark gray tabby tom with white mark on his chest

SUN SHADOW—black tom with amber eyes

JAGGED PEAK—small gray tabby tom with blue eyes

HOLLY—she-cat with prickly, bushy black fur

MOUSE EAR—big tabby tom with unusually small ears

MUD PAWS—pale brown tom with four black paws

KITS

STORM PELT—gray tom-kit with blue eyes

DEW NOSE—brown tabby she-kit with white tips on nose and tail

EAGLE FEATHER—brown tom-kit

WIND RUNNER'S CAMP

LEADER

WIND RUNNER—wiry brown tabby she-cat with yellow eyes

GORSE FUR—thin, gray tabby tom

SLATE—thick-furred gray she-cat with one ear tip missing

GRAY WING—dark gray tom with golden eyes

SPOTTED FUR—golden-brown tom with amber eyes and a dappled coat

MINNOW—gray-and-white she-cat

REED—silver tabby tom

KITS

DUST MUZZLE—gray tabby tom-kit

MOTH FLIGHT—white she-kit with green eyes

ROGUE CATS

SLASH—mangy, scarred brown tabby tom with white slash across front legs

FERN—jet-black she-cat

PROLOGUE

❧

The long sweep of clouds that lingered beyond Highstones began to tear apart, and the dying sun cut through and set the peaks ablaze. Far below them, crow-black shadows reached up to swallow the stone. Gray Wing, sitting at the edge of the moor, his pelt ruffled by the evening breeze, lifted his gaze toward the horizon and narrowed his eyes against the sun's fiery glare. Turtle Tail shifted beside him, purring softly.

His heart swelled with love as her fur brushed his. "This moment is perfect. I never want to leave," he murmured.

She stiffened sharply, and he turned to meet her gaze, puzzled by her reaction. Didn't she want to be here with him?

Her green eyes shone wistfully. "Your life has already changed," she told him.

"Has it?" Gray Wing struggled to remember. With a jolt, he recalled Slate. His heart quickened. *She* was his mate now, not Turtle Tail. This was a dream.

He blinked, guilt weighing down his belly. How could he forget his beloved Slate?

Turtle Tail pressed her cheek against his as grief surged in his chest. For a moment, the gentle queen's death seemed as fresh as when Thunder had first told him she'd been killed in Twolegplace by a monster.

"I still miss you," he mewed hoarsely.

"I miss you too." Turtle Tail drew away slowly. "But I'm glad you have Slate now. You shouldn't be alone."

"Are you sure you don't mind?" Was Turtle Tail hurt that he'd fallen in love again?

"It comforts me to see you happy." Turtle Tail's tortoise-shell pelt rippled in the breeze. "I love you so much. You gave me such happiness when I was alive. And you raised my kits. I will always be grateful that they had you to take care of them." Sadness flashed in her eyes. "Leaving them was even harder than leaving you."

Gray Wing sensed her grief. It stabbed through his heart. Though he had never had his own kits, Pebble Heart, Sparrow Fur, and Owl Eyes had *seemed* like his, and he still missed them now that they'd left the moor to live among the pines and the oaks. Yet he was proud that they'd followed their instincts and chosen their own homes.

Turtle Tail went on. "You have been like a father to so many." Her eyes glowed. "To Thunder, as well as to my kits. To any cat who has needed comfort and guidance. No other cat is as well loved as you, Gray Wing. You will be remembered." She paused, her eyes suddenly glistening. "Even after you—"

The screech of an owl cut into Gray Wing's dream. Ears twitching, he jerked awake.

Even after what? Turtle Tail's words lingered in his mind as he blinked in the darkness of his nest.

Beside him, Slate rolled onto her back, her paws limp with sleep. He nuzzled her cheek softly. Turtle Tail's scent was still in his mouth, and happiness moved like sunshine beneath his pelt. He was lucky to have been loved by two mates. *No cat is as well loved as you.* He snuggled deeper into the nest to escape the leaf-bare wind, which whipped across the camp, making the heather shiver.

"Gray Wing?" Slate's mew was sleepy. Her eyes opened, glinting in the darkness. She was staring at him. "Are you okay?"

"I'm fine," he promised. "I was dreaming."

"What about?"

"About how lucky I am." He nestled closer and purred as her musky scent mingled with his memory of Turtle Tail. "Let's go back to sleep."

CHAPTER 1

Dawn sunshine filtered through the canopy. The clouds were clearing at last. Snowmelt dripped from the branches and splashed onto the forest floor. Soggy leaves squelched beneath Clear Sky's paws as he hurried along a trail between the oaks.

Star Flower had been missing since moonhigh. It felt like a lifetime.

He lifted his muzzle warily and tasted the air. Pausing, he glanced over his shoulder. Was some cat watching him? His fur pricked along his spine as he remembered Slash's warning. *There are more of us than you can imagine.* Beyond his borders, rogues lurked in the shadows like foxes, preying on the weak.

Clear Sky growled. *I'm not weak!* But how could he fight Slash's gang? They'd taken Star Flower. He could do nothing but agree to Slash's demands. The mangy tom's threatening stare flashed in his thoughts. Fury rose in his chest. "Coward!" he hissed under his breath as he remembered how he'd woken to find Slash standing beside Star Flower. Two vicious toms had flanked them, snarling. The tang of blood had soured the air. A wound had glistened on Star Flower's cheek where Slash had raked his claws.

She'd looked so scared. Clear Sky shuddered, his heart twisting. And Quick Water had just watched without offering to help! She'd been his Tribemate and was his campmate now. And yet she'd hidden in the bracken and watched. If she'd joined him, they could have fought off the rogues. Star Flower would be with him now instead of a hostage.

He'd challenged Quick Water after Slash and his rogues had dragged Star Flower away. The mountain cat had accused Star Flower of being one of them—of *wanting* to go with Slash. Clear Sky had scratched her muzzle angrily. *Dumb old fool!*

He turned now toward camp, energy fizzing suddenly beneath his pelt. He was wasting time. He needed to act. Slash had demanded that the leaders of every group meet him at the four trees hollow at the half-moon. It had been hard to get him to give Clear Sky even those few extra days to talk to the other leaders, but there was no way Clear Sky could have convinced them in the one day Slash had originally allowed him. Slash would release Star Flower if they agreed to give the rogues a share of their prey—not just once, but always. Clear Sky fluffed out his fur against the early morning chill. Leaf-bare had only just begun to grip the forest, and prey was already scarce. Persuading Thunder, Tall Shadow, River Ripple, and Wind Runner to promise a part of their catch would be hard. Would they even agree to *meet* Slash?

Surely they would feel some sympathy for Star Flower. Tall Shadow and Thunder had seen how loyal and supportive she'd been when Clear Sky's mother had died. So what if she was the daughter of a cruel and bloodthirsty cat? Star Flower was nothing like One Eye. She had made poor decisions in the past, but she was different now. *And she's carrying my kits.*

Clear Sky broke into a run, his paws pattering over the wet earth. He would form a patrol to visit each group in turn and persuade Thunder, River Ripple, Tall Shadow, and Wind Runner to meet with Slash. They only had to agree to the rogue's terms long enough to get Star Flower back. *That isn't so much to ask, surely?* Bursting through the bramble barrier, he skidded into camp.

Thorn and Alder spun around as he scrambled in. Nettle and Sparrow Fur circled the edge of the leaf-strewn clearing, their eyes narrowing as he stopped in the middle. Blossom hung back behind Acorn Fur and Birch, watching uneasily.

Quick Water paced beside the yew, her tail flicking.

Clear Sky heard paws shift on earth. Breath billowed around him. Ears and whiskers twitched. But no cat spoke.

She's told them. His gaze flicked toward Quick Water. "What have you said?" he demanded.

She faced him, her eyes glittering with rage. Blood had dried on her nose where Clear Sky had scratched her. "I told them the truth."

Clear Sky curled his lip. "The truth is that you were too cowardly to fight for your campmate!"

"Star Flower's not my campmate!" she snapped. "She's gone back to her true friends."

"They *kidnapped* her!" Clear Sky dug his claws into the ground, swallowing back fury. He scanned the other cats, trying to read their expressions. Alder was watching through slitted eyes. Birch had tipped his head to one side, his gaze thoughtful. Nettle blinked, giving nothing away, while Thorn fidgeted beside him, shifting his weight from one paw to another.

Only Acorn Fur and Blossom met his gaze.

Sparrow Fur sat between them, her tail twitching. "Quick Water said one of the rogues used to be Star Flower's mate."

"That's not true." Clear Sky's tail bristled. "Slash was a friend of One Eye's. Star Flower knew him, that's all."

Quick Water padded forward. "The other two knew him as well! They're all from the same group of rogues. I bet Star Flower knows them all."

Alder blinked at Clear Sky. "How big is this group?"

"I don't know." Panic sparked in Clear Sky's chest. He pictured the rogues' camp: Star Flower alone, surrounded by mangy cats. "We have to get Star Flower away from them."

Nettle frowned. "But Quick Water says she went with them freely."

"She had no choice!" Clear Sky snapped. "Slash ripped open her cheek. She was terrified!"

"Then why didn't she fight?" Quick Water demanded.

"You *saw* why!" Clear Sky turned on her. "She was outnumbered. And she's carrying kits. How could she risk their safety?"

Acorn Fur widened her eyes. "So these three rogues took her against her will."

"Yes!" Clear Sky felt a flash of hope. Did someone believe him at last?

"Couldn't *you* stop them?" Sparrow Fur asked.

"Not on my own!" Clear Sky felt shaken by the barrage of questions.

"*Why* did they take her?" Birch blinked at him.

Clear Sky steadied his breath. "Slash wants to speak with the leaders of all the groups. They're going to keep Star Flower until I persuade Tall Shadow, Wind Runner, Thunder, and River Ripple to meet with him."

"What does Slash want with the other leaders?" Thorn asked.

Clear Sky hesitated. "He wants a share of our prey."

Thorn's ears twitched. "Just like the old days." He swapped looks with Nettle. "When we were loners, we left offerings at the edge of the woods. It kept the rogues happy. They'd stay away from our land."

Nettle nodded. "We traded prey for peace."

Clear Sky met his gaze hopefully. "We can do it again! We need peace."

Quick Water's eyes flashed. "Do you really think we'll make it through leaf-bare if we have to give away half our prey?"

Nettle flicked his tail. "It doesn't have to be *half*," he reasoned. "Just enough to keep them happy."

Thorn snorted. "Cats like Slash and One Eye aren't happy until they have *everything!*"

Despair weighed like a stone in Clear Sky's belly. "You're right," he muttered. "But we only have to give Slash what he wants until Star Flower comes home. After that, the rogues can hunt for their own prey."

"And where do you think they'll hunt?" Birch demanded.

"On *our* land," Blossom muttered darkly.

"That's why we have to get the other groups to help," Clear

Sky urged. "We have to get Star Flower back first, and then decide what to do."

Blossom glanced away, staring anxiously between the trees. "What if they refuse to help?"

"They can't!" Clear Sky's pelt pulsed with fear. He'd fought the other groups in the past. He'd even turned against his own kin. Had Thunder, Gray Wing, and Jagged Peak forgiven him? "You have to help me persuade them!" He blinked hopefully at his campmates.

Quick Water huffed. "The other leaders won't risk *their* cats for Star Flower. She betrayed them."

"That was moons ago!" Clear Sky argued. "And who can blame her for siding with her own father?"

Birch sniffed. "Would you be so forgiving if she wasn't your mate?"

"Or so desperate to get help if the rogues had taken a *different* cat?" Thorn chimed in.

Clear Sky glared at the brown tom. "I'd fight just as hard for any of you! You're my campmates!"

Acorn Fur lifted her tail decisively. "I'll come with you," she told Clear Sky.

Relief flooded beneath his pelt. "Thank you!"

"But what if Quick Water's right?" Birch argued. "What if Star Flower went with them freely?"

"Even if she did, she's carrying Clear Sky's kits," Acorn Fur told him firmly. "Her kits are part of our group. We must get them back."

Alder glanced at Birch, her gray-and-white fur rippling. She blinked at her brother. "Don't you remember how the group protected us after our mother died?"

Guilt pricked at Clear Sky's belly. *He'd* killed their mother when she'd fought to protect her nest. Petal had brought the kits into the group and raised them as her own.

Birch nodded, his gaze softening. "We've always had a safe nest to sleep in and prey to eat." His gaze flicked around the gathered cats. "Star Flower's kits deserve the same. They haven't done anything wrong."

Quick Water narrowed her eyes. "But can we trust their mother?"

Thorn frowned. "She may just be setting another trap."

"Never!" Clear Sky bristled.

"She's done it before," Nettle reminded him. "She led us into One Eye's ambush."

Anxious murmurs rippled around the cats.

"What if she set up her own kidnapping?" Thorn gasped. "To gather the group leaders together."

Blossom's eyes widened in alarm. "They must be planning an attack!"

"Why would they do that?" Clear Sky snapped. "They only want prey."

"Are you sure?" Quick Water's tail swept the ground. "If they kill our leaders, we'll all be vulnerable."

Clear Sky stiffened as he saw fear bristling in the pelts of his campmates. He fluffed out his fur. "You talk as though we're helpless rabbits!" he snapped. "But our claws are as long as any rogue's. No one will get killed!"

Alder nodded. "We can't let them scare us."

"We have to fight to keep what's ours!" Sparrow Fur agreed.

Clear Sky looked at her hopefully. "Then will you come with me to persuade the other leaders?"

"Yes." Sparrow Fur padded forward.

Alder followed her. "I'll come too."

As Clear Sky blinked at them gratefully, Thorn cut in. "Is it wise for so many cats to leave camp? It leaves us prone to attack. What if the rogues come back?"

"They already have Star Flower," Clear Sky told him. "What else would they want?"

Quick Water growled ominously. "The food from our mouths."

Clear Sky glanced at her bitterly. "Then you'll have something to fight for, won't you?" He headed for the camp entrance, looking back with relief as he saw Sparrow Fur, Alder, and Acorn Fur at his heels.

He ducked through the bramble barrier and took the trail that led toward Thunder's camp. Would his son be more understanding than his campmates? Worry churned in his belly. Thunder had plenty of reasons not to help him. Clear Sky knew he'd never been a good father. And Thunder had loved Star Flower before she'd chosen Clear Sky as a mate. As the path steepened toward a rise, he steadied his breath. After everything that had happened between them, could he count on Thunder's support?

CHAPTER 2

Thunder pricked his ears at the sound of tiny paws pattering over wet leaves. He stopped, heart quickening, and signaled to Lightning Tail with a twitch of his tail. As Lightning Tail froze behind him, Thunder dropped into a hunting crouch and opened his mouth. Through the scent of musty leaves, he tasted mouse. It was the first ground prey he'd smelled since they'd left camp at dawn. The dripping forest canopy rustled as birds flitted from tree to tree, but the forest floor seemed dead, as though the recent snows had frozen all life.

The mouse moved again, and Thunder glimpsed fur beneath a trailing bramble, which spilled over the top of a rise. Keeping low, he crept forward. The mouse darted deeper into the bramble. Thunder's belly tightened with anticipation. He quickened his pace, then leaped, sailing through the air, his claws outstretched. He narrowed his eyes as he plunged through the spiky branches and landed squarely on the mouse. It struggled beneath his claws as he curled them around it. Tail lashing with triumph, he jerked his muzzle forward and bit through its spine. It fell limp, and he hooked it between his teeth. Barging out of the brambles, he ignored his scratched muzzle and proudly held up his catch.

Lightning Tail purred when he saw it. "I was starting to think there were no mice left in the forest."

Thunder dropped the mouse at his friend's paws. "The cold weather came too early." He glanced at the frost-scorched berries, shriveled on the brambles around them. "It destroyed their food."

Lightning Tail stared at the mouse. "Hungry prey won't last long."

Anxiety tugged at Thunder's belly. What if the prey didn't last until newleaf? "Perhaps they managed to store enough food before the snows came," he meowed hopefully.

Lightning Tail glanced around. "The mice and squirrels might only be hiding until the thaw's finished."

"I guess." Thunder tried to push away his doubts. "Let's keep hunting." He was leader. He was supposed to know what to do. But he couldn't make prey appear out of thin air. He picked up the mouse and followed the rise, climbing over the roots that snaked across the earth. He knew there was a crop of boulders near the top of the ravine. Prey might have burrowed deep into the crevices there. As he headed toward them, glancing wistfully up at the treetops, Lightning Tail fell in beside him.

Early sunlight glowed between the bare branches. Thunder's thoughts flashed to the previous day. He had helped move the heavy stone in the four trees hollow and watched as Clear Sky, Gray Wing, Jagged Peak, Sun Shadow, and Tall Shadow had laid Quiet Rain to rest beneath it. The old she-cat's body was safe now from prowling foxes, finally at peace after her long journey and painful sickness.

He'd been privately glad to leave grief behind and return to the ravine. His friends had welcomed him happily, listening solemnly as he'd shared the news of Quiet Rain's death, and murmuring with surprise when he'd told them that Gray Wing had left Tall Shadow's group to return to the moor. *I hope he has finally found his true home.*

Thunder had never regretted leaving Clear Sky's group and starting his own. Leaf, Pink Eyes, Owl Eyes, Lightning Tail, and Milkweed were loyal and brave, and he was grateful that they'd decided to come with him to the new camp. For the first time, Thunder was where he felt he belonged. On the moor, Gray Wing's kindness had never eased Thunder's craving for the love and approval of his father, Clear Sky. In Clear Sky's camp, he'd never felt fully accepted. Now he knew that he no longer needed either of them. He was guided only by the needs of his group. They depended on him, and he was determined not to let them down. He was a leader.

As they neared the rocks, Lightning Tail's mew cut into his thoughts. "The group should practice tree climbing." The black tom stopped and gazed up the wide trunk of an oak. A blackbird was hopping along a lower branch.

Thunder stopped and laid the mouse on the ground. "Try it," he encouraged.

Lightning Tail circled the tree, then reached up and hooked his claws into the mossy bark. Hauling himself up, he sent fuzzy pieces showering down. The blackbird jerked around, eyes sparking as it caught sight of Lightning Tail. With a squawk it fluttered upward and landed easily on a branch overhead.

Lightning Tail growled. "Why does the best prey have wings?"

Movement caught Thunder's eye. His gaze snapped toward the rocks. A thrush was strutting over the top, stopping every few steps to peck at the cracks in the stone. Thunder froze. There was no undergrowth between him and the thrush. One move and he'd be spotted. He stared, paws rooted to the ground. A thrush would make a good meal for Clover and Thistle. They were only four moons old and the bird would fill their bellies easily. He watched it hungrily. How could he get near enough to pounce without being seen?

Slowing his breath, he crouched and slithered like a snake along the forest floor. Wet leaves soaked his belly fur. Heart pounding, he fixed his gaze on the thrush.

Suddenly a black shape dropped from above.

Thunder gasped, pelt bushing. *Lightning Tail!* Had the tom fallen? Panic flashed beneath Thunder's fur. Then it melted as he caught his friend's eye. Lightning Tail's gaze was fixed on the thrush. He'd *jumped* from the branch!

The bird spread its wings, eyes wild with alarm. Too late. Yowling with triumph, Lightning Tail landed with a thud beside it and snapped his jaws around its neck.

Thunder broke into a purr. "Impressive!"

Lightning Tail bounded toward him, the thrush swinging between his jaws. He dropped it beside Thunder, then shook out his front paws, one at a time, wincing. "Ow! Stone is *hard*!" His whiskers twitched proudly as he glanced at the thrush. "Let's take it back to the camp so the others can have a bite while it's still warm."

Thunder nudged his friend's shoulder playfully. "You just want to boast about how you caught it."

Lightning Tail winked at him. "I might mention that I swooped on it like a hawk." He scooped up the thrush between his paws and hurried toward the ravine.

Thunder grabbed his mouse and followed. As they neared the edge, familiar scents of home rose from the camp. Thunder slipped past Lightning Tail and scrambled down the steep cliff, following the route from ledge to ledge until he reached the soft earth at the bottom. Lightning Tail landed beside him and raced for the gorse barrier. He ducked first through the tunnel.

Thunder followed, the gorse scraping his pelt. As he burst into camp, Clover and Thistle raced from the bramble bush where they shared a nest with their mother, Milkweed. They were growing bigger each day. Thunder wondered whether he should bring live prey back to camp and start to teach them how to hunt.

Thistle skidded to a halt in front of Lightning Tail as the black tom stopped in the middle of the clearing. Early sunshine speared between the branches at the top of the ravine and dappled the camp with light. Clover raced past her brother and ran to Thunder. "Did you catch any shrews?" Her yellow eyes shone hopefully. Her ginger-and-white fur prickled along her spine.

Thunder dropped the mouse. "Just this, I'm afraid."

"And my thrush," Lightning Tail called, nodding to the bird at his paws.

Thistle was already nosing through the feathers, his orange tail twitching with excitement.

Milkweed called from the bramble. "Slow down, Thistle! The others might be hungry."

Pink Eyes slid from his nest beside the fallen tree. "Let the youngsters eat," he mewed huskily. "I can wait." He blinked through the sunshine as though trying to see. His pale eyes had never been very sharp. The passing moons seemed to dull his eyesight even more.

Thunder noticed with a frown how skinny the old tom looked. Starting leaf-bare so thin wasn't healthy. "Have this mouse, Pink Eyes." He carried his catch to the white tom and dropped it at his paws. "Thistle and Clover can have the thrush. I'll send out another hunting patrol soon."

"I'll go." Leaf padded from the bramble, his fur still ruffled from sleep.

Owl Eyes scrambled from his nest beneath the yew. "Can I go too?"

Thunder purred, pleased to see his campmates so eager. "How would you like to lead it?"

"Yes, please!" Owl Eyes lifted his tail excitedly.

Thunder glanced at Leaf. The black-and-white tom was older and more experienced. Would he understand that it was important for younger cats to practice leading as well as following?

Leaf whisked his tail happily. "That's a great idea."

Cloud Spots padded from the fern tunnel, which led to a small clearing among the fronds where he'd made his nest. The ferns were dying back now, but bracken crowded behind, sheltering the den with stiff orange leaves. Cloud Spots still looked bleary with sleep. "I smell prey." He glanced at the thrush. Then his gaze flicked toward the mouse at Pink Eyes's paws. "Is that all you found?" There was worry in his mew.

Thunder shook out his fur. "I'm sure Owl Eyes and Leaf will find more," he answered breezily. He didn't want the group to know how concerned he was. "They're about to leave on patrol."

"I'll go with them," Cloud Spots told him. "Six eyes are better than four."

Thistle looked up from the thrush. "If I come too, there'll be *eight* eyes!"

Leaf touched his nose to the kit's head. "You can come another time."

"You can check the ravine for mice while we're gone!" Owl Eyes was already hurrying to the camp entrance, Cloud Spots at his heels.

"I already checked yesterday!" Thistle complained. "There aren't any!"

"Try again," Leaf told him, turning to follow Cloud Spots.

Milkweed crossed the clearing. "We need you here, Thistle," she meowed. "If everyone goes hunting, who's going to guard the camp?"

Thistle snorted. "You're just saying that to stop me from going."

Clover trotted toward her brother. "Of course she is," she sniffed. "If she doesn't make you feel special, you'll sulk all morning."

"I never sulk!" Thistle glared at his sister.

"You sulked all afternoon yesterday because Milkweed wouldn't let you play in the rain."

Thistle stuck his tail in the air crossly. "It was only *rain*!"

Thunder padded between them, swapping glances with Milkweed. He could hear grit showering down the ravine side as Owl Eyes led his patrol up to the forest. "When everyone's had something to eat, I'll take you into the forest with Milkweed," he promised Thistle.

Milkweed looked at him gratefully.

Thistle's fur rippled with excitement. "Like a real patrol?"

"Can I come too?" Clover asked eagerly.

"Of course." Thunder gazed at her warmly.

Lightning Tail picked up the thrush and carried it to a patch of sunshine beside the tree stump near the edge of the clearing. "Come and eat this," he called to the kits. "And I'll tell you how I caught it."

Thistle and Clover raced toward him.

Milkweed glanced at the fallen tree, her gaze flicking over Pink Eyes's nest. The squashed pile of bracken looked limp, soggy after the recent rain. "Should I make Pink Eyes a new bed?" She glanced at Thunder.

As Thunder nodded, Pink Eyes looked up sharply from his mouse. "I can make my own nest," he grunted.

"I know," Milkweed answered. "But why don't I get it

started and you can help me when you've finished eating. I can gather fresh bracken, and you can scrape moss from the fallen tree and spread it in the sunshine to dry." She didn't wait for a reply, but crossed the clearing.

As she disappeared into the bracken, Lightning Tail's pelt caught Thunder's eye. The black tom was diving across the clearing, forepaws outstretched.

Thistle and Clover stared at the tom, wide-eyed, their mouths full.

"The thrush didn't even see me," Lightning Tail told them as he demonstrated his move. "I just swooped on it as silently as an owl."

"Will you teach me how to climb trees?" Clover asked.

"We're not squirrels!" Pink Eyes swallowed the last morsel of his mouse. Thunder felt a flicker of relief that the old cat had not lost his appetite.

Thistle sniffed. "That doesn't mean we can't climb."

Pink Eyes gave his forepaws a quick lick and stood up. "Don't blame me if you fall out and twist your tail." He headed for the fallen tree and began to strip moss from the rotting bark.

Behind him, bracken rustled. Thunder heard roots tear as Milkweed hauled up fresh stems.

Thunder glanced at the pale blue sky. Moons of cold weather lay ahead. How would he keep his cats well fed if prey was already scarce? He hoped Owl Eyes, Cloud Spots, and Leaf would find better hunting than he and Lightning Tail had. *If they don't, I'll go out again later.* He was determined he would *never* let his cats go hungry.

Never? His pelt pricked. Was that a promise he could make? He suddenly pictured Quiet Rain lying in her shallow grave. Then his thoughts flashed to Lightning Tail's leap from the tree. He'd thought for a moment that his friend had fallen. An accident could befall any of them at any time. *What if I die? Could these cats manage without me?* The thought struck him like cold water. Would the group stay together? He'd led them here. They looked to him to decide what was best. Without him, would Leaf hunt for anyone but Milkweed and her kits? Would Milkweed worry that Pink Eyes had a dry nest? Would Lightning Tail spend his time telling stories to Clover and Thistle? They were good-hearted cats. But without a leader, would they think of themselves as a group, or would they drift back to being rogues? What if they rejoined Clear Sky's group?

They mustn't! The thought chilled him. He got to his paws and began to pace. Clear Sky had mellowed these past moons, but Thunder knew what his father was capable of. Cats had died at his claws.

I won't die! Thunder told himself. *I can't. These cats need me too much.* As he tried to push worry away, stones clattered down the side of the ravine.

He looked up, straining to see over the gorse barrier. Was the hunting party back already?

Thistle and Clover jumped to their paws. They raced toward the camp entrance.

"It's Owl Eyes!" Clover called, her nose twitching. "I can smell him!"

"You're just guessing," Thistle scoffed. "How can you smell him from here?"

"I can smell nearly as well as Pink Eyes!" She looked toward the old tom expectantly.

"Clover's right," Pink Eyes confirmed, his gaze fixed on the long strip of moss he was peeling from the fallen tree.

Paws thumped onto the ground beyond the barrier.

Thunder crossed the clearing, weaving in front of the kits. Whoever was approaching the camp was in a hurry. He pricked his ears as Owl Eyes burst through the gorse tunnel. Alarm sparked in the young tom's gaze. "Clear Sky's coming!" he puffed. "He has a patrol. Acorn Fur, Sparrow Fur, and Alder are with him."

"Did you speak to them?" Thunder demanded.

"Cloud Spots and Leaf are talking to them now. Leaf sent me back to camp to warn you."

Lightning Tail hurried to Thunder's side. "What's the problem? Is Clear Sky starting another fight?"

"Why would he?" Pink Eyes blinked at them from across the clearing. "There's nothing to fight about."

"Clear Sky can *always* find something to fight about," Lightning Tail growled darkly. "Why else would he bring a patrol here?"

Thunder's ears twitched. Clear Sky had shown no hostility the last time they had met. He'd been stricken with grief at Quiet Rain's death. "He's probably just bringing news," he told Lightning Tail.

"He doesn't need to bring *three* campmates to share news," Lightning Tail argued.

Paws scrabbled down the ravine beyond the gorse.

Thunder lifted his chin. "Why don't we just wait and see?" He shot Lightning Tail a warning look. His friend could be hotheaded and was a bit wary of Clear Sky. "I don't want unnecessary arguments."

The gorse shivered, and Clear Sky hurried in. His gray fur was ruffled, and his eyes glittered with panic. Acorn Fur, Alder, and Sparrow Fur hurried in behind him, their gazes solemn.

Thunder blinked at his father. "Are you okay?" Anxiety sparked in his pelt.

"I need your help." Clear Sky's tail swished restlessly.

Thunder frowned. "Why?"

"Slash has taken Star Flower," Clear Sky told him. "He's holding her hostage."

Slash. The name rang in Thunder's mind like the call of a distant bird. He'd heard it before. But where? He stiffened. *Fern.* She was a young rogue she-cat that he'd met with Gray Wing. Gray Wing had been taking her to Tall Shadow's camp to escape Slash! She'd confessed that Slash had been forcing her to spy on the cats in the pine forest. And she'd sounded scared.

Thunder suddenly became aware of Clear Sky's gaze probing his.

"Star Flower's in danger!" Clear Sky meowed urgently.

Thunder met his gaze. "We must save her."

"I don't know where she's being held," Clear Sky told him.

Acorn Fur chimed in. "Who knows how many rogues are guarding her?"

"Slash said there were more than we could imagine," Sparrow Fur added.

Thunder stared at his father. Didn't Clear Sky have a plan? "What do you want me to do?"

Thunder's eyes narrowed as Clear Sky explained what Slash had demanded: to meet with all the group leaders to discuss a way to share their prey with the rogues.

As Thunder shook his head in disbelief, Clover and Thistle pushed their way forward.

"Hi, Acorn Fur!" Clover blinked at the she-cat who'd once been her campmate. "Do you remember me?"

Thistle nudged his sister aside. "I bet she doesn't," he sniffed. "We're nearly grown up."

Clear Sky growled. "This is no discussion for kits." He flicked his tail toward them and glared at Thunder. "Shouldn't they be doing chores, or something *useful*?"

Thunder felt a prickle of irritation with Clear Sky. Even now, when he needed their help, he couldn't stop bossing other cats around. "This is my camp, Clear Sky," he meowed firmly. "I decide who does what."

The bracken rustled at the back of the camp. "What's happening?" Milkweed asked as she hurried across the clearing, her eyes sparking with worry when she saw Clear Sky, Acorn Fur, Sparrow Fur, and Alder.

Clover stared at her mother. "Clear Sky said we should be doing chores."

"He thinks kits aren't allowed to *talk*," Thistle added indignantly.

Milkweed bristled, shooting Clear Sky an angry look as she guided Clover and Thistle away.

Paw steps sounded beyond the gorse, and Cloud Spots hurried into camp, Leaf at his tail.

Tension prickled in the air like a coming storm. Forcing his ruffled fur flat, Thunder padded to the center of the clearing and faced Clear Sky. "I want to help you," he began, "but prey is scarce already. We can't give what we catch to rogues."

Clear Sky stepped forward, tail twitching angrily. "*You have to!* Slash will kill Star Flower if we don't do as he says."

Lightning Tail growled. "If we agree to their demands, these rogues will think we're weak, and they'll keep pushing us around!"

Leaf nodded. "He's right. Rogues like that are worse than foxes. Too lazy to hunt for themselves, but happy to bully other cats into doing it for them."

Milkweed moved closer to her kits, wrapping her tail around them. "Perhaps we *should* give them a little of our prey, just to keep them quiet."

Pink Eyes glanced sympathetically at the queen. "I know you're frightened for your kits, but the rogues are just trying their luck. If we give in now, they'll keep pushing until they drive us away. We've worked hard to make this land our own."

"Exactly!" Lightning Tail snapped.

Thunder kneaded the ground anxiously. He glanced at Lightning Tail. His friend's eyes shone with rage. Leaf circled the visitors, his black-and-white pelt spiking along his spine. Cloud Spots watched through narrowed eyes.

Clear Sky's gaze fixed desperately on Thunder. "You have to help me."

Why? Bitterness suddenly rose in Thunder's throat. *You never helped me!* Why hadn't Clear Sky ever shown as much concern for *his* mother? If he had, Storm and his littermates might still be alive.

He pushed the thought away. The past was over. Clear Sky needed his help. No matter how bad a father he'd been, he was still a cat who deserved to be heard.

And yet Thunder knew that he must put his campmates first. He met Clear Sky's gaze. "I can't promise prey to these rogues. We need it as much as they do."

Clear Sky leaned forward, whiskers trembling. "You don't have to *give* them prey. Just meet Slash and promise so they return Star Flower."

Lightning Tail growled. "Meeting these rogues is hunting for trouble."

Leaf lashed his tail. "We should stay out of it."

"It's not our problem," Cloud Spots agreed.

Clear Sky kept his gaze on Thunder. "Help me, please!" His mew was hoarse with despair.

Thunder shook his head, guilt jabbing in his chest. "I can't," he murmured. "I must think of my campmates. I can't sacrifice their well-being for yours."

Clear Sky's tail bristled. "What kind of son are you?"

Thunder's heart sank as anger hardened his father's gaze. He'd seen it countless times before. Wearily, he held his ground as Clear Sky went on.

"How long are you going to resent me for taking Star Flower as my mate?" Clear Sky snarled. "Must you punish her as well? If my kits die, I'll never forgive you!"

Thunder swallowed back fear. "I'm punishing no one," he meowed steadily. "Star Flower chose you, and I respect her decision. I'm sorry she's in trouble, and I'd help if I could, but I can't let my campmates starve to save her. You must solve this problem yourself."

Clear Sky stared at him, eyes wide with disbelief.

Acorn Fur leaned toward her leader. "Come on," she murmured. "Let's go."

"Perhaps Tall Shadow will help," Alder mewed encouragingly.

"River Ripple will know what to do." Sparrow Fur shot Thunder a sharp look. "The river's always full of fish. He'll be happy to share some of *his* prey."

Clear Sky turned away. "You're right," he muttered. "The others will help. They have to." He hurried through the gorse tunnel, his campmates following.

As Thunder heard them scramble up the ravine, he realized he was trembling. Should he have agreed to help? He wasn't convinced the other leaders would really support Clear Sky. And if they didn't, what would happen to Star Flower?

He shivered as a damp wind spiraled into the hollow. Star Flower had softened his father. He shuddered to think how Clear Sky might react to her death. Would a refusal now lead them into another Great Battle?

CHAPTER 3

❧

Gray Wing scanned the moorside, a damp wind tugging at his whiskers. His belly growled with hunger as he tasted the air. But there was no scent of prey, only the musty smell of dying heather. Below him, Gorse Fur stalked across the slope, grass streaming around his paws. Where the moor began to dip toward the forest, Wind Runner sniffed at the edge of a swath of heather.

As she stretched her muzzle forward, Spotted Fur burst through the heather. "The prey-scents are stale even here." Gray Wing heard the young tom's mew on the wind.

Spotted Fur was a new member of the group—a golden brown tom whose mother had hunted with Slate in her rogue days. Spotted Fur had left his mother and littermates when they'd moved on to new territory. He'd watched the moorland cats hunting and racing through the heather and wanted to join them. Wind Runner hadn't been keen to accept a rogue as a campmate, but Slate had vouched for him, swearing that his mother was a kindhearted cat and a good hunter. And Spotted Fur had quickly proven the gray she-cat right. He'd caught as much prey as Wind Runner, and the group leader had soon forgotten that she'd ever had doubts about the young tom.

But even Spotted Fur's skill and enthusiasm couldn't make prey appear where there was none.

Gray Wing narrowed his eyes, unnerved by the empty slopes. Surely the thaw should have brought the prey from their burrows by now? Had the early snowfall killed this year's young? He shifted his paws anxiously. If it had, leaf-bare would be long and hungry. He saw Gorse Fur freeze, and stiffened. Had the gray tom spotted prey? He followed Gorse Fur's gaze, disappointed as he saw it fall on Moth Flight.

Wind Runner and Gorse Fur's scatterbrained kit had wandered away from the patrol again and was staring at the sky. The small white she-cat was five moons old, but she was as easily distracted as a kit half her age. Gray Wing frowned as he watched her scamper forward to sniff a withered stem poking from the grass before resuming her cloud gazing. Curiosity was natural in kits, but by now Moth Flight should have learned to concentrate on what she was doing.

"Moth Flight!" Gorse Fur called to her. "You can watch clouds later! We're supposed to be hunting!"

Gray Wing flicked his tail irritably. If any prey *had* crept from its burrow, Gorse Fur's yowling would send it running back for shelter.

Moth Flight dipped her head apologetically and began to stalk the hillside.

Behind Gray Wing, paw steps thumped against the ground. He caught a trace of Slate's scent a moment before she stopped beside him, her thick, soft pelt brushing his. "Caught anything yet?" She was out of breath. Her pelt still carried the warm, heathery smell of their nest.

Gray Wing glanced past her to the hollow in the hillside where the camp sheltered. She must have come from there. "There's nothing to catch," he told her gloomily.

"Of course there is!" Slate lifted her chin and headed toward the others.

Gray Wing's dream flashed in his thoughts. *It comforts me to see you happy.* He remembered Turtle Tail's words, fondness swelling in his chest. He was glad she didn't begrudge the warmth Slate had brought to his life, relieved that he wouldn't have to spend the cold leaf-bare nights alone. With Turtle Tail dead and her kits in different groups, he missed the closeness of family. He was lucky to be starting a new life with Slate.

He watched her walk toward Wind Runner. Spotted Fur had slid from the heather and was gazing hopefully across the hillside. Slate stopped beside them, dipping her head to the leader.

As the two she-cats exchanged greetings, movement caught Gray Wing's eye. A rabbit had darted from behind a tussock and was speeding across the grass. It was too far away for Wind Runner and Spotted Fur to reach. But Gorse Fur had seen it and was charging up the slope. The rabbit streaked toward Moth Flight.

Moth Flight, look! Gray Wing tensed. The young she-cat was still gazing into the sky. Silently he urged her to turn her head. The rabbit was veering away, heading upslope to the safety of the moortop burrows. Moth Flight didn't move. Couldn't she hear its paws? Frustration surged in Gray Wing's belly. He broke into a run. If he cut off the rabbit's escape, he could steer it straight into Moth Flight's path. She'd *have* to see it then. He ran, the damp air searing his lungs. The breathlessness he'd suffered for moons had grown worse with the coming of leaf-bare. Pain gripped his chest, but he kept running, pelt fluffed as he tried desperately to make an imposing silhouette against the skyline, enough to scare the rabbit into changing course.

It's working! Hope surged through his fur. The rabbit's eyes sparked with fear, and it skidded wildly away from him.

Moth Flight stood, face to the sky, and stared dreamily upward.

She must hear it's close by now! The ground seemed to tremble with the thrumming of its paws. Even Wind Runner, Spotted Fur, and Slate had turned to watch. Gorse Fur was still chasing, too far behind, eyes fixed on the rabbit.

"Moth Flight!" Gray Wing yowled as the rabbit streaked past her. She turned and blinked at him, oblivious as the rabbit shot past her and disappeared over a rise.

Gray Wing pulled up, his paws slithering on the wet grass, and stopped a tail-length away from Moth Flight. He glared at her. "What in all the stars are you doing?" His lungs burned as he struggled for breath.

She blinked at him anxiously. "Are you okay?" She hurried toward him and sniffed at his muzzle. "Does your breathing hurt again?"

"I'm fine," he gasped. Didn't the foolish young cat even *realize* what she'd done?

Her eyes widened. "You should sit down and rest."

As she spoke, Gorse Fur thundered past her, his eyes fixed on the rise where the rabbit had disappeared. He chased it, tail streaming behind.

Moth Flight stared after her father, confusion showing in her round gaze.

"Didn't you *see* it?" Gray Wing puffed.

"See what?"

Anger flared in Gray Wing's belly. "Taste the air! Its scent is everywhere."

Obediently, Moth Flight opened her mouth, her pink tongue showing between her teeth. "A rabbit!" she gasped, her eyes widening suddenly.

Gray Wing could hardly believe his ears. "How did you miss it?"

"I'm so sorry!" She jerked her head around, scanning the grassy moorside, but the rabbit had long disappeared over the rise, followed by Gorse Fur.

Wind Runner charged toward them.

Moth Flight shifted her paws self-consciously as her mother stopped and stared at her accusingly. "I was watching clouds," she murmured. "One looked just like a rabbit."

Gray Wing glanced at the sky, where the clouds were piling so thickly now that he was amazed she could make out any shape at all. "If you'd been watching the moorside, you'd have seen a *real* rabbit," he snapped.

Wind Runner growled. "Moth Flight! How many times have I told you that when you're hunting you have to *concentrate?*"

Moth Flight bowed her head. "I'm sorry."

"*Sorry* doesn't feed your campmates!" Wind Runner's ears twitched.

"I'll try harder next time," Moth Flight promised.

"You said that *last* time!" Wind Runner hissed.

Gray Wing felt a sudden wave of sympathy for Moth Flight as she gazed pitifully at her mother. Perhaps the young cat just wasn't cut out to be a hunter. She might be more use in camp, clearing out bedding and building new dens. He flicked his tail toward the hollow. "Why don't you see if Reed and Minnow need you to fetch more heather?" He had left the pair weaving a shelter against the camp wall, threading heather stems into the gorse to make a den. Dust Muzzle was helping them. Perhaps he should have brought Dust Muzzle on the patrol instead of Moth Flight. The young tom was a far more accomplished hunter than his sister.

Moth Flight blinked at him eagerly. "Let me follow the rabbit's trail. Please! I have a good nose. I'm sure I can find where it's gone."

Wind Runner snorted. "It'll be deep in a burrow by now. You're probably mouse-brained enough to follow it in and get lost. Then we'll have to send a search party to find you."

Moth Flight seemed to shrink inside her pelt.

Gray Wing's heart twisted. "Perhaps we can follow its trail together—"

As he spoke, Gorse Fur appeared on the rise. The rabbit was clamped between the tom's jaws.

"You caught it!" Gray Wing purred.

Gorse Fur slowed as he neared them, and laid the rabbit beside Wind Runner.

Moth Flight's gaze shone with guilt. "I'm sorry for being such a mouse-brain."

"No harm done," Gorse Fur meowed breezily.

Wind Runner lashed her tail. "What if *you* hadn't been here to fix Moth Flight's mistakes?" She glared at her mate.

Gorse Fur met her stare calmly. "She's still young."

"She's old enough to stop a rabbit when it practically trips over her," Wind Runner snapped.

Moth Flight glanced anxiously from her mother to her father. "I promise, I won't do it again."

Wind Runner snorted. "You will, so long as your father keeps making excuses for you."

"You're too hard on her, Wind Runner," Gorse Fur objected.

"Somebody needs to be, or she'll never learn to hunt."

Gray Wing turned away, leaving the family to settle their squabble in private, and headed back along the slope.

Slate padded to meet him. "Is everything okay?" She glanced toward Wind Runner.

Gray Wing kept walking. "Gorse Fur caught the rabbit." He spoke slowly, trying to disguise his breathlessness.

Slate fell in beside him. "Wind Runner doesn't look too pleased."

"She thinks *Moth Flight* should have caught it."

"We all make mistakes."

"I shouldn't have chased the rabbit right toward her," Gray Wing murmured. "I should have known Moth Flight was unreliable."

Slate nudged his shoulder gently with her muzzle as they walked side by side. "Don't blame yourself for a kit's mistake."

He shot her a look, his worry over Moth Flight melting as he saw warmth in her gaze. "I guess she'll grow out of her day-dreaming eventually," he conceded.

"Of course she will." Slate glanced toward the hollow. "Should we go back to camp?" There was anxiety in her mew.

Gray Wing tensed. Had she heard him wheezing? "We should catch more prey first."

"The others can manage without us for a while," Slate argued. "Besides, it's a good chance for Moth Flight to prac-tice hunting."

Ahead, Spotted Fur was sniffing the roots of a gorse bush. He lifted his muzzle as they neared. "The prey-scent is so stale I can hardly smell anything."

"Look by the high burrows," Gray Wing suggested. He pointed his nose toward Moth Flight, her white pelt moving over the grass like a tiny cloud as she trailed behind Wind Runner and Gorse Fur. "You can show Moth Flight how to spot fresh rabbit trails."

Spotted Fur's gaze lit up. "Do you think she'd like that?"

Slate purred. "I think she'll appreciate your company."

Spotted Fur hared away, cutting across the slope to catch up to the young she-cat.

Gray Wing realized that Slate had gently steered him

onto the trail that led to the hollow entrance. Perhaps he *should* rest for a while and catch his breath. He could always go out again later. Dusk often lured fresh prey from its hiding places.

As they crossed the smooth grass outside the camp entrance, familiar scents touched his nose. His pelt prickled with curiosity. Clear Sky and Tall Shadow had passed this way. What had brought them here? He quickened his step, hurrying into camp.

His brother was pacing the clearing. Tall Shadow sat at the edge, her gaze dark. Reed and Minnow were working on their den beside the wall, their gazes flicking nervously toward the visitors as they wove heather into the rough frame jutting from the gorse. Dust Muzzle sat near them, his gray tabby pelt prickling as he stared at Clear Sky from beside a pile of heather sprigs.

Clear Sky jerked his gaze expectantly toward Gray Wing. "Is Wind Runner with you? I must speak with her." He slid past Gray Wing and peered through the gap in the gorse. "Reed told me you were hunting together."

"She's on the moortop," Gray Wing told him.

Slate blinked at Clear Sky. "Should I fetch her?"

"Fetch her?" Clear Sky echoed, his thoughts clearly distracted.

Gray Wing noticed his brother's unkempt pelt. The fur around his neck clumped in thick spikes. Something was wrong. He nodded to Slate. "Go and get Wind Runner." She clearly recognized the urgency in his mew and dashed from the camp. Gray Wing searched Clear Sky's gaze, alarmed to see fear sparking in its blue depths. Something was *very* wrong. "What's happened?"

"They've taken Star Flower!" Clear Sky kept pacing.

"Who's taken Star Flower?" Gray Wing's heart quickened.

Tall Shadow padded forward. "Slash and his rogues."

Gray Wing's thoughts whirled. *Slash!* The cat who had been using Fern to spy on Tall Shadow's group! He'd left Fern in Tall Shadow's care, though he hadn't told the black she-cat why. He hadn't wanted to worry her. Had he been foolish to leave one of Slash's rogues among the forest cats? "Where's Fern?"

"Fern?" Tall Shadow blinked at him. "She left us soon after you did."

Alarm pricked beneath Gray Wing's pelt. Had she been spying for Slash all along? "Did she say why?"

"No." Tall Shadow tipped her head curiously. "She just disappeared. I wasn't surprised. She couldn't seem to settle. It was like she had something on her mind. As though she was frightened."

Why hadn't Fern stayed with Tall Shadow's group? Hadn't she felt safe, even there? Fear wormed beneath Gray Wing's pelt. Slash was clearly more dangerous than he'd imagined.

Clear Sky stepped between Gray Wing and Tall Shadow. "Why are you talking about Fern? What's she got to do with this?"

"She was one of Slash's campmates," Gray Wing explained. "I tried to help her escape from him."

Tall Shadow shot him a look. "Why didn't you tell me?"

Clear Sky flexed his claws. "I didn't come here to talk about Fern!" he snapped. "They've taken Star Flower! Don't you understand?"

As he spoke, Wind Runner burst into the camp, breathless. Slate and Gorse Fur skidded to a halt at her heels. "What's happened?" Wind Runner demanded.

Clear Sky turned to her eagerly. "I need your help," he blurted. "A gang of rogues has taken Star Flower. They're holding her hostage."

Wind Runner frowned, confusion clouding her gaze. "Why?"

"They want a share of our prey for her safe return." Clear Sky stared at her urgently.

Wind Runner narrowed her eyes. "Who are these rogues?"

Gray Wing's ear twitched anxiously. "Their leader's called Slash. He's an old friend of One Eye."

Wind Runner bristled. "And you want us to share our prey with them?"

"Just talk to him," Clear Sky pleaded. "He wants all the group leaders to meet with him at half-moon to discuss terms."

Gorse Fur padded forward, ears twitching warily. "Star Flower is One Eye's daughter," he reminded her. "How do we know she's not a *friend* of Slash?"

Wind Runner's tail quivered. "It might be *her* plan."

"Never!" Clear Sky glared at the wiry she-cat. "She loves me. She's carrying my kits! Her loyalty lies with her campmates."

Wind Runner's gaze slid past Clear Sky and rested on Tall Shadow. "Do *you* support Clear Sky?"

Tall Shadow's gaze was dark. "Star Flower spent time in our camp while Quiet Rain was dying. I believe she has the heart of a forest cat, not a rogue. She has turned her back on the life she knew as One Eye's daughter."

Gray Wing nodded. "Tall Shadow's right. I watched Star Flower care for Clear Sky with kindness and loyalty. She's being held against her will, I'm sure of it."

Wind Runner glanced at him uncertainly. "That doesn't mean we have to share our prey with this bunch of fox-hearts."

Panic flashed in Clear Sky's gaze. "You *have* to help!"

Wind Runner looked at him coldly. "We don't have to do anything for you."

"What if it were you?" Clear Sky demanded. "Imagine they were holding Gorse Fur hostage. I'd help you free *him*."

"Really?" Wind Runner sniffed. "You've never helped *anyone* but yourself."

"That's not true." Gray Wing felt a surge of loyalty toward his brother. "He rescued Holly's kits when they went missing!"

Wind Runner kept her gaze fixed on Clear Sky. "This is *your* problem, not ours."

Gray Wing blinked at her. Surely they had to help save Star Flower.

Clear Sky's eyes widened. "You'd let harm come to Star Flower and my kits?"

Wind Runner hesitated, her fur rippling.

Gray Wing sensed a moment of doubt. "I think we should help," he murmured softly.

Slate moved closer to Gray Wing. "It's too risky," she breathed. "These rogues are dangerous."

"So are we," Gray Wing growled.

Gorse Fur stepped forward, tail flicking. "But we can't spare any prey!"

"We don't *have* to," Gray Wing countered. He looked at Clear Sky. "Slash just wants to meet with the group leaders, right?"

Clear Sky nodded. "After he's met with you, he'll return Star Flower."

"Then it's simple," Gray Wing urged.

Wind Runner stared at him. "Why should we get involved?"

Gray Wing returned her gaze gravely. "It is our duty to protect Star Flower and her unborn kits."

Slate moved beside him. "But she's not part of our group."

Gray Wing met her amber eyes. "If it were you and our unborn kits in danger, I'd want every cat I knew to help save you."

Her gaze softened.

Wind Runner grunted. "I guess there are kits involved." She dipped her head. "Very well," she conceded. "I trust your judgment, Gray Wing. We will meet with these rogues."

Joy burst in Clear Sky's gaze. "Thank you!"

Tall Shadow got to her paws and shook out her fur. "I'm glad you've chosen to help, Wind Runner." She began to head for the entrance.

"Are you leaving straightaway?" Wind Runner glanced at her. "Shouldn't we come up with a plan?"

"We can do that later." Clear Sky began to follow Tall Shadow. "First we need to speak with River Ripple."

"Hasn't he agreed yet?" Wind Runner's fur pricked along her spine.

"No." Tall Shadow paused. "But he will."

Gorse Fur's gaze darkened. "Has Thunder agreed to meet with the rogues?"

Clear Sky glanced at Gray Wing. "He refused."

Wind Runner exchanged glances with Gorse Fur. "I thought Slash wanted to meet with *all* the leaders. What's the point in going if Thunder won't be there?"

Gray Wing lifted his tail. He could understand why Thunder might be reluctant to help a father who had rejected him so many times, but he knew Thunder had a good heart. He couldn't truly want to risk harm to Star Flower and her unborn kits. "I'll speak to Thunder."

"Do you think he'll change his mind?" Clear Sky lifted his chin hopefully.

"Thunder will listen to reason," Gray Wing reassured him. *Especially if I'm the one who reasons with him.* But what would they do at the meeting?

Clear Sky's eyes brimmed with gratitude. "Thank you."

"Come on," Tall Shadow urged as she slid out of camp.

As Clear Sky disappeared after her through the gap in the gorse, Gray Wing had an idea. *That's it!*

Wind Runner frowned at him. "Do you really think it's a

good idea to meet with these rogues and promise them a share of our prey?"

Gray Wing's whiskers twitched. "We only promised to *meet* the rogues. We never promised our prey."

Wind Runner's eyes widened. "But what will they do when we refuse—"

Gray Wing interrupted her. "They won't be able to do anything," he told her. "I have a plan."

CHAPTER 4

Clear Sky's pelt rippled along his spine. Above him, the half-moon shone in a crow-black sky. The last leaves of leaf-fall fluttered around him as a bone-deep chill gripped the forest. He pricked his ears, listening for the reassuring patter of prey or the call of an owl. But the forest had been silent since he'd left camp. It was as though everything was waiting for the outcome of tonight's meeting.

Who would come?

Clear Sky quickened his pace as he neared the rim of the four trees hollow.

Tall Shadow had promised she'd be there; Wind Runner, too. He knew River Ripple would be true to his word. The leader of the river cats was probably already waiting for him beneath the great oaks. But what about Thunder? Had Gray Wing managed to persuade him?

Fear sparked through Clear Sky's blood. The long quarter moon of sleepless nights had exhausted him. Fear was his only energy now. And hope. He longed to see Star Flower's face. He hurried faster as he imagined her waiting beside Slash in the four trees hollow. Would she be okay? Had the rogues treated her well? He tried not to think what she might have suffered at their paws.

What if she wasn't there? What if Slash didn't show up? *It might be a trick.* He tried to silence the echoing doubt that had nagged him day and night. What if calling the leaders to a meeting was part of a scheme to leave the camps vulnerable?

Clear Sky narrowed his eyes. He'd made sure his camp-mates were prepared, assigning each cat to a position and warning them to be on their guard. Nettle and Thorn were stationed at the camp entrance. Birch and Alder stalked the woods for signs of intruders. Sparrow Fur and Blossom watched from the oak bough that overhung the clearing, while Acorn Fur and Quick Water hid in the shadows below. If any rogue tried to invade, they would meet fierce resistance. He hoped the other leaders had taken similar precautions.

"Clear Sky?"

As he neared the top of the four trees hollow, a call echoed through the trees. He stopped, his heart quickening.

The voice sounded again. "Is that you?"

He recognized Tall Shadow's mew. Tasting for her scent, he hurried forward, his apprehension easing as her familiar smell bathed his tongue.

She slid out of the darkness, hardly more than a shadow herself. "River Ripple's waiting at the other side of the hol-low." She led him from the cover of the forest and stopped at the top of the slope. Clear Sky padded after her and followed her gaze toward the shape at the hollow's rim on the far side. It was River Ripple, a pale silhouette against the undergrowth.

Tall Shadow plunged over the edge of the slope and

threaded her way through the bracken. Clear Sky followed, nosing through the fronds as he tracked her zigzagging route to the bottom.

Grass swished on the far side as River Ripple hurried to meet them, his long silver fur rippling in the moonlight.

Clear Sky broke from the bracken and padded into the clearing. Cold washed over his face. Chilly air had pooled at the bottom of the hollow, and he moved through it like a fish through icy water. Heat pulsed beneath his pelt as he struggled against fear. He scanned the clearing quickly, his heart beating so hard that he could hear his blood pulsing in his ears. At one end, the great rock rose in the moonlight like a massive curled claw. Beyond it he saw, with a surge of gratitude, Wind Runner's wiry frame. She was heading toward him.

He strained to see past her through the darkness. Had Gray Wing persuaded Thunder to come too?

Bracken rustled on the forest slope behind him. Clear Sky jerked his head around and recognized his son's broad shoulders as Thunder pushed his way into the clearing. His orange pelt glowed blue in the moonlight.

"Thunder!" Joy flooded Clear Sky's belly. He ignored the prick of resentment he felt at the fact that Gray Wing had persuaded his son to help him when he had failed. But how could he begrudge Gray Wing his influence? He had been more of a father to Thunder than Clear Sky ever had.

Tall Shadow and River Ripple stopped beside Clear Sky and waited for Thunder to join them.

"I can smell rogue scent," Thunder growled.

"Is it fresh?" Wind Runner asked.

A voice rang from the great rock. "Of course it's fresh." There was amusement in the mew.

Clear Sky spun and stared up at the rock. His breath caught in his throat. He'd waited a quarter moon for this moment. Dread spiked his pelt. He could smell rogue stench, and the scent of the other leaders, but something was missing.

Slash stood on top. Six rogues flanked him. They watched, as unmoving as stone in the moonlight, their dull pelts clinging to their lean bodies. The gleam in their eyes betrayed menace behind their stillness.

"I hoped you would come." Slash padded to the edge of the rock and looked down, scorn flashing in his gaze.

Clear Sky curled his lip as anger swept his fear away. "You gave us no choice."

Slash snorted. "I gave *you* no choice, Clear Sky." His gaze flicked to the other leaders. "*They* have no reason to be here. What do they care if you never see Star Flower or your kits again?"

Clear Sky's heart lurched. "Then why did you insist I bring them with me?"

Amusement flickered through Slash's whiskers. "I just wanted to see if you could persuade them."

Wind Runner flicked her tail angrily. "What if he hadn't?"

"I'd have dealt with Star Flower and found another way to make you share your prey," Slash told her.

Dealt with Star Flower? Clear Sky's tail twitched with fear. What did he mean? He suddenly felt as helpless as a kit. Where *was* she? He opened his mouth, reaching for her scent and realizing with a jolt which scent had been missing. *Hers!*

Thunder bristled. "How dare you threaten us!"

Slash flicked his tail, his gaze flashing toward the other rogues. They moved forward, hissing, and stood at the edge of the rock. "Do you really want to argue with me, Thunder?" Slash asked.

Thunder flattened his ears. "What makes you so sure we'll agree to share our prey?"

Slash's gaze flicked over the leaders. "The same thing that made you come tonight. You don't want to see Clear Sky lose his mate and his kits."

Clear Sky darted forward, snarling up at the great rock. "Where *is* Star Flower?" Panic quickened his thoughts. Terror hollowed his belly. "Is she okay?"

Slash paused, his gaze burning into Clear Sky's.

Rage seized Clear Sky. The rogue was playing with him like prey, prolonging his suffering for his own warped enjoyment. *"Where is she?"* he repeated.

Fur brushed his flank. He jerked around, bristling.

River Ripple stopped beside him. "Don't let him rile you," the silver-furred tom murmured. "He wants to cloud your thoughts, but you need to keep a clear head."

Clear Sky took in River Ripple's soothing gaze. He felt his breathing ease and his heart slow as the silver tom's calmness seemed to seep into him. Steadying his paws, he turned back to Slash. "You promised to return Star Flower if I brought the other leaders here."

Slash tipped his head. "If I gave you Star Flower now, what

incentive would you have to honor the agreement we will make tonight?"

Clear Sky dug his claws into the cold earth. "No one will agree to anything until Star Flower is safely returned."

Slash flattened his ears and peered over the edge of the rock. "I'm afraid that isn't something you get to decide. If you want to see your mate or your kits alive, you will meet my demands."

Cold fear seeped beneath Clear Sky's pelt. Words dried in his mouth.

"What are your demands, exactly?" Thunder's steady mew sounded behind him.

"For every five pieces of prey you catch, I want one," Slash told him simply. "My rogues will visit you each day to collect our share."

Wind Runner glared at the rogue. "We'll starve!"

Thunder growled. "We're not going hungry to feed you!"

Slash narrowed his eyes. "Why should *you* grow fat on prey from *our* land?"

"No one will grow fat this leaf-bare," Tall Shadow spat. "There's hardly enough prey for ourselves. There's certainly not enough to share with you."

"That's not my problem," Slash answered back. "If you want to live on our land, then you must share what you catch there."

"It's not your land!" Thunder hissed.

"It's not your land either. You took it without asking," Slash snapped. "You force us to roam the edges and live off your scraps."

"You've *always* roamed the edges of other cats' land," Wind Runner snarled. "You know no other way. Your kind has been bullying others to hunt for them since I was a kit."

Clear Sky's thoughts whirled. Why were they arguing over *land*? This meeting was about Star Flower. Why weren't the other leaders trying to save her?

River Ripple eyed Slash coldly. "Why do you stay? The moor, the river, and the forest mean nothing to you. New lands stretch as far as the horizon. Why not go and hunt somewhere else?"

"Why should we bother when we have you to hunt for us?" Slash began to pace the edge of the rock, his rogues moving back to let him pass. "You pride yourself on your hunting skills. Isn't this a perfect chance to show them off? And I think I've given you enough incentive. . . . Remember, if you don't share your prey, Star Flower will die."

No! Clear Sky's breath caught in his throat. "What if we gave you one piece of prey in ten?" he blurted.

Slash's ears twitched. "That's not very generous."

"One in seven?" Clear Sky's mew was husky with desperation. He glanced over his shoulder at the other leaders, silently pleading for them to back him up. "One in seven isn't much to ask," he rasped. "It'll be newleaf before we know it, and the land will be prey-rich again."

Thunder avoided meeting his eyes. Tall Shadow blinked at him apologetically. Wind Runner's gaze was too narrow to read.

River Ripple stepped closer to the great rock and stared up

at Slash. "Our campmates will not go hungry to feed yours."

Clear Sky felt sick. Didn't they care if Star Flower died? He broke from River Ripple's side and hurried to Thunder. "You can't do this!" He snapped his gaze to Wind Runner. "You have to help save her!" Tall Shadow backed away as he glared at her. "You promised that you'd help me!"

A low growl sounded in Slash's throat. Clear Sky turned to face him. The rogues paced menacingly around their leader.

"Give me a chance to persuade them," Clear Sky begged.

Slash scowled. "Clearly your friends don't care if Star Flower dies," he snarled. "But don't worry. You won't be the only one to pay for this." His claws scraped the stone. "None of you realize the danger you face. My rogues outnumber you. They are more savage than any of you can imagine. If you value your prey more than the lives of your kits and your campmates, then you are free to refuse me."

Thunder lifted his chin. "You're bluffing."

Tall Shadow hissed at Slash. "Why should we believe a word you say?"

"For all we know," Wind Runner added, "every one of your campmates is beside you right now."

"Are you willing to take that chance?" Slash eyed her menacingly.

She didn't flinch. "Yes."

"Yes." Thunder stepped forward.

"Yes." Tall Shadow lashed her tail.

"No!" Clear Sky looked desperately at River Ripple. Surely *he* wouldn't let this happen. "Don't you understand? He's

going to kill Star Flower!"

River Ripple's eyes rounded with sympathy. "We can't give in to this bully," he meowed softly. "He will only return with more demands until we *all* starve."

"So you're going to sacrifice my mate?" Clear Sky could hardly believe his ears. "The mother of my kits?"

"Very well." Slash's mew was hard with rage. "If that is your decision."

"No!" Clear Sky looked up at him pleadingly. "*I'll* hunt for you! You can have *all* my prey. Just give me Star Flower!"

Slash's gaze flashed with contempt. Then he turned and disappeared down the back of the great rock. His rogues filed after him. Clear Sky stood, motionless as rock, as he listened to them swish away through the bracken. *Star Flower!*

Grief tore at his heart. Paws trembling, he stumbled and slumped onto his side. A sob choked his mew. Horror closed in around him so that he hardly heard the paw steps moving around him.

"Clear Sky." River Ripple's soft mew sounded in his ear.

"You've killed her. And my kits." He buried his nose beneath his paw. "Leave me alone!" *Everyone has betrayed me. Even my own son!* "I never want to see any of you ever again."

Sharp claws raked his ears. "Clear Sky!" Wind Runner's breath billowed over his face. "Sit up and stop acting like a kit."

Shocked, Clear Sky jerked up his head. Wind Runner, River Ripple, Thunder, and Tall Shadow were gathered around him, their eyes bright. "Don't you understand?" he pleaded. "Star Flower's going to die!"

"You fool," Wind Runner hissed. "Do you think we have no hearts?"

Thunder leaned down and nudged Clear Sky's shoulder with his muzzle. "Get up."

"Why?" Bewildered, Clear Sky let Thunder help him to his paws.

Tall Shadow lifted her tail. "Come with us," she told him. "We have something to show you."

CHAPTER 5
❧

Gray Wing peered through the shadowy pines. Scrubland stretched ahead of him, bathed in moonlight. In the distance, he could hear the rumbling of the Thunderpath. Beyond the scrub, the carrion place rose against the star-specked sky. Gray Wing shuddered as the stench of the mountain of Twoleg trash touched his nose. Was Slash really keeping Star Flower so close to such a filthy place?

Lightning Tail shifted beside him. The forest cat's musky scent seemed strange to Gray Wing now. Leaf and Reed fidgeted in the shadows behind them.

Leaf and Lightning Tail had volunteered to join the patrol when Gray Wing had traveled to Thunder's camp to discuss his plan. Reed had insisted on coming right from the start, and Gray Wing had been grateful to his campmate. The silver tom's knowledge of healing might be useful. Who knew what state they'd find Star Flower in?

Lightning Tail wrinkled his nose. "Are you sure this is the place?"

Gray Wing kept his gaze fixed ahead. "Fern said it was."

Leaf glanced over his shoulder uneasily. "Where *is* Fern?

You said she'd meet us here."

"She has to slip away from her campmates without being seen," Gray Wing reminded him.

"Let's hope she hurries," Reed muttered. "We need to get Star Flower away before the meeting is finished and Slash leaves the four trees. If he's willing to kidnap a queen, what in the stars will he do to *us* if he finds us trying to help her escape?"

Gray Wing glanced at the half-moon. It was still rising. How long would the meeting last? Wind Runner had promised to stretch it out as long as she could. Hopefully there was still plenty of time. He glanced back into the shadows anxiously. Was Fern coming? Perhaps they should start searching the scrubland for Star Flower without her.

Gray Wing had spent the last quarter moon tracking Fern, scouring the pine forest for some sign of her scent as he tried to figure out where she'd gone after she'd left Tall Shadow's camp. He'd ranged farther and farther, trekking through the oak forest and even beside the river in the hope that he could catch up with her. She was his only link to Slash and his only chance of finding out where Star Flower was being held.

At last, he'd found her scent, beyond the pines. He'd tracked it, growing wary as it mingled with rogue stench. The scents had thickened as he'd followed her trail, until he could smell nothing else. He had halted, his pelt pricking with fear. He had located the rogues' camp. It was a dip where the pines thinned onto boggy land, hidden by a thick wall of marsh grass. He'd circled it gingerly, then climbed the slope beyond. Hazel thickets crowded between willow trees, which stretched toward denser forest. It was a perfect hiding place from which to observe the comings and goings of the rogues. Gray Wing had found a patch of rotting moss and rolled in it to disguise his scent, then crouched at the heart of the most tangled thicket and waited.

A long day and night passed before he glimpsed Fern. As dawn washed the marshland in watery light, he saw her. She was following a patrol along a trail toward the camp. Gray Wing's heart had lurched as he wondered how to attract her attention without being spotted by her campmates.

He was lucky that she had such a keen sense of smell. She'd paused as she padded along the bottom of the slope, her nose twitching. She had pricked her ears. Gray Wing's heart had quickened as she turned and glanced toward the willows.

"I'll catch up to you!" she'd called to the patrol.

As soon as they were out of sight, Fern had hared up the slope, darting between the hazel thickets, her pelt rippling.

She'd guessed he'd come about Star Flower but swore she didn't know where the queen was being held. "Slash won't tell anyone but her guards," she'd confided. "He's keeping her away from the camp so no one can find her."

"But we have to know where she is," Gray Wing had pressed.

Fern had promised to find out where Star Flower was being held. "But you mustn't come back here," she had told him. "I'll find *you*. It's safer for both of us." He'd left her, feeling more anxious than relieved. Was it fair to let Fern put herself at risk? He'd pushed the worry away. Clear Sky's unborn kits were at greater risk.

Days had passed, with the meeting at the four trees looming ever closer. At last Fern had come, slinking at dawn from a patch of heather as he passed on hunting patrol, her eyes round with fear. "I know where she's being held," she'd breathed. "I can't show you now. Slash will already be wondering where I am."

They'd arranged to convene at the edge of the pine forest on the night of the meeting.

The night had arrived and Gray Wing glanced at the half-moon again. Where *was* she? Hadn't she been able to get away? He shifted his paws, feeling stiff from crouching on the damp earth.

"What if Fern doesn't come?" Lightning Tail glanced at him.

"We'll find Star Flower ourselv—" Gray Wing broke off as the brambles rustled behind them.

He spun, signaling with a twitch of his tail-tip for the others to be silent.

"Gray Wing?" Fern's frightened whisper sounded between the trees.

Gray Wing felt a flicker of relief, then stared anxiously into the shadows. "Are you alone?"

"Of course I am." She slid from the tangled branches, wincing as the thorns tugged her black, knotted fur.

Leaf straightened. "We thought you weren't coming."

Fern glared at him. "I said I would, didn't I?"

Reed dipped his head. "We're just glad you made it here safely."

Lightning Tail blinked at her expectantly. "Where's Star Flower?"

"Follow me." Fern brushed past him and padded from the trees. Keeping low, she led them across the scrubland.

Short, wiry grass jabbed between Gray Wing's claws. Frost-blackened bushes crowded on either side. The stench of the carrion place grew stronger as they neared it.

Fern slowed her pace. She nodded toward a dense patch of bracken. "She's in there," she breathed. "Swallow and Snake are guarding her."

Lightning Tail padded closer, tasting the air.

Gray Wing saw Fern hesitate, fear-scent wafting from her pelt.

"You'd better get back to your camp," he whispered.

She glanced at him gratefully. "If Slash finds out I led you here—"

"I know." Gray Wing touched his nose to her head gratefully. "You've been very brave, and we will remember your kindness and courage for many moons."

She blinked at him expectantly. "I hope you get her away from here. It's no place for a queen who's carrying kits." Dipping her head quickly, she hurried back toward the cover of the pines.

Gray Wing turned to Lightning Tail. "Are you ready?"

"Of course!" Lighting Tail lifted his chin.

Gray Wing nodded toward Leaf. "Do you remember what to do?"

Leaf nodded.

Gray Wing tasted the air. Rogue scent touched his tongue. The bracken swished in the light breeze. He signaled Lightning Tail and Leaf forward with a flick of his tail, then crouched, pressing his belly to the earth. Reed dropped down beside him as the two forest cats padded closer to the bracken.

Gray Wing held his breath as they neared the shadowy fronds. Leaf glanced at him quickly, then ducked beneath the cover of a juniper bush. Lightning Tail lifted his chin and marched straight on.

"Who are you?" An angry snarl sounded from the bracken patch as Lightning Tail disappeared behind it.

"Just a loner looking for prey," Lightning Tail answered breezily.

"Go hunt somewhere else!" A second snarl cut through the night air.

Lightning Tail sniffed. "Where's the best place to hunt around here?"

A threatening growl sounded from behind the bracken.

Gray Wing stiffened as he saw Lightning Tail back away, his ears twitching uneasily. Two cats stalked toward him, hackles high. One was an orange tabby she-cat with amber eyes, the other a gray tabby tom with broad shoulders. Their tails twitched aggressively.

"I'm sorry I bothered you." Lighting Tail was leading them farther away from the bracken. "I'll leave you in peace."

As he spoke, Leaf let out an anguished wail.

The rogues jerked around, pelts bristling.

"What's going on?" The gray tom flattened his ears.

"I don't know." Worry flashed in the tabby's eyes.

"Go find out what that noise was and I'll get rid of this loner." The gray tom turned toward Lightning Tail, his teeth glinting as he drew back his lips.

The tabby stalked cautiously toward the bush where Leaf was hiding.

Leaf let out another anguished wail.

"Who is it?" the tabby asked nervously. "What's wrong?"

"Quick!" Gray Wing hissed in Reed's ear. With both guards distracted, this was their chance. He slunk forward, keeping low, and crept toward the bracken. Reed's breath warmed his tail-tip. He reached the wall of stiff fronds and pushed through, emerging into a small clearing.

Star Flower lay at one edge. Her matted fur clung to her body. Her swollen belly jutted out from a bony frame. Hadn't they been feeding her? Gray Wing stared at her, shocked, as she lifted her head.

She gazed at him dully. "Who is it?" She sounded numb.

"It's Gray Wing." He hurried to her quickly and crouched at her side. "We've come to take you home."

The bracken rustled as Reed slid in behind. "How is she?"

"She looks weak," Gray Wing told him.

Star Flower was staring at him, confused. "Where's Clear Sky?"

"He's keeping Slash busy." Gray Wing tucked his nose under her shoulder and began to nudge her to her paws. "We have to get you out of here. We haven't got long."

As he spoke, a yowl sounded outside camp. "If you want a

fight, you've got one!" Lightning Tail's snarl echoed through the air.

"Hurry!" Gray Wing urged.

A second shriek sliced through bracken wall. *Leaf!*

Star Flower's eyes seemed to spark into life as she heard it. Suddenly she was hauling herself to her paws, "There are two guards," she warned Gray Wing.

"I know," he told her. "Lighting Tail and Leaf are taking care of them."

"No." Star Flower stared at him. "Two *more!* Slash sent extra because of the meeting."

Gray Wing's chest tightened. "Where are they?"

"They went to hunt rats in the carrion place." Star Flower glanced fearfully at a gap in the bracken. "They'll hear the fighting!"

"Come on." Gray Wing nudged her toward the twisted fronds where he'd broken in.

As she pushed through, Gray Wing nodded Reed after her.

Paw steps were pounding over the ground outside.

He pushed through the bracken as Star Flower and Reed began to run for the pines. Lighting Tail was wrestling with the gray tom. Leaf was pummeling the tabby with churning hind legs.

The paw steps grew louder. Two burly shapes loomed from the shadow of the carrion place. One veered toward Star Flower and Reed with a yowl of rage. The other leaped for Gray Wing.

Paws slammed into his side. He lost his footing and fell to

the ground. Claws raked his muzzle. Teeth sank into his hind leg. Pain seared like fire through him as a ginger tom bit down through his fur.

He strained to see if Star Flower had gotten away.

Reed was rolling across the ground, writhing with a tortoiseshell she-cat. Beyond him, Star Flower had stopped and turned back to look.

"Run!" Gray Wing wailed. As he spoke, the ginger tom let go and hared away, charging after Star Flower.

Gray Wing scrambled to his paws and chased after him. He felt a twinge in his chest. It sharpened as he saw the tom reach her first. Star Flower's eyes lit with fury. She reared and met the attack with outstretched claws, but the tom hit her like a barreling wind. Grunting, Star Flower staggered backward and fell, her swollen belly thumping onto the ground.

"You thought you could escape." The ginger tom lunged, his claws flashing in the moonlight. Star Flower tried to find her paws, her eyes wild with fear, but the rogue hooked his claws into her neck.

Gray Wing's pelt bristled. "Get off her!" He grabbed the tom's scruff between his teeth and hauled him away.

Star Flower shrieked as fur tore from her pelt.

The tom struggled free and leaped again at Star Flower. "You won't escape!"

Moving as fast as a snake, Gray Wing darted between them.

The ginger tom crashed into him, his gaze flaming. He stretched a paw around Gray Wing, reaching for Star Flower, but Gray Wing thrust him away and sent him reeling backward.

He threw Star Flower a quick, desperate look and saw her freeze, panic showing in her eyes. Blood dripped from her cheek. Clumps of fur stuck out of her pelt.

"Run!" Gray Wing yowled. "We can hold them off!"

She stared at him for a moment, then turned and fled for the pines.

Reed struggled from beneath the tortoiseshell. "Is Star Flower hurt?"

"Go with her!" Gray Wing ordered. He reached out a paw and swiped at the tortoiseshell's tail.

The tortoiseshell turned on him as Reed raced away, but Gray Wing hardly saw her. The ginger tom had found his paws. He dived for Gray Wing, knocking him down. As the rogue spun to chase after Star Flower, Gray Wing hooked a paw around his leg. Sinking in his claws, he held on tight, the claws of his other paw holding fast to the tortoiseshell's tail. "Lightning Tail!" Panic flared through Gray Wing. The rogues were struggling from his grip.

Lightning Tail was driving the gray tom back with a flurry of blows. He turned just as the ginger tom broke free and chased after Star Flower and Reed.

Lightning Tail pelted after the rogue.

Gray Wing twisted around and slammed a paw into the tortoiseshell's flank. He dug in his claws and scrambled up. Pinning her with one paw, he slashed her nose with the other. Terror shone in her eyes. She fell limp beneath his grip.

"If I let you go, will you leave Star Flower alone?" he hissed.

The tortoiseshell blinked at him desperately. "Yes!"

Backing off, he let her go. She scrambled to her paws, her pelt bushed. Her gaze flitted from him to the others. Lightning Tail writhed on the ground, the ginger tom in his grasp. Leaf battered the tabby's muzzle as he cowered against the earth. The tortoiseshell blinked at Gray Wing in disbelief.

"Go home," he snarled.

Her gaze lingered on him for a moment; then she turned and fled toward the carrion place.

Gray fur flashed at the edge of Gray Wing's vision. The gray tom was zigzagging between the bushes, heading for the pines.

Gray Wing plunged after him, his lungs screaming as his chest tightened. The world seemed to close around him, but he pushed onward, his vision narrowed to a tunnel, fixed only on the gray tom.

The tom slowed as he reached the pines, stumbling on the brambles that snaked between the trees. Gray Wing began to catch up. He raced into the shadow of the trees, leaping easily between the brambles. He'd spent too much time in forest to let them trip him. The tom raced on, but Gray Wing was gaining. As the trees opened into a clearing, Gray Wing flung himself forward. Stretching his claws, he dug them deep and dragged the tom to a screeching halt. Blood roared in his ears, but he kept his claws curled deep into the gray tom's pelt. The tom shrieked and tried to struggle free, but Gray Wing held him hard.

Closing his eyes, he fought to breathe, the tom writhing in his claws. *I mustn't let go.* The single thought throbbed in his mind.

Then the tom stopped struggling.

Gray Wing opened his eyes and peered at the rogue. The tom was lying on the ground, as still as dead prey.

Slowly, Gray Wing released him and stepped away.

The tom grunted. Then, pelt rippling, he staggered to his paws and glared reproachfully at Gray Wing.

"You're wasting your time," Gray Wing puffed. "I won't let you get her."

The gray tom growled. His tail dragging, he limped away between the pines.

Gray Wing drew in a shuddering breath. In the distance he heard Lightning Tail screech.

Then another yowl cut through his ear fur.

He stiffened.

The cry was filled with pain. Not the furious pain of battle, but a deep and frightened yowl.

Star Flower!

Something was wrong.

He forced himself to run, his lungs aching with every step. Swerving out of the trees, he broke onto the verge of the Thunderpath. A monster thundered past, and he flattened his ears against the wind as it whipped by his face.

Its roar faded and he heard the desperate yowl again.

Ahead, on the grass, he saw Reed crouching over a fallen body.

Had Star Flower been hit by a monster?

His thoughts reeled as he remembered Turtle Tail. A monster had killed her. He'd never seen her body, but he had imagined her over and over again, lying stricken beside a strange and distant Thunderpath. His heart seemed to burst inside his chest, but he forced himself to keep moving toward the huddled figure of Reed.

"What happened?" His mew was trembling as he neared.

Reed tuned to him, his eyes wide with fear. "The kits!" he breathed. "They're coming!"

CHAPTER 6

Gray Wing struggled to steady his breathing. "Are you sure?"

"Of course!" Reed snapped his gaze back to Star Flower.

She lay on her side, a low moan rolling in her throat. Her flanks convulsed. "But it's so early," she croaked, fear flashing in her green eyes.

A monster growled on the Thunderpath. Gray Wing glanced up, blinded as its eyes drenched them in light. Instinctively, he lunged forward, protecting Star Flower with his body as the monster tore past. The grass streamed around them, and an acrid wave of stench blasted over him. It burned inside his chest, but Gray Wing ignored the pain. Fighting back a cough, he glanced over his shoulder. Had Lightning Tail and Leaf managed to drive the other guards away? Had news of the rescue reached the rogue camp? Was a bigger patrol coming? "We have to get Star Flower away from here."

"How?" Reed stared at Star Flower. "She can't *walk!*"

Star Flower screeched as another convulsion seemed to grip her.

"I'll get help." Gray Wing tried to ignore his wheezing. There wasn't time.

Reed looked at him, his ears twitching. "I'll go," he growled. "You need to catch your breath."

Gray Wing shook his head. "You know more about herbs than me," he told the silver tabby. "Find her something to help her pain."

"Here?" Reed stared at the grass verge, then flicked his gaze toward the pines. "I don't know anything about forest herbs."

"Then guess!" Gray Wing was already on his paws. He leaped across the verge and pelted between the pines. Tall Shadow's camp was closest, and he knew the quickest route. Dodging brambles and leaping ditches, he raced through the darkness. He struggled for breath, wondering if he could keep going. He felt as though he were underwater, trying to swim for the shore before he ran out of air.

I can't let Star Flower die. Or her kits!

He had to get help.

The forest thickened, the branches blocking out the moonlight. Gray Wing dodged past trees, the rough bark scraping his flanks. Running on instinct, he managed to skim the jutting roots, leap ditches, and swerve past trailing brambles. At last, the trees thinned. The camp was near. He strained to see, trying to ignore the desperate pain in his chest. In the weak moonlight that filtered through the branches here, he saw the camp's shadowy walls. He veered around them and burst through the entrance, his lungs on fire.

"Jagged Peak!" He caught sight of the gray tabby tom limping across the clearing.

Jagged Peak spun, pelt bushing. Shock showed in his eyes. "Gray Wing!"

"Help!" Gray Wing gasped and dropped to his belly. Dragging in air, he felt dizzy, the camp swimming around him.

"Where's Star Flower?" Jagged Peak was at his side in a moment. He knew about Gray Wing's plan. "Did you save her? Are you hurt?"

"The kits," Gray Wing wheezed.

"Kits?" Jagged Peak looked puzzled.

Twigs rustled around Gray Wing as the forest cats scrambled from their nests. Eyes glinted in the entrances of the dens. Sun Shadow poked his head out. Mouse Ear slid into the moonlight. Holly hurried into the clearing.

Pebble Heart raced toward Gray Wing. "Is Tall Shadow okay?" He scrambled to a halt. "Are you okay?"

Gray Wing fought to find enough breath to explain. "Star Flower's kits," he rasped.

"Her *kits*?" Pebble Heart ducked close, his pelt rippling. "Are they coming?"

Gray Wing nodded mutely.

"It's too soon!" Pebble Heart looked at Jagged Peak, panic flashing in his gaze.

Jagged Peak ignored him and stared at Gray Wing. "Where is she? Did you get her away from the rogues?"

"Yes, but she collapsed. Rogues . . . following." Gray Wing managed to blurt out the words, hoping Jagged Peak would know what to do.

Jagged Peak lifted his head. "Mouse Ear! Sun Shadow!

Holly! Go and find Star Flower. Bring her here."

"There may not be time if the kits are coming!" Pebble Heart flicked his tail as the three cats started for the camp entrance. "Let me come too! I might be able to help."

Jagged Peak glanced at him. The young tom looked determined. "Okay."

Gray Wing pushed himself to his paws, the air slowly returning to his lungs. "I'll show you the way," he wheezed.

"You need to rest," Pebble Heart told him sharply.

"I know where she is," Gray Wing gasped, Star Flower's desperate yowl ringing in his mind. "She's suffering. If you follow the wrong trail, she might die."

Mouse Ear stopped at the entrance. "He's right."

"He can rest when he's shown us where to go," Holly agreed.

Pebble Heart looked anxiously at Gray Wing. "Will you be okay?"

"I have to be," Gray Wing told him grimly. He headed after the others, struggling to hide the shakiness of his paws.

Holly waited for him to catch up and pressed against him. "Lean on me," she murmured.

"I can manage—"

"Just lean!" she told him firmly.

He relaxed against her, relieved to feel some of the weight leave his paws as she moved beside him, her shoulder supporting his.

Mouse Ear hurried ahead as they left camp. "Which way?" His gaze scanned the shadows.

"Toward the ditches," Gray Wing puffed. He jerked his

nose toward the thickening pines. "She's beside the Thunder-path."

Mouse Ear hared away, Pebble Heart at his heels. Their pelts were quickly swallowed by the darkness.

"Hurry!" Gray Wing pushed on harder, relieved to feel Holly keeping up. Sun Shadow pressed against his other flank. Together they took his weight so that his paws seemed to skim the earth.

"Is this the right way?" Pebble Heart's mew echoed from the blackness ahead.

"Wait," Gray Wing puffed as Holly and Sun Shadow steered him toward the young tom's voice. They caught up to him in a pool of moonlight where a fallen tree had left a hole in the canopy. Mouse Ear was circling Pebble Heart, his gaze scanning the forest. Gray Wing stretched his nose forward. "Cross the ditches and head straight," he ordered. "She's beyond the thickest part of the forest."

Pebble Heart and Mouse Ear hared away again.

Holly and Sun Shadow pressed harder against Gray Wing. Frustration clawed at his belly. He felt like an ancient, lumbering badger. He shouldn't need help like this. Why did his breathing have to be so bad? He let them lead him after Mouse Ear and Pebble Heart until they reached the ditches.

Sun Shadow and Holly broke away. "You need to leap these yourself," Holly warned him.

Gray Wing drew in a shuddering breath, realizing with relief that his breathing had eased. He leaped the first ditch and crossed the short stretch of ground to the next. He leaped again, then again, until he'd crossed the rutted clearing, then veered toward the trail he'd followed from the Thunderpath.

He halted as Holly and Sun Shadow caught up. There was no sign of Pebble Heart or Mouse Ear's scent. "They've gone the wrong way!"

"Pebble Heart!" Holly yowled through the trees. "Over here!

Paws pounded across the ground, and a moment later Mouse Ear crashed from the darkness. Pebble Heart pulled up beside him.

"It's this way," Gray Wing told them, ducking onto the bramble-strewn trail he'd followed earlier. He led them as the trees thickened around him. The foul stench of the Thunderpath touched his nose. He pricked his ears, hearing nothing but the distant rumble of a monster. Hope pricked in his heart for a moment. *No battle cries.* The rogues hadn't reached Star Flower yet. But why wasn't she yowling with pain? *What if she . . . ?* He pushed fear away as it threatened to swamp him and hurried faster between the trees.

Holly was at his tail as the trail narrowed between the brambles. He could hear her campmates pounding behind her. Ahead the monster's roar grew. He broke from the trees as it passed, blinding him with its blazing eyes.

He blinked, startled for a moment, and then, as the monster pounded away, scanned the verge.

Reed was still crouching where he'd left him. Star Flower lay on the grass beside him.

"Is she okay?" Gray Wing hurried to his side. The queen

was panting hard. He stiffened as he saw Reed's paws glistening darkly. "Is that blood?"

"Yes." Panic showed in the silver tom's eyes. "I found some thyme to help with the shock, and she's focusing on her breathing to help with the pain, but I can't stop the bleeding."

Pebble Heart nosed past him. "Any sign of the kits?"

Reed met the young tom's gaze. "Not yet, but I hope it won't be long. There's too much blood."

Holly pushed past Gray Wing. "We must get her back to the camp." She nodded to Sun Shadow.

The black tom leaned down and shoved his nose beneath Star Flower's shoulders. She grunted as he heaved her up onto his back.

Mouse Ear quickly ducked beneath her. Reed pressed against her flank. Pebble Heart darted to her other side. Supporting the queen between them, the four cats began to head into the forest.

Star Flower groaned. She dipped and rose like a leaf being carried downstream as they moved.

"Stay close to each other," Holly ordered. "You mustn't let her fall."

"We won't," Sun Shadow grunted.

Gray Wing followed, recovering his breath as they moved slowly between the trees.

They swerved to avoid the ditches, taking the long trail around. As they neared the bramble wall of the camp, Gray Wing heard paws pounding the earth behind them. His heart lurched as he stopped and scanned the shadows. Were the rogues following their trail?

Eyes glinted between the trees.

"Gray Wing!" Lightning Tail's mew rang out. He hurried closer, his black pelt dappled by moonlight. Leaf was at his heels.

"Where are the rogues?" Gray Wing glanced past the two cats anxiously.

"We chased them off," Leaf told him.

Lighting Tail blinked at Star Flower as the others carried her into camp. "Is she hurt?"

"The kits are coming," Gray Wing told him, "and they're *very* early."

Leaf frowned. "Does Clear Sky know?"

Gray Wing stiffened. *Clear Sky!* He'd been so panicked about Star Flower that he hadn't thought about his brother. Had the other leaders told him of the plan to rescue Star Flower yet? He dashed away, calling over his shoulder. "Tell Jagged Peak I'll bring Clear Sky as soon as I find him!" His mind whirled. Where was he? At the four trees hollow? On his way to get Star Flower?

I have to cut him off. Gray Wing quickened his pace. Slash might have learned about Star Flower's escape by now. What if he'd sent out a patrol? Clear Sky mustn't run into a band of angry rogues. He imagined Clear Sky backed against a tree, hackles up, teeth bared, rogues closing in on him.

Fear spiraling, Gray Wing cut through the woods, trying to guess the fastest route from the four trees hollow to the carrion place. *He must be heading through the pines.* Wheezing,

Gray Wing zigzagged, covering as much ground as he could, ears pricked for the sound of paw steps. The tightness in his chest hardened, but he pressed on. As he reached the bottom of the slope that led to the border between Clear Sky's land and Tall Shadow's, he heard voices.

"We should have rescued her as soon as we knew where she was!"

It was Clear Sky.

Gray Wing stopped. Clear Sky stood at the top of the rise. Wind Runner was beside him, while River Ripple, Tall Shadow, and Thunder crowded behind.

"Clear Sky!" Gray Wing puffed.

Clear Sky's eyes widened. He bounded down the slope. "Did you rescue her? Is she safe?"

"We got her away from the rogues," Gray Wing told him. "But the kits are coming."

Clear Sky's pelt bushed. "Already?"

"It's too soon!" Tall Shadow raced to join them.

"Where is she?" Clear Sky demanded.

"We took her to Tall Shadow's camp," Gray Wing told him. "Pebble Heart and Reed are with her."

Tall Shadow frowned. "Have *they* had kits? Have they even *seen* a kitting?"

"Holly's with her too," Gray Wing reassured her. "*She's* had kits."

"So have I." Wind Runner scrambled down the slope. "I know what to do."

She darted past Gray Wing and headed for the camp, Tall

Shadow close on her heels. Clear Sky blinked at Gray Wing, then followed the two she-cats.

River Ripple hesitated at the top of the slope. "Too many paws at a kitting will just get in the way. Please send word that Star Flower and the kits are all right."

Thunder padded closer. "Are Lighting Tail and Leaf okay?"

Gray Wing nodded. "They helped carry Star Flower to Tall Shadow's camp. They're there now."

Thunder flicked his tail, looking relieved. "Send them home when they're ready. I must go. Their campmates will be worried." His gaze fixed on Gray Wing, earnest in the moonlight. "I hope Star Flower's okay."

Gray Wing blinked at the tom. "Thanks for agreeing to meet with Slash tonight," he meowed. "It gave us the time we needed to rescue Star Flower."

"It was a good plan, Gray Wing," Thunder answered. "I'm glad I got the chance to help."

River Ripple dipped his head. "Let's hope the stars are on our side," he meowed solemnly. "Early kits rarely survive."

Gray Wing's belly tightened. He glanced meaningfully toward Thunder. "Clear Sky's kits are strong," he murmured. "This litter will be fine."

He headed after his brother, quickening his pace as he neared the camp. Nosing through the bramble entrance, he scanned the clearing. Mouse Ear and Mud Paws paced the far end nervously. Jagged Peak sat and watched, his pelt prickling along his spine.

Shapes were huddled at the edge of the camp, beneath a

dome of woven brambles. He hurried toward them, tensing as he scented blood.

Blinking through the darkness, he saw Pebble Heart hanging back beside Reed and Tall Shadow. Lightning Tail shifted from one paw to another, watching as Wind Runner and Holly moved around Star Flower. He could hear the desperate panting of the queen.

Clear Sky crouched by her head. "It's okay, my love," he murmured. "Everything will be okay."

Gray Wing slowed to a stop beside Pebble Heart. "Isn't there anything you can do?" Pebble Heart had always had a natural skill for healing.

The young tom shook his head. "They know far more than me about kitting. But I'll learn all I can." He didn't take his eyes from the she-cats as Wind Runner ran her paw over Star Flower's belly, while Holly lapped at the queen's cheek.

"Just one more push," Wind Runner murmured.

"You're doing really well," Holly crooned.

Star Flower's body convulsed as though a fox had grabbed her. She yowled a long, deep yowl, her eyes rolling with pain.

Clear Sky winced and pressed his muzzle to her head.

"It's a she-kit!" Wind Runner's mew of triumph rang through the air.

Gray Wing leaned forward and saw a glistening scrap of fur, slick and wet and half covered in a pale membrane. The kit squirmed on the ground, tiny paws churning.

Tall Shadow purred. "Is . . ." She hesitated. "Is she *okay?*"

"She looks like any newborn kit," Wind Runner proclaimed

happily. "Only smaller." Quickly she scooped up the kit and placed her beside Star Flower's muzzle. "Give her a wash and keep her warm," she ordered.

But Star Flower had already stretched out her nose and was lapping her newborn kit, her eyes shining with joy. Then she stiffened as another convulsion gripped her. As she writhed, growling with pain, Holly snatched the she-kit from beside her muzzle and tucked her safely beneath her own belly.

"Push!" Wind Runner ordered.

Star Flower shuddered and moaned. Wind Runner leaned back, her eyes lighting up. "Another she-kit!"

Star Flower convulsed again.

"And a tom!" Wind Runner purred loudly as she picked up both kits between her jaws and placed them beside Star Flower. She ran her paw over Star Flower's belly. "That was the last, I think. And the bleeding's stopped."

Pebble Heart darted forward. "May I feel?"

Star Flower lifted her head groggily and stared at the young tom.

"I want to learn how to help if any of my campmates have kits," Pebble Heart told her.

Star Flower gave a deep purr, amusement lighting her weary gaze. "Go ahead." Her mew was slurred with relief.

Pebble Heart tentatively ran his paw over her belly, tipping his head to one side, his eyes glazing as he disappeared into his own thoughts.

Gray Wing knew that look well. Pebble Heart had always been wise beyond his years, staring into the distance as though lost in another world when his littermates had wanted to play. Gray Wing's thoughts flitted to Moth Flight. *Perhaps some cats are born to see beyond hunting and fighting.*

"What do you think?" Star Flower's mew cut into his thoughts. She was staring at Clear Sky, her three kits squirming at her belly.

"They're beautiful." Clear Sky buried his muzzle in his mate's neck fur.

Pebble Heart stepped away. Holly and Wind Runner withdrew to Tall Shadow's side.

Gray Wing stared at his brother.

Clear Sky had lifted his head and was staring at the tiny, slick-furred kits with a look of wonder that Gray Wing had never seen in his eyes. Pure love melted his ice-blue gaze. He leaned gently forward and lapped at one of the she-kits, who was nuzzling deeper into Star Flower's belly.

Gray Wing felt his chest soften and his breathing ease. A deep longing tugged in his chest. How he wished to feel the love that was clearly sweeping Clear Sky now. He had felt like a father to Turtle Tail's kits, and he loved them all. But the pure joy glowing in his brother's eyes took him by surprise, and he wished that he could one day feel the same.

Wind Runner shifted her paws. "They all look perfectly healthy, but they're very small."

Pebble Heart glanced at his leader. "Can they stay here for a while, Tall Shadow? Just until they're a little stronger."

Tall Shadow nodded. "Of course."

Pebble Heart blinked at Clear Sky. "Will you let them stay?

A trip through the forest might expose them to unnecessary risks."

Clear Sky glanced at Wind Runner. "What do you think?"

"For a few days," Wind Runner advised.

Holly's ears twitched. "I've never seen kits so small. Make sure they stay warm, and don't let them have too many visitors."

Pebble Heart flicked his tail anxiously. "Don't let any sick cats near them for at least a moon!"

"Of course not!" Clear Sky looked alarmed.

"You'll be able to take them home soon," Wind Runner promised Clear Sky. "Kits grow fast."

Clear Sky looked at the two she-cats, his gaze brimming with gratitude. "Thank you for getting her safely through this." He glanced at his kits, his mew growing husky. "And them."

Gray Wing followed his brother's gaze, marveling at Star Flower's strength and courage. Only a short while earlier, she had been fighting rogues! Now she was curled around her first litter.

"Gray Wing?"

He realized that his brother was talking to him. "What?" He met Clear Sky's gaze, surprised by its warmth.

"Thank you for rescuing Star Flower."

"It was the right thing to do."

Clear Sky tipped his head to one side. "Why did you keep your plan secret from me?"

Gray Wing blinked. "If you'd known where she was,

nothing would have kept you from her. But we needed to wait until Slash was distracted."

"And *I* was the distraction." Clear Sky grunted.

"You had to be convincing." Gray Wing dipped his head apologetically. "It seemed the best way to get her back safely."

"I will always be grateful."

"It's nothing." Gray Wing shrugged. "You'd have done the same for me."

Doubt flickered in Clear Sky's moonlit gaze, then dissolved. He padded closer and rubbed his muzzle against Gray Wing's. His fur was warm against his cheek, his scent so familiar that, for a moment, Gray Wing's thoughts flashed back to his kithood, when they'd snuggled side by side at Quiet Rain's belly.

He suddenly realized that Clear Sky was purring. "Congratulations," he breathed.

"Thank you, brother," Clear Sky murmured, his mew cracking. "I will never forget this."

CHAPTER 7

❧

Frost-whitened leaves crunched beneath Thunder's paws. Sunshine dappled the forest floor. Although it was the coldest season, leaf-bare brought light to the forest; blue sky showed between the branches now that the lush green canopy had gone.

Thunder felt a prickle of excitement. Pebble Heart had come to the camp earlier to visit with his littermate Owl Eyes. He'd brought news that Clear Sky and Star Flower had returned to their camp in the forest with the kits. In the days since her escape, Star Flower had recovered from the trauma, and the kits were growing strong.

When Lightning Tail had returned from the rescue mission, Thunder had been shocked by his injuries. Wounds scarred his flank, and his ear tip had been torn. A scratch near one eye was still swollen. Thunder wasn't convinced by Lightning Tail's assurances that it had been an easy fight. The sight of his friend, so battered by his encounter with the rogues, unnerved Thunder. Had Slash's boast been true? Were his rogues more numerous and more savage than the forest cats?

He pushed the thought away now. Why spoil such a crisp leaf-bare morning with worry? He was on his way to meet his newest kin—Tiny Branch, Dew Petal, and Flower Foot.

As the forest sloped down toward Clear Sky's territory, Thunder kicked his white paws through the drifted leaves and hopped over fallen branches brought down by leaf-fall storms. When the brambles thinned and gave way to swaths of bracken, Thunder began to smell the scents of Clear Sky's cats. Nettle and Birch had passed this way recently. Instinctively, Thunder opened his mouth and tasted for prey-scent. Were the woods here any richer than his own? He smelled only cat scent and the musky odor of fungus. The voles and mice, which had scuttled beneath every root and bush during greenleaf, were clearly as scarce here as near the ravine. And with the squirrels taking to their dens until newleaf, there had been little to hunt besides a few careless birds.

As he neared Clear Sky's camp, he recognized fresh scents. Blossom and Birch must be nearby. He slowed, scanning the bracken crowding the bramble entrance.

"Hello?" he called out tentatively. He hadn't warned Clear Sky he was visiting.

"Thunder?" Blossom slid out from the bracken and lifted her tail amiably.

Birch hopped from the steep bank that edged the track. "Is anything wrong?" Worry darkened the ginger tom's eyes.

"No." Thunder pricked his ears. *Should there be?*

"Clear Sky put us on guard," Blossom told him. "He's sending out patrols day and night."

Thunder's fur rippled uneasily. "Is he worried Slash will retaliate?"

Birch scanned the forest quickly. "He took Star Flower once. Why wouldn't he do it again?"

Blossom snorted. "He'd better not try," she growled. "We're ready for him this time."

Birch thrust his muzzle toward Thunder. "Have you seen any of his rogues?"

Thunder shrugged. "Our part of the forest has been quiet."

"Good." Blossom padded a few tail-lengths farther into the forest and looked around. She glanced back at Thunder. "Are you here to visit the kits?"

Thunder whisked his tail. "Yes, if that's okay."

Blossom exchanged looks with Birch. "No one's allowed near them yet," she warned Thunder. "But I'm sure Clear Sky will be pleased to see you. He's so grateful for everything the others did to rescue Star Flower."

Her gaze wavered for a moment, and Thunder wondered whether *she* was pleased that Star Flower was back. He knew that many cats still did not trust One Eye's daughter. Hopefully, now that she was mother of Clear Sky's kits, there would be no doubts about her loyalty.

Birch nodded toward the entrance. "Clear Sky's in his den," he told Thunder. "He hardly comes out now. You may as well go and find him."

Thunder dipped his head. "Thank you." He slid through the prickly tunnel. The branches rattled around him.

Quick Water looked up from beneath an oak as he padded into the clearing. "Hi!" The gray-and-white she-cat looked pleased to see him.

"Hi," he answered. "I've come to visit my kin." He noticed that her fur clung to her frame, and realized suddenly that Birch and Blossom had looked leaner than usual too. He wondered if he seemed skinny to them. He had gone to his nest hungry more than once over the past quarter moon.

Acorn Fur and Thorn were sharing tongues beside a yew. Acorn Fur looked up. "Hi, Thunder. Did you see any prey on the way?"

"I wish I had," Thunder told her.

Thorn straightened, his ears still wet, and sighed. "It looks like more freezing weather's on the way. That won't help the prey return."

"At least it's not raining," Thunder answered, determined to be optimistic. He refused to believe that prey would stay hidden all leaf-bare. A few more days and the forest would be teeming with mice and voles scavenging for food. Surely they must be hungry too?

He crossed the clearing and leaped the bank, pushing through the bracken that shielded Clear Sky's den from the rest of the camp. The small clearing beyond was empty, but he heard mewling from the shadowy opening in the brambles.

The kits! His heart quickened. They sounded so tiny, their shrill squeaks more like mouse cries.

"Clear Sky?" he called across the stretch of leaf-strewn earth.

His father's face appeared in the den entrance. Clear Sky's eyes lit up as he saw Thunder, and he squeezed out of the den. "It's good to see you!"

"Hi." Thunder blinked. Warmth shone in his father's gaze. His cheery welcome took him by surprise. He'd expected to find Clear Sky anxious and still angry about Star Flower's ordeal. Instead, he seemed at ease with the world, for the first time ever. "How's Star Flower?"

Clear Sky glanced fondly back toward the den. "She's had a hard time, but now that she's home and safe, she'll be fine."

"And the kits?" Thunder peered around him toward the den. "May I see them?"

"They're too small, I'm afraid," Clear Sky told him apologetically. "They're to see no one until they're stronger."

Stronger? Anxiety pricked in Thunder's belly. "They *are* okay, aren't they?"

"They're fine," Clear Sky told him. "But they're small. They're staying near Star Flower's belly until they're older. Pebble Heart said we have to keep them away from other cats for a moon. It's hard to believe they're so helpless." His gaze glistened with warmth as he went on. "I'm never going to let anything bad happen to them."

A pang of grief took Thunder by surprise. Why hadn't Clear Sky been this concerned when *he* was born? His father had left his own mother to kit alone, beside a Twoleg camp. She'd died when the nest she'd made for them had been crushed. He'd only been saved because Gray Wing had come searching for them. Thunder couldn't help feeling that his life might have been very different if Clear Sky had rescued Storm before she'd kitted, just as he'd rescued Star Flower.

He shook out his fur. What was the point in wondering?

He wasn't going to feel sorry for himself. Everything that had happened to him had made him the cat he was now. His cats were loyal, and he had friends in every group. He was as much a leader as Clear Sky.

He changed the subject. "Blossom said you were sending out patrols day and night. Are you worried about Slash?"

Clear Sky's tail twitched. "I won't make the same mistake twice," he grunted. "Slash and his rogues aren't going to get anywhere near my kits."

"Good." Thunder wondered if patrols were enough to keep Slash from stirring up trouble. But at least Clear Sky wasn't talking about revenge. He felt sure that, in past moons, his father would already have been planning an attack. But then he stiffened. Perhaps Clear Sky *was* thinking about going after Slash. . . .

He eyed Clear Sky uncertainly. "You're not thinking about causing any trouble with the rogues, are you?"

A loud squeal sounded from the shadows, and Clear Sky glanced toward his den. "Why poke a hornets' nest? Slash deserves to suffer for what he's done. But I'm not risking the safety of Star Flower and my kits. They are more important now."

"You're right." Thunder understood. After all, he'd refused to help Clear Sky at first, to keep his own group safe. "Protecting the cats we care about is more important than starting battles."

Another squeal sounded from the den.

"I'd better go back to them." Clear Sky's gaze shifted, and

he began to back away. "Star Flower's still very tired. I don't like to leave her alone too long."

"I'll come back and see the kits when they're bigger," Thunder called.

But his father was already disappearing into the den. "You do that." Clear Sky's mew sounded distant.

Thunder turned away, relieved when, this time, no grief jabbed his belly. Clear Sky seemed truly content for the first time in his life. His father had found happiness, and Thunder was happy for him, and for the kits who would know nothing but love.

Purring softly to himself, he leaped down the bank and crossed the clearing.

"Did he let you see them?" Acorn Fur called to him as he headed for the entrance.

"Not this time," he answered, ducking out of camp. "But I'll be back."

Birch and Blossom were sniffing through a patch of frost-scorched nettles as he headed along the trail toward the rise.

"See you soon!" he called to them.

Birch looked up, clearly distracted. "Yeah, sure."

As he headed for the ravine, Thunder tasted the air. Clear Sky might be sure he could guard his camp, but Blossom and Birch had seemed edgy. Perhaps they were right to be wary. Slash didn't seem the sort of cat to give up easily.

Unease wormed beneath Thunder's pelt. Slash would stir up more trouble, he was sure of that. He just wondered when it would begin.

* * *

Warmed by his run through the forest, Thunder paused at the top of the ravine. A cold wind ruffled his fur as he peered over the edge. Familiar scents rose from the sheltered hollow, and he leaped down onto the first ledge, glad to be home.

Hopping lightly from one jutting rock to the next, he heard angry mews from beyond the gorse barrier. He tensed as he pricked his ears. His campmates rarely argued. Had an unwelcome visitor barged into camp? He smelled no strange scents as he reached the bottom of the cliff and hurried for the gorse tunnel.

"How could we fight them off?" Cloud Spots sounded indignant. "We were outnumbered!"

"It would have been better than creeping away like mice!" Leaf snapped back.

"They caught us unprepared, that's all," Lightning Tail reasoned.

Alarm fizzed through Thunder's pelt. He ducked through the tunnel and hurried into camp. "What's happened?"

Leaf, Cloud Spots, and Lightning Tail turned to face him. Their fur was fluffed out, clumps sticking out here and there as though they'd been fighting.

Clover dashed across the camp to meet Thunder. "They were robbed!"

Thistle scampered between Lightning Tail and Cloud Spots. "The rogues attacked them while they were hunting," he told Thunder.

Lightning Tail shooed the kit away with his tail. "Five

rogues jumped us beside the big sycamore tree," he told Thunder. "We were gathering up our catch, ready to come home. We'd caught three mice and a thrush. We fought the best we could, but we were outnumbered. It seemed best to back off and let them take the prey. No one's really hurt—only our pride is wounded."

Leaf snorted. "Our pride would be fine if we'd fought them properly!"

Thunder's ears twitched uneasily. "Pride heals faster than scratches."

Milkweed paced beside the tree stump. "Does this mean the woods aren't safe anymore?" She glanced at Thistle and Clover.

Pink Eyes sat at the edge of the clearing, his tail flicking. "There have always been rogues, and there always will be."

"Not like these rogues," Cloud Spots muttered darkly. "They came looking for us, and they took our catch just to prove they could."

Leaf nodded. "They didn't want it because they needed it; they just wanted us to go hungry."

Owl Eyes pawed at the earth beside Pink Eyes. "I wish I'd been there. I'd have clawed their ears off."

Thunder padded to the middle of the clearing and gazed around at his campmates. "You were right to let them take the prey," he told them. "Never fight a battle when your enemy is the only one prepared." *Were these definitely Slash's rogues?* "Did they say anything, Lighting Tail?"

Lighting Tail met his gaze gravely. "One of them told us

that if we wouldn't *give* them our prey, they'd have to take it."

"And next time they'd take our pelts as well," Leaf growled.

Milkweed's fur rippled along her spine.

Owl Eyes hurried to her side. "Don't worry. I'll keep an eye on Thistle and Clover."

"I can look after Clover!" Thistle puffed out his chest.

Clover flicked her fluffy tail indignantly. "I don't need *any* cat looking after me!"

Thunder hardly heard them. His thoughts were whirling. He shifted his paws. "This is only the beginning," he warned his campmates. "Slash said he would take our prey, and he clearly means to."

Lightning Tail frowned. "Perhaps we can outwit them, as we did with Star Flower."

"We can't just let them rob us," Cloud Spots growled in agreement.

Leaf flexed his claws. "We need to do something about it."

Thunder saw expectation in his campmates' eyes. What could he say? He didn't know how many rogues Slash had, or where their camp was. He had no idea how to outwit the rogues.

Lightning Tail blinked at him suddenly. "I've got an idea."

Thunder lifted his tail. "Share it with us."

Lighting Tail padded to the tree stump and leaped on top. "We need to train," he announced. "Those cats wouldn't have stolen our prey so easily if we'd known what to do. We must practice fighting moves. We must learn new skills so that we're always prepared. We're strong and we're smart. If we practice, we can win even when we're outnumbered. Slash's rogues are just kittypets nobody wants. If we train hard and grow strong and learn fighting moves they've never seen, we will always be ready to defend what is ours."

Leaf lifted his chin, his eyes shining. "That's a great idea."

"We can start training at once!" Owl Eyes put in.

"I already know a few moves I can share," Cloud Spots offered.

"Can we train?" Thistle gazed eagerly at Lightning Tail.

"We must *all* train," Lightning Tail told the kit.

Thunder gazed at his friend, his chest swelling with pride. It seemed that with the passing moons, his friend had become wise. *I've been worrying about what will happen to the group when I'm not around anymore, and the answer has been with me all along!* Lightning Tail should be the next leader. Thunder's shoulders loosened as relief washed his pelt. Suddenly the weight of leadership seemed to ease. The group would be safe even after he was gone.

But Thunder intended to live a good while yet! Shaking out his fur, he padded toward the tree stump. "Thanks, Lightning Tail." He looked up at his friend. "I'm putting you in charge of training."

He glanced around at the others. Their eyes were shining with excitement. Milkweed lifted her chin defiantly.

They were no longer angry or afraid, Thunder mused. *They are ready to fight.*

CHAPTER 8

"I hope we're not the only group the rogues are stealing from." Wind Runner's angry mew rang through the cold night air. A full moon bathed the moor with light.

Gorse Fur padded beside her. "Why would they target us?"

"Thunder hinted that was why he called tonight's meeting," Gray Wing reminded them as they headed toward the four trees hollow.

Thunder had visited the moor camp the day before, asking Wind Runner to bring a patrol to a meeting at the four trees. The orange tom had looked troubled. And thin. But he had said he didn't want to discuss what was wrong until all the leaders were present.

Gray Wing followed Wind Runner and Gorse Fur between the wide swaths of heather. Slate was at his side. He relished the warmth of her pelt as it brushed against his.

Minnow padded at their tails. "I should have stayed behind with Spotted Fur and Reed," she fretted. "Moth Flight and Dust Muzzle are too young to fight if the rogues attack the camp."

"The rogues won't attack the camp," Gorse Fur reassured

her. "They're not that mouse-brained."

Gray Wing hoped she was right. He'd suggested to Reed that he shelter with Spotted Fur and the kits in Wind Runner's den for the night. If the rogues did cause any trouble, its narrow entrance and thick walls would make it easy to defend.

Wind Runner glanced over her shoulder, her eyes flashing in the silver moonlight. "Why can't the rogues leave us alone?"

Gray Wing could understand Wind Runner's frustration. Twice in the past half-moon, rogues had come onto their land. Once, they'd hunted rabbits on the high moor. The second time, they'd simply swiped prey from Moth Flight and Dust Muzzle, leaving the two young cats shaken.

Slate glanced at him. "Do you think Thunder has a plan?" she whispered.

"I hope so." Gray Wing swished his tail-tip along her spine. "We can't keep losing prey like this." Rabbits had started venturing farther from their burrows in search of grazing, which made them easier to catch. But Gray Wing knew that the more rabbits they killed now, the fewer there'd be when leaf-bare really began to bite. He was thankful that snipe and grouse still roamed the moor. At least they wouldn't starve. Unless the rogues kept taking their food.

The oaks loomed ahead, their ancient branches reaching above the rim of the hollow. Bare now, they stretched like claws toward the star-speckled sky. Gray Wing tasted the air and smelled pine and river scents. "Tall Shadow and River Ripple are here," he told Slate softly.

"What about the others?" Her nostrils twitched.

"I'm not sure." Thunder's and Clear Sky's musky scents were masked by the damp forest smell drifting from the trees beyond.

He followed Wind Runner and Gorse Fur over the rim of the hollow and squinted into the shadows below. Shapes moved between the trees. As he threaded his way down the bracken-covered slope, he heard the murmuring of voices. Gradually, more scents touched his nose.

"We're the last to arrive," he told Slate.

Minnow growled from the back. "Unless the rogues are planning to join us. We can't seem to go anywhere these days without tripping over them."

"Wind Runner!"

Gray Wing heard Thunder greet Wind Runner as she padded into the clearing.

He followed her out of the bracken, blinking as icy air bathed his face.

Thunder was standing between Leaf and Milkweed in the shadow of the great rock, while Lightning Tail walked the edge of the clearing, sniffing warily at the undergrowth. Clear Sky paced in a pool of moonlight beside Blossom and Nettle. River Ripple was sitting in the middle of the clearing, Shattered Ice beside him. Gray Wing dipped his head in greeting, noticing how calm the river cats seemed, so still beside the restless pacing of the others.

Tall Shadow, Jagged Peak, and Mouse Ear stayed near the edge of the clearing, weaving around one another, their ears pricked, their gazes darting to any small stirring of the bracken on the slopes. Tall Shadow lifted her tail as Wind Runner approached. Thunder moved from the shadow of the great rock to join them as they stopped beside River Ripple.

Thunder glanced around at the cats. "Our prey is being stolen by rogues."

"Ours too!" Wind Runner's eyes shone angrily in the dark.

"They've taken half our prey since Star Flower was rescued." Tall Shadow sounded weary.

Clear Sky blinked at her sympathetically. "In the past few days, they've attacked two of our hunting parties. We're all suffering."

River Ripple's tail swished over the ground. "They haven't stolen our prey yet. Perhaps they don't like fish."

"Or getting their paws wet," Shattered Ice added, a glint in his eyes.

Wind Runner turned on the gray-and-white tom. "This is no joking matter! Cats are going hungry, and leaf-bare is only just beginning!"

Shattered Ice dipped his head respectfully. "You're right. I'm sorry."

River Ripple met Wind Runner's angry stare. "There are plenty of fish in the river. We are happy to share what we have."

"Fish!" Lightning Tail snorted. "Who wants to eat fish?"

"Hungry cats must eat what they can," River Ripple answered.

Thunder swished his tail. "River Ripple's offer is kind, but his fish can't feed us all."

"And what if the river freezes over?" Wind Runner added. "Then there'll be no fish at all."

Thunder stepped forward. "This is everyone's problem. We need to find a solution."

Clear Sky's gaze flicked around the other cats. "This trouble started when the rogues kidnapped Star Flower," he meowed. "And I'm sorry I got you involved, but I had no choice. You did the right thing in rescuing her. She's safe, and my kits are growing stronger with each day. You know as well as I do that none of you would have slept soundly in your nests if you'd let them die."

Gray Wing caught his brother's eye. For once, Clear Sky had judged them perfectly. Not one of the cats who stood bathed in moonlight could have found peace knowing that Star Flower and her kits had come to harm because of their inaction. Pride surged beneath his pelt, and he padded closer to his brother. "Star Flower was just Slash's excuse to start stealing from us." He glanced around the leaders. "He is determined to hate us, and he must find a reason to justify his hate. It is deep in his bones, just as it was with One Eye."

Thunder growled. "Some cats need an enemy to make them feel strong."

River Ripple nodded. "Their bellies don't feel full unless they are eating another cat's food."

Wind Runner's pelt pricked impatiently along her spine. "What are we going to do about it?"

Tall Shadow's ears twitched. "We've been sending out larger hunting patrols, but we're always outnumbered."

"How many rogues does Slash have?" Leaf lashed his tail, looking toward Gray Wing. "Has Fern given you any idea?"

"I haven't seen her since we rescued Star Flower," Gray Wing told him. "But I've seen their camp and smelled the scents. He seems to have a large group, but I'm not sure how big."

Wind Runner flexed her claws. "You need to find out."

Fear spiked Gray Wing's belly as he imagined sneaking back to the marsh. It would be risky. And even if he found Fern again, he'd be putting her in danger just by talking to her.

Thunder blinked at him. "I'll come with you. We can take a patrol."

He felt Slate's pelt pricking against his and scented her fear. "I'm coming too."

Gray Wing shook his head. "I'm going alone. Sending a patrol might cause a battle."

Wind Runner grunted. "Perhaps we *should* have a battle and end this once and for all."

"No." Clear Sky paced between the cats. "It would be mouse-brained to fight a battle against an enemy we don't know. First we need to know how many rogues there are."

Gray Wing nodded. Clear Sky was right. "I'll find out what I can."

"Meanwhile, we must prepare to defend what is ours." Thunder glanced toward Lightning Tail. "We've been train-ing to fight and practicing battle moves. I think you should all start training so that you can fight off any rogue attack. There may be many of them, but they're not very skilled. If they were, they wouldn't have to travel in such big groups."

Milkweed's eyes glittered. "Lightning Tail has been teaching Clover and Thistle how to defend themselves."

Tall Shadow flicked her tail-tip. "Storm Pelt, Dew Nose, and Eagle Feather each have their own trainer. They've only been learning to hunt so far, but they could learn some battle moves too." She nodded to Mouse Ear. "You've formed quite a bond with Eagle Feather, haven't you?"

"He's a fast learner." Mouse Ear glanced around at the other cats. "And it's easier if I train him alone. I can learn his strengths and weaknesses and build on what he already knows."

Lightning Tail blinked. "That's a good idea." He glanced at Thunder. "Maybe I should assign trainers to Clover and Thistle."

"I'd be happy to train either of them," Leaf offered. "They're both bright and eager to learn."

Milkweed fluffed out her pelt proudly.

Wind Runner exchanged looks with Gorse Fur. "Perhaps if Moth Flight had her own trainer, she'd learn faster. She certainly doesn't seem to have learned much from us."

"She's doing fine—" Gorse Fur began to defend their kit, but Jagged Peak interrupted.

"I got nowhere trying to train Eagle Feather," he admitted. "I was either too soft on him or too hard. We ended up squabbling."

Mouse Ear shifted his paws. "It's easy for me to see Eagle Feather's progress with a clear eye. It seems more difficult to train one's own kit."

"Very well." Clear Sky dipped his head. "Let's all begin battle training, and give each kit their own trainer."

Wind Runner nodded. Tall Shadow dipped her head. As River Ripple blinked his approval, shadows darkened the clearing.

Gray Wing glanced at the full moon. Clouds were beginning to drift across it. Thicker clouds lurked on the horizon. Night was coming, and it would be easier to reach Slash's camp in the dark. "I'll go and find Fern now." The sooner they knew what they were facing, the faster they could prepare. *For what?* His ears twitched uneasily. Was there really going to be a battle? He shuddered, remembering the Great Battle, fought right where they were standing. So many cats had died.

Slate moved closer and lowered her voice. "Are you sure you don't want me to come with you?"

"I'm sure." He wasn't going to put her in danger.

She gazed at him, worry darkening her eyes. "Be careful," she breathed.

"I'll be okay," he promised, hoping it was true. He knew what it was like to wait for a loved one who never returned, and he wouldn't wish it on Slate for anything. Stiffening, he determined that he was going to be back at her side by dawn. "I promise."

He nodded to the others, then turned and headed for the slope. Breaking into a run, he plunged into the bracken and headed toward the pine forest.

As he neared the edge of the pines, he tasted the air. He winced as he smelled the dank odor of decaying mushrooms and followed the scent, moving silently through the shadows, until he found a patch of wilted ink caps at the foot of a tree.

Wrinkling his nose, he lay down on the mushrooms, shuddering as he felt their rotting flesh collapse beneath his weight and squish into his fur. He stood up and shook out his pelt. The rankness of their scent would disguise his.

Gray Wing headed for the edge of the pines, ducking as he emerged from their shelter. The moon and stars were covered by cloud. Fern would be curled up in her nest, fast asleep. Would he have to wait like last time, to catch her on patrol? As the grass beneath his paws turned to mossy peat, he slowed. He could just make out the marsh grass rising ahead. The wall of the rogues' camp was half-hidden by the dip. He veered away, heading for the willow copse, and climbed the slope, then crouched between the hazel thickets once again.

Blinking in the darkness, he pricked his ears and listened. He stiffened as an owl's hoot echoed across the stretch of marshland. Wings fluttered far above his head, and the owl swooped, dipping over the boggy land, silent as it glided across the grass. Gray Wing watched it as it pulled up. It seemed to stall, turning its wings to slow itself and stretching out its claws. The shriek of prey cut through the air as the owl grabbed something and lifted into the sky, tracing a long, slow circle against the dark night as it headed back to the trees. Gray Wing strained his neck, following the owl with his gaze, his belly rumbling as he glimpsed a small shape wriggling in its claws. As the owl disappeared among the branches overhead, the grass below Gray Wing rustled.

Gray Wing snapped his head around, pelt bristling. A shape was moving up the slope toward him. He drew back into the hazel thicket, pressing his belly to the ground, and unsheathed his claws.

"Gray Wing!"

His heart seemed to burst with relief as he recognized Fern's mew. Two green eyes flashed at him through the darkness. He began to slide out of his hiding place, hesitating suddenly. Was this a trap? He glanced beyond Fern, scanning the slope for other shapes. Then he tasted the air, frustrated as the stench of rotting ink caps bathed his tongue.

Fern snorted. "You smell foul," she hissed as she stopped a tail-length from the hazel thicket. "It was the stink that woke me up. I guessed it was you. We don't get many walking mushrooms around here."

"Are you alone?" Gray Wing breathed, hoping he could still trust her.

"Of course I'm alone!" Her mew was indignant. "Do you think I risked my pelt just to betray you now?" Her eyes flashed with anger.

Gray Wing slid out of the thicket and stopped in front of her. "I'm sorry," he breathed. "It's just that I don't like coming here."

"You should try living here," she grunted.

"Why don't you leave if you hate it?" Gray Wing stared in wonder at the young she-cat.

"I would if I thought there was anywhere safe from Slash." She glanced over her shoulder, then slunk past Gray Wing and headed deeper into the copse. She led him to a clearing beyond the hazel thickets. "The farther away we are from camp the better," she whispered. "If your stink woke *me* up, it might wake up someone else."

"I was trying to disguise my scent." Gray Wing's pelt felt hot with embarrassment.

"It worked," Fern snorted. "You smell worse than a badger."

"At least I found you," Gray Wing pointed out. "I thought I was going to have to wait."

"Smelling like death is a great signal," Fern muttered. "But you might want to tone it down a bit next time." She blinked at him through the darkness. "Why are you here?"

"I need information," he told her.

"What about?" Fern tipped her head to one side. "You rescued Star Flower, didn't you?" She leaned closer. "Is she okay?"

"Yes."

"Has she had her kits yet?"

Gray Wing's tail bristled as he remembered the traumatic escape. "Yes. Two she-kits and a tom."

Fern purred. "I'm glad. I wish I could tell Juniper and Willow. They've been worried about her."

Gray Wing frowned, confused. "Who are Juniper and Willow?"

"Just campmates." Fern shrugged.

"Why do they care about Star Flower and her kits?" They'd helped hold her captive, hadn't they?

Fern lifted her chin indignantly. "We're not all fox-hearts, you know!"

Gray Wing shifted his paws, even more confused. "Then why do you stay with Slash?"

Fern narrowed her eyes. "Why do *you* give him your prey?"

"He steals it!"

"Why not fight for it?" Fern pressed.

"He . . ." Gray Wing hesitated. He didn't want to admit that Slash's rogues outnumbered them.

"Slash knows how to make other cats do what he wants," Fern growled. "If you go against Slash, you take a big risk. It's easier to go along with whatever he says."

"But you could *leave*."

"I tried that, remember?" Fern glared at him. "I couldn't sleep at night. Every time I heard a rustle in the brambles, I thought it was Slash coming to get me. He doesn't like disloyalty."

Gray Wing stared at her, his heart twisting as he realized what a huge risk she was taking just by talking to him.

She went on. "He also doesn't like it when his plans are ruined. He's been all wound up since you rescued Star Flower. He keeps going on about making you all pay."

"We guessed," Gray Wing growled darkly. "He's been stealing our prey again."

"I know." Fern dropped her gaze. "I've never eaten so well."

"We're going hungry."

Fern stared at him, her eyes widening with worry. "He won't stop, you know. Not until he's driven you out."

"No one's driving us out," Gray Wing growled.

"Are you going to fight him?

"If we have to." Gray Wing held her gaze. "But we need to know how many cats we face."

Fern glanced away.

"I understand if you don't want to help us." Gray Wing guessed that she was scared of telling him anything that would make her campmates vulnerable. "But if we just had some idea of how many we were fighting . . ."

Fern turned back, her gaze intent. "If you stood up to Slash, some of us might stand up to him too."

"Really?" Gray Wing's pelt prickled with hope. "Do you think your campmates would actually help fight him?"

Fern drew away. "It's hard to say. He has some loyal friends, but a lot of us think it was cruel to hold Star Flower in her condition. He risked the lives of unborn kits. A cat who'd do that is capable of anything. We're scared to stay but even more scared to leave. Who knows what he'd do if he ever found us again?"

"Will *you* fight with us?" Gray Wing pressed.

Fern looked away. "I can't promise anything. Slash is powerful. And he's hungry for revenge. Standing up to him means risking our lives. None of us want to die."

Gray Wing's heart sank. "Especially for cats you've never met."

Fern glanced up at him. "I wish I could promise to help you, but I can't even do that. I just wanted you to know that Slash may not be as powerful as he thinks."

"I understand." Gray Wing wished he could persuade this young cat to leave with him. He felt sure he could keep her safe. But it wasn't enough for him to believe it. *She* needed to believe it too.

Fern was gazing at him with frightened eyes. "If your groups fight together, you'll outnumber us," she confessed. "But Slash is determined and cruel, and he will make us pay for cowardice and disloyalty with our own blood. If there is a battle, it will be a hard one. Slash will fight to the death, and he'll expect us to do the same."

"What if we just waited?" Gray Wing suggested hopefully. "Do you think he might move on?"

Fern snorted. "Slash enjoys his anger. He'll hold on to it for as long as it makes him feel powerful and he gets your prey." She lowered her voice to a whisper. "I think he *wants* a battle, and if stealing your prey doesn't make you fight him, he'll find another way to start it." She shrugged apologetically. "Either way, you're going to lose."

"Not if some of your campmates join us."

"I can't promise that. If it looks like a battle you can't win, none of us will dare join you."

The owl hooted again.

Fern's tail quivered. "I should get back. If anyone notices I'm missing, they'll want to know where I've been."

Gray Wing gazed at her. "Come with me."

She shook her head. "I have kin here who will suffer if I leave."

Gray Wing blinked. "Why would *your kin* suffer?"

"He'll blame my sister for my disloyalty." Fern turned to leave. "Be careful, Gray Wing. Slash is determined to make you pay."

"What for?" Helplessness swamped Gray Wing.

Fern stared at him blankly. "For being happy, I guess."

He watched her disappear between the trees. *Is that how our groups seem to Slash? Happy?* He thought of the hollow on the moor and his nest. Slate would be there, staring into the darkness as she waited for his return. A purr rumbled softly in his throat. He couldn't imagine any cat waiting hopefully for Slash. His campmates lived in fear of him. He stole to feel powerful. No cat who lived like that could be happy.

Gray Wing wove between the willows, quickening his pace as he slipped from the copse and began to cross the marshland. Breaking into a run, he raced for the pines, relieved to slip into their shadow. He skirted Tall Shadow's camp and headed for the moor. His chest tightened with every step. But he had to get home. Slate would be worried. Ignoring his wheezing, he pushed on. Anger surged beneath his pelt. Why couldn't he *breathe?*

It must be the cold night air, he reasoned. With a sudden pang, he longed for the days when he could race from forest to moor and back again with ease.

By the time he reached the hollow, he was struggling for every breath. He slowed as he crossed the grass outside the entrance. He wanted to catch his breath before he padded into camp. He glanced at the forest behind him. The treetops were turning pink beneath the rising sum.

"Gray Wing!" Slate's call took him by surprise. She darted from the camp and wove around him, purring loudly. "I was so worried."

"I told you I'd be okay," he puffed.

"You need to rest." Slate began to guide him into camp.

"I have to talk to Wind Runner first." He struggled to speak. "Did you find Fern?"

"Yes." He headed for Wind Runner's den.

The brown she-cat slid out as he neared, her eyes bright. "What did she say?"

"She . . ." Gray Wing stopped, panting for air.

"Wait until you get your breath back," Wind Runner ordered.

Gray Wing sat down, feeling the moments pass as he willed his chest to loosen.

Slate settled beside him, her eyes clouding with worry. Wind Runner paced around them, the fur pricking around her neck.

At last, Gray Wing found breath enough to speak. "Fern says that if the groups join together, we'll outnumber them. And she says that Slash's campmates fear him. They might not fight for him if there was a battle."

Wind Runner's eyes lit up. "Then we can beat him?"

Gray Wing shook his head. "She couldn't promise that they'd betray him. They're scared of him, and with good reason. Slash is out for revenge, and he's dangerous. We need to be on guard."

Slate pressed against Gray Wing. "Is he going to *attack*?"

"She said he might," Gray Wing told her. "We must have patrols watching the camp at all times. We need to be prepared for anything."

Wind Runner glanced toward the camp entrance. "I'll post guards day and night."

"I'll take first watch." Slate blinked at her eagerly.

Wind Runner shook her head. "You've been up all night waiting." Her gaze moved to Gray Wing. "You both need to rest. Spotted Fur can stand guard." She flicked her tail toward Gray Wing's nest. "Go and get some sleep."

Grateful, Gray Wing heaved himself to his paws. Slate pressed against him as he padded to their nest. The heather felt fresh as he climbed inside. "Did you line it while I was gone?" he asked.

"I knew you'd be tired when you got home, and I wanted you to have somewhere comfortable to rest."

Gray Wing purred as he curled up in the soft heather. Slate climbed in after him and snuggled down beside him.

Exhausted, Gray Wing closed his eyes, relieved to feel Slate's warmth against him. For a moment he pitied Slash. No cat that cruel could have felt love like this. Then his pity gave way to anger. Why did Slash want to make others suffer? His mind began to drift as tiredness pulled him toward sleep. Images of the moor, bright with heather, flashed in his mind. His thoughts jumbled; the pink heather turned red with blood as Gray Wing slipped into troubled dreams.

CHAPTER 9

❧

Clear Sky scuffed at the leaves that had drifted into the crook of an oak root. He sniffed their moldy scent, and his heart sank. Not even a trace of fresh prey. He glanced at Sparrow Fur, who was wriggling her way beneath a bramble. "Any sign of prey over there?" he called. Sparrow Fur backed out, whipping her tail free as it snagged on a thorn. She sat up and stared at Clear Sky. "All I can smell are rotting leaves."

Clear Sky frowned. "Me too." He glanced over to where they'd hidden the scrawny rabbit they'd caught earlier. It was hardly enough to feed one cat, let alone the whole group.

Sparrow Fur shook out her pelt. "We should have brought Blossom and Acorn Fur."

"I want the camp well guarded," Clear Sky reminded her. "Besides, more hunters leave more scent. They might have frightened the prey away."

Sparrow Fur snorted. "*What* prey?"

Clear Sky didn't answer. She was right. They had been out since dawn, and now the sun was shining high above the trees, against a cloudless sky. He wondered if Star Flower had let the kits leave the den. They had been begging to explore the camp, but they were still so small. And he wanted to be there when they took their first steps beyond the nest. He had almost sent Thorn hunting with Sparrow Fur and stayed behind. It had been hard enough leaving Star Flower and the kits the night before for the meeting at the four trees hollow. He longed to be with them now. But he was the group's leader. He couldn't stay in his den and let his campmates do every patrol.

"Clear Sky! Look!" Sparrow Fur hissed under her breath.

He jerked his muzzle toward her. The tortoiseshell she-cat was staring at a patch of dry ferns a tree-length away. He followed her gaze. A fat squirrel was sifting through the leaves with its forepaws. After scrabbling deep, it dragged up a nut and began to inspect it.

Clear Sky's heart leaped. He dropped into a hunting crouch. Leaves rustled softly as Sparrow Fur tiptoed to his side.

"You head to that side of the beech," he told her, jerking his muzzle to show her the way. "I'll take the other. We mustn't let it escape."

Sparrow Fur nodded and began to slowly creep forward, her belly fur skimming the ground.

Clear Sky's pelt prickled with excitement. The warm scent of squirrel filled his nose. His belly growled with hunger as he slunk forward. Tail down and spine low, he moved as silently as a snake, placing his paws on the dampest leaves so no crunch would betray his approach.

He felt for the breeze with his ear tips, relieved when he found he was upwind of his quarry. Glancing out of the corner of his eye, he saw Sparrow Fur's tail as she disappeared around the other side of the beech. He skirted the roots, veering wide. Whichever way the squirrel ran, they'd catch it.

A twig cracked. Clear Sky tensed. Sparrow Fur must have crushed it beneath her paw. The squirrel straightened, snapping its head one way, then the other. Panic flashed in its eyes, and it darted forward.

As Sparrow Fur pelted after it, excitement surged beneath Clear Sky's pelt. He leaped, kicking out leaves behind him. The ground blurred beneath him as he hared after the squirrel. It was racing for the base of an oak. It bobbed over the jutting roots and shot upward.

Clear Sky jumped, throwing his forepaws up. He unsheathed his claws and hooked them into the squirrel's pelt, plucked it from the bark before it could escape his reach, and dragged it to the ground. Ducking quickly, he gave it a killing bite. Its spine crunched between his jaws. The sweet warmth of blood bathed his tongue as the squirrel fell limp.

Thank you. He was grateful to the forest. He would have enough prey for Star Flower and more to share with the others.

"Great catch." Sparrow Fur was panting. She stared at the squirrel, her eyes shining.

"Let's collect the rabbit and take our catch back to camp," Clear Sky decided.

"Okay." Sparrow Fur licked her lips, still gazing at the squirrel.

"Do you want to carry it?" Clear Sky pawed it toward her. She'd been hunting all morning. She deserved a taste of blood on her tongue before they reached camp.

Sparrow Fur purred, hooking the squirrel between her jaws. Lifting her head, she trotted away, the squirrel's bushy tail trailing behind her.

Clear Sky followed. The group could share the squirrel, and Star Flower could have the rabbit to herself. It was small, but it would be enough. She needed prey to stay strong. Their kits were growing fast on her milk. *I'll take care of you all.* Joy warmed his pelt, taking him by surprise. He'd never felt so protective of anyone before. Then he remembered the grief that had flashed momentarily in Thunder's gaze when he'd come to see the kits. Clear Sky shifted his paws guiltily. He'd never felt this way about his firstborn son. He realized now that *Thunder* had once been as helpless as Tiny Branch, and he'd had no father to protect him. His mother, Storm, had cared for him alone, hunting for her own prey. A chill swept Clear Sky's pelt. *How could I have been so cruel?*

He felt Sparrow Fur's gaze on him. She'd stopped and was staring at him, the squirrel hanging from her jaws.

There wasn't time to dwell on the past now. Star Flower hadn't eaten since yesterday. And he wanted to organize another hunting patrol. If *one* squirrel had decided to come down from the trees, there might be more. He hurried after her.

Sparrow Fur led the way to the leaves where they'd buried the rabbit. He slid past her as they reached it and began to sift through them, feeling for the soft body beneath. He touched bare earth. *Where is it?* He sat back on his haunches, worry sparking in his belly. "It's gone."

"It can't be." The squirrel thumped the earth as Sparrow Fur dropped it. She plunged her paws into the leaves and scrabbled beneath them.

"Could a fox have stolen it?" Clear Sky tasted the air. He lowered his voice to a whisper. "Sparrow Fur, watch out."

Sparrow Fur stopped searching for the rabbit and shot him an alarmed look. "What's wrong?" Her eyes glittered with worry as she read his warning gaze. She opened her mouth to taste the air.

A drawling mew rang from between the trees. "Are you looking for something?" Slash strolled out from behind an elm, his eyes shining with amusement.

Clear Sky turned, hackles up. "Where is it?"

Slash glanced to one side and a black-and-brown rogue padded out. The scrawny rabbit dangled from his jaws. "Beetle found your pitiful catch," Slash sneered.

Another rogue followed Beetle from behind the tree, his black-and-white pelt rippling.

Slash went on. "Poor Splinter was upset that you'd only caught one." He glanced at the black-and-white rogue. "Weren't you, Splinter?"

Splinter flicked his tail. "I thought you were supposed to be great hunters." He glanced derisively at the scrawny rabbit as a fourth rogue padded out.

Snake. Clear Sky shifted his paws uneasily as he recognized the striped tabby. Snake had belonged to Clear Sky's group once, but his true loyalties had been with One Eye.

He narrowed his eyes. They were outnumbered. Perhaps he should have brought a bigger patrol after all.

Slash's gaze flashed to the squirrel at Sparrow Fur's paws. "I guess it's better than nothing."

Sparrow Fur hissed. "We didn't catch it for *you*. We caught it for our campmates."

Slash padded forward and circled Clear Sky and Sparrow Fur slowly. "You're sharing your prey with us, remember?"

"We told you at the meeting that you'd have to catch your own," Clear Sky snarled.

"Really?" Slash eyes lit up with a malicious glint. "I think I remember you promising that you'd give me all your prey." The mangy brown tom suddenly dropped into a cowering crouch and mimicked a desperate mew. "Oh, Slash. *I'll* hunt for you! You can have *all* my prey. Just give me Star Flower!"

Clear Sky felt his pelt burn as he remembered pleading desperately at the meeting. He didn't dare look at Sparrow Fur. Instead he glared at Slash. "I got her back," he hissed. "Which means I don't have to give you anything!"

Slash straightened and stalked back to his campmates. "You got what you want, and so now I get what *I* want." He stared at the prey at Sparrow Fur's paws. "Give it to me." His gaze burned into Sparrow Fur's.

Sparrow Fur lifted her chin. "Never!"

Clear Sky curled his claws into the ground. Blood roared in his ears. Every instinct told him to hurl himself at Slash and rip his fur off. *But what about Star Flower? If you're hurt, who will protect her and your kits?* Heart pounding, he forced himself to stay still.

Sparrow Fur looked at him in surprise. "We're not going to let them take it, are we?"

Slash padded closer. "It belongs to us."

Sparrow Fur placed her paw on the squirrel protectively. "No, it doesn't!"

Slash stopped a muzzle-length from Clear Sky and glared at him. "Give us the squirrel and we'll leave you alone."

"For now," Splinter growled softly behind him.

Snake purred with amusement. "Poor Clear Sky. You never *were* much of a leader."

Rage boiled in Clear Sky's belly. Every hair on his pelt itched to fight these rogues. But he couldn't take risks. He backed away, nodding to Sparrow Fur. "Let them take it."

Sparrow Fur blinked at him in disbelief. "Really?"

Clear Sky gazed coolly at Slash as he answered her. "We're outnumbered, Sparrow Fur. Fighting would be a waste of energy. Let these lazy fox-hearts take our prey. We can catch more while they're growing fat and soft."

Slash flattened his ears.

Satisfaction washed over Clear Sky's pelt. He'd angered the rogue. "Here." He pawed the squirrel toward Slash. "This should fill your bellies until you learn how to catch your own."

Slash's eyes blazed. Showing his teeth, he lashed out with a paw. Clear Sky saw the blow coming and began to duck. But Sparrow Fur was faster. Diving like a hawk, she caught Slash's paw on her shoulder. She heaved it away, unbalancing Slash, then spun and raked her claws across the rogue's scarred muzzle.

Slash yowled with rage, and Snake darted forward and

slashed at Sparrow Fur's tail. As she twisted to face the yellow-eyed tom, Slash reared and slammed his paws onto her spine. Hooking his claws into her pelt, he dragged her onto her side.

Snake hissed. "Kill her!"

Beetle and Splinter split apart, their eyes widening with excitement as Slash leaped onto Sparrow Fur and began lashing at her with his forepaws.

"Get off!" Clear Sky tensed, ready to drag the rogue from his campmate, but he hesitated. If he joined in, then the others would too, and he wanted to *avoid* a fight. He grabbed the squirrel and tossed it at Snake. "Just take this and go!"

Slash paused. Sparrow Fur squirmed beneath him, lashing out clumsily as he leaped clear and landed beside Splinter. The squirrel lay at Beetle's paws. Slash looked at it, then glanced at Sparrow Fur.

The she-cat scrambled to her paws, hackles high. She glowered at Slash, a low growl rolling in her throat.

Clear Sky stepped in front of her and guided her away. "It's not worth the fight," he murmured.

She frowned, anger clear in her gaze. "But they've taken everything we caught," she whispered.

Clear Sky stared in dismay as Splinter picked up the squirrel between his jaws. Beetle scooped up the scrawny rabbit.

"Thanks, Clear Sky." Slash curled his lip. "Next time, be a little more polite, or you might get hurt." He turned and stalked away. Snake followed, Beetle and Splinter falling in behind.

Clear Sky could feel himself shaking with rage as he

watched them walk away with his catch. "You might have won this time!" he spat at Slash. "But one day you will feel my claws in your throat." He froze as Slash turned and stared at him coldly.

For a moment the sounds of the forest disappeared. He could only hear his own heart pounding, and a voice in the back of his mind: *Think of Star Flower and your kits. They need you.*

Slash snatched the scrawny rabbit from Beetle and carried it back to Clear Sky. With a snort, he flung it near Clear Sky's paws. "Give this to Star Flower." His growl was thick with derision. "Tell her it's a gift from me."

Rage throbbed in Clear Sky's belly. He dug his claws deep into the ground as Slash turned and stalked away. *One day, you will pay for this.*

As the rogues disappeared between the trees, Sparrow Fur glanced at the pitiful rabbit. "I guess we ought to take it. It won't feed many mouths, but it's better than nothing."

Clear Sky hardly heard her, but he turned as the fresh scent of blood reached his nose. The fur on her cheek was dark and wet. "You're hurt," he meowed, shaking himself from his thoughts. "Let's head back to camp so you can clean your wounds properly." Gratitude stirred in his chest. "Thanks for defending me," he added. It wasn't the first time the feisty young she-cat had leaped to save him. She'd fought for him when One Eye had tried to drive him from the group, too.

Sparrow Fur shrugged and poked the rabbit with her paw. "It's not much to show for a morning's hunting."

"I'll send out another patrol this afternoon," Clear Sky told her.

"And what if Slash steals from them too?" Worry clouded the she-cat's gaze.

"We'll deal with that if it happens." He scooped up the rabbit, swallowing back the resentment that rose in his throat. How dare Slash give him his own catch as though it were a gift? He wanted to toss it away and catch fresh meat. But with so little prey running in the forest, he had no choice. Star Flower needed every morsel she could get.

Growling softly to himself, he headed toward camp.

Star Flower refused to touch the rabbit until the afternoon patrol returned. As the sun sank slowly behind the trees, Clear Sky paced outside the den, listening for the sound of the hunting party. They should be back soon. He'd sent out a big patrol—Blossom, Birch, Nettle, Quick Water, and Thorn. He wanted to make sure that if the rogues attacked again, they wouldn't be able to steal whatever the patrol had caught.

Clear Sky stopped pacing. He poked his head into the den once more. "Please take just a mouthful." He pushed the rabbit closer to Star Flower.

She shook her head. "I can't eat while the others go hungry."

Tiny Branch clambered onto his mother's flank. "We're not hungry."

Dew Petal and Flower Foot were wrestling beside her belly. Dew Petal struggled free of her sister's paws and grabbed her tail. "I win!" she squeaked.

Star Flower purred. "See?" She blinked at Clear Sky. "They're getting plenty of milk, and they're as strong as badgers."

Clear Sky frowned. He could see bones showing sharply through Star Flower's pelt. "But what about you?"

"I've been through worse," she assured him.

Clear Sky glanced at the scrawny rabbit lying untouched at her side. Was it cruel to leave it where Star Flower could smell its fresh-kill scent? He'd been trying to tempt her, but if she refused to be tempted, perhaps he should move it away so she didn't have to look at it.

As worry wormed in his belly, the bramble entrance rattled. Paw steps thrummed into camp. "They're back." Hope flashed beneath his pelt. He turned eagerly from the den, pushed through the bracken, and leaped down the steep slope.

Blossom was standing in the middle of the clearing, two mice at her paws. Clear Sky looked past her hopefully at Birch, Nettle, Quick Water, and Thorn. Were they carrying any prey?

A vole hung from Nettle's mouth.

Was that it?

Clear Sky tried not to look disappointed. At least they'd caught something. Perhaps they'd caught more and been ambushed by Slash. "Did you see the rogues?"

Blossom shook her head. "No sign of them."

Nettle padded forward. "I know it's not a big catch," he apologized. "But we did our best."

"Of course you did." Frustration rippled through Clear Sky's pelt. Where had all the prey gone?

Quick Water shook out her pelt. "It's leaf-bare," she reminded him. "Don't you remember the cold seasons in the mountains? There was a time when the Tribe didn't eat for five days."

Clear Sky twitched his tail crossly. "That's why we came to the forest! So we'd have prey no matter what season it was."

Thorn padded across the clearing and settled in his favorite spot between the roots of the beech. "Sometimes prey doesn't make it through the first snows," he meowed matter-of-factly.

"We'll survive," Nettle chipped in. "River Ripple will share his fish. Or we could scavenge in Twolegplace. Don't forget, most of us have lived as loners. We know what it's like to suffer through difficult times."

Clear Sky gazed around his cats. "But living as a group, surely life should be easier?"

Quick Water blinked at him sympathetically. "Hunger is easier to bear when you're surrounded by campmates. Why do you think the Tribe survived so long despite the hardship of the mountains?"

Thorn sat down and began to wash. "We have warm nests," he mewed between laps. "And the hope that tomorrow's hunting will be better."

Unless the rogues take it, Clear Sky thought darkly.

Blossom glanced toward the bracken that shielded Clear Sky's den. "Did Star Flower eat the rabbit?"

"She won't eat until she knows the rest of you have food," Clear Sky told her.

"Then give her this." Blossom tossed him one of the mice. "We can share the rabbit and the rest of our catch. Tell her we have plenty. We'll make sure she doesn't go hungry."

Clear Sky blinked at her gratefully. He knew that one scrawny rabbit, a mouse, and a vole wouldn't fill every belly. But if Star Flower was well fed, the kits would have milk. "Thank you."

Quick Water purred. "It's good to have kits in the camp again. They bring hope."

Clear Sky dipped his head, grateful for his campmates' optimism. He picked up the mouse. It swung from his jaws as he leaped up the slope and headed for his den.

"Blossom says you should eat this." He dropped the mouse beside Star Flower.

She blinked at him through the shadows of the den. "Did they catch much?"

"Enough for everyone to eat something." Even if it *was* just a mouthful each.

Star Flower narrowed her eyes suspiciously. Did she know he was exaggerating?

"I think they would appreciate the rabbit," he told her quietly, avoiding her eye.

Star Flower nosed it toward him. "Then they should have it. Make sure Birch and Alder get a bite. I know rabbit is their favorite."

He purred, pressing his cheek to hers, then picked up the rabbit. Anger pricked in his belly as Slash's words rang in his mind: *Give this to Star Flower.*

How would he stop the rogues from stealing their prey?

He lifted his chin. Tomorrow they would start training to fight, as Thunder had suggested. But would that be enough? He hurried to the clearing and dropped the rabbit beside the meager prey pile, then headed back to his den.

"Aren't you eating anything?" Birch called after him.

He shook his head. "I'll eat tomorrow," he replied without looking back. His belly felt tight with hunger, and as he reached his den, he smelled fresh mouse blood. Star Flower had eaten it already. She must have been starving. Tomorrow he would hunt again. He slid into the nest and settled beside Star Flower. She was lying drowsily in her nest while the kits clambered over her.

"Clear Sky?" Tiny Branch leaped onto his flank. "Can we leave the den tomorrow?"

"Yes." Clear Sky stretched his muzzle forward and nudged the kit's cheek.

Tiny Branch's tail quivered excitedly. "Did you hear that?" he squeaked, leaping onto Dew Petal and Flower Foot. "We can go outside tomorrow!"

"Finally!" Dew Petal cheered.

She tumbled into the mossy depths of the nest, tugging Flower Foot and Tiny Branch with her.

Happiness filled Clear Sky's empty belly as they wrestled beside him. And yet he couldn't relax. The idea of his kits training to go out into the world made him uneasy. Because as long as Slash and his rogues roamed the forest, none of his cats were safe.

CHAPTER 10

Thunder gazed across the four trees hollow. The cats from the other groups milled around him, waiting for the meeting to start. The sun glittered through the bare branches of the oaks, bathing the hollow in cold, bright light.

Lightning Tail's breath brushed his ear fur. "This place looks bigger in the daylight."

Thunder purred softly. "Are you missing the dark?" He knew that Lightning Tail enjoyed melting into the shadows and watching the other cats. His friend often teased him about his white paws and orange pelt. *Too white to hide in shadow and too orange to hide in snow.*

Lightning Tail leaned closer. "I don't know why Clear Sky called a meeting so soon after the last one."

"We'll find out soon enough," Thunder answered.

His father was pacing one edge of the clearing. Star Flower watched him, a few tail-lengths away, through green eyes. Thunder's pelt pricked with curiosity. How had he persuaded the queen to leave her kits?

Wind Runner and Gorse Fur were shifting impatiently from paw to paw. Wind Runner had explained that Gray

Wing had wanted to come, but his breathing was bad today. Thunder pictured the gray tom in his nest; he must be very ill to miss a meeting. *Why?* Had he worn himself out hunting? Or was his breathing growing steadily worse? Whatever sickness ailed him, Gray Wing seemed unable to escape its slowly tightening grip. Thunder pushed the thought away, his gaze flicking to Tall Shadow. The forest cat sat as still as stone beside Jagged Peak, while River Ripple and Shattered Ice gazed calmly at Clear Sky.

Wind Runner whisked her tail. "So?" She stared questioningly at Clear Sky. "Why did you ask us to come?"

Thunder pricked his ears as Clear Sky stopped pacing and faced the moor cat.

"My cats are growing hungry." His gaze flicked around the others. "We've tried defending our prey, but the rogues fight like foxes."

Tall Shadow curled her lip. "They fight like *cowards!*"

"But they win," Wind Runner growled. "We've lost half our catches to them in the past few days."

Thunder narrowed his eyes thoughtfully. "Then *we* must learn how to fight like foxes too."

"No." River Ripple's tail swept the ground. "Foxes have cruel hearts. If we fight like foxes, we will become like foxes."

Jagged Peak snorted. "Then how do we beat the rogues?"

River Ripple's eyes gleamed. "We must learn to fight better than foxes."

"How?" Thunder blinked at him. Lightning Tail had been training his campmates how to rear higher and swipe harder. What else could they do?

Lightning Tail blinked excitedly at Thunder. "Do you remember the trick we use when we run into a Twoleg dog in the forest?"

Thunder paused. "The thunder-and-lightning move?"

Lightning Tail nodded eagerly. "We could use it to fight the rogues."

Thunder frowned, confused. "How? We only use it to escape."

"But if we changed it a little—"

Thunder interrupted, his heart lifting as he understood. "Of course! A bunch of rogues is no worse than a dog. I pull them one way," he began.

"And I attack from behind!" Lightning Tail finished.

Wind Runner leaned forward. "Show us."

Thunder nodded toward Gorse Fur, River Ripple, and Shattered Ice. "You pretend to be the rogues. Imagine I've just caught a juicy pigeon." Thunder's belly growled as he imagined the plump bird at his paws.

River Ripple, Shattered Ice, and Gorse Fur padded toward him, ears flattened menacingly.

Thunder blinked at them, snatched up the imaginary bird, and turned. Running across the clearing, he heard paws pattering after him. He ran long enough for Lightning Tail to get in position; then he spun, his paws skidding, and reared.

Shattered Ice, River Ripple, and Gorse Fur scrambled to a surprised halt in front of him.

Snarling, Thunder backed away. He could see Lightning

Tail racing up behind the three cats. With a yowl, the black tom flew past Shattered Ice, sliding his paws over the river cat's gray-and-white flank.

Shattered Ice turned in surprise, but Lightning Tail was already circling away toward Gorse Fur. He leaped the moor cat, kicking his spine with his hind paws as he sailed over him. Thunder dived on River Ripple as the river cat blinked in confusion. It was even easier than Thunder had expected to unbalance the stocky tom and tackle him to the ground.

He leaped off and blinked at the three ruffled toms as River Ripple scrambled to his paws.

Lightning Tail raced to his side. "They looked as confused as any Twoleg dog," he purred.

Gorse Fur shook out his pelt.

Shattered Ice shifted his paws, his pelt pricking. "Nice move!"

Thunder flicked his tail happily. "Surprise is the sharpest claw."

River Ripple nodded approvingly. "And it works even when we're outnumbered."

"Exactly." Lightning Tail lifted his chin.

Gorse Fur's eyes lit up. "It's a bit like the move we use on rabbits." He was staring excitedly at Wind Runner.

She hurried toward him. "Of course!"

Clear Sky pricked his ears. "Show us."

"It's easier to catch a rabbit if we can separate it from its group and tire it out," Wind Runner explained. She marched around Thunder, Lightning Tail, Shattered Ice, and River Ripple, nudging them closer together. "You can be the rabbits—" She paused. "I mean the *rogues*."

She backed away as Thunder flattened his ears, pretending to be Slash. Shattered Ice hissed beside him, while River Ripple and Lightning Tail lifted their hackles menacingly.

Wind Runner nodded toward Gorse Fur. He seemed to read her thoughts and broke into a run. Thunder twisted his head as the tom circled them, moving fast. Frowning, he wondered what in the stars Gorse Fur was doing. Dirt sprayed beneath Gorse Fur's paws as he hared around the bunched toms; then suddenly he veered and barged between Thunder and Lightning Tail. Thunder blinked as he found himself separated from the others. A paw batted his cheek. He spun in surprise and saw Wind Runner dash past him.

He froze. *What do I do now?* Gorse Fur was still circling Lightning Tail, Shattered Ice, and River Ripple, dodging as they aimed clumsy blows at him. *What would a rogue do?* Wind Runner raced past him again, grazing his cheek with a second swipe. *Chase her!*

Thunder hared after the wiry brown she-cat as she plunged into the bracken. Diving after her, he pounded up the slope. Suddenly he heard paws behind him. He glanced backward and saw Gorse Fur on his tail. *Am I chasing or being chased?* Confused, he kept running, tracking Wind Runner up the slope and then down until he was breathless. She burst into the clearing. He followed, Gorse Fur at his heels. Thunder ran harder, chasing Wind Runner toward the oaks. As he neared, she spun and faced him. He skidded to a halt and she started to pummel his muzzle. He reared to fight her off, realizing suddenly how breathless he was. Paws thumped him from behind. Thunder gasped as Gorse Fur leaped onto his back and tussled him to the ground.

Panting, Thunder thrashed his tail. "I give up!"

He struggled to his paws as Wind Runner and Gorse Fur backed away and fought to catch his breath. "You two are fast!" he puffed.

"We spend our days running the moors," Wind Runner reminded him.

Gorse Fur nodded, raising his voice so the others could hear. "You must *all* practice running. The rogues are lazy. I bet we are fitter than them already. With some training, we can be even stronger."

"That's not enough." Star Flower's mew took Thunder by surprise.

She padded past Jagged Peak and Tall Shadow and faced the group. "You have to learn how rogues fight."

Thunder frowned. "But I thought we weren't going to fight like foxes."

Star Flower met his gaze. "If you fight a fox, you must know how it thinks."

"How?" Jagged Peak tipped his head. "We can't see their thoughts."

Star Flower flicked her gaze toward him. "I am One Eye's daughter, remember? I know how they fight—using trickery and deceit. I can show you the kind of moves they use. I can teach you what to expect."

Clear Sky hurried to her side. "You're in no condition to teach battle moves."

Star Flower halted him with an emerald stare. "I'm as fit as the rest of you. If I can give birth to three kits, I can certainly teach battle moves." She nodded at Thunder. "Attack me."

Thunder blinked at her, his gaze flicking uncertainly to Clear Sky.

Clear Sky's tail twitched nervously. "Be careful," he warned.

Star Flower glared at her mate. "I'm not made out of cherry blossom," she snapped. She turned to Thunder, holding his gaze as she backed away from the group. She came to a stop in the middle of the clearing. "*Attack* me!"

Thunder shifted his paws uneasily. He would go easy on Star Flower. She must still be weary after her ordeal, and she wasn't used to fighting. He approached her slowly.

Her gaze flashed with impatience, but she said nothing.

Nearing her, Thunder lifted a forepaw, preparing to swipe lightly at her muzzle.

She lunged at him. A forepaw struck him hard on the top of his shoulder. Another slammed the same shoulder from the side. Thunder stumbled, shocked as his leg buckled beneath him. He thumped onto his chest, his shoulder numb where Star Flower had hit him. His leg was as limp as fresh-kill. He could hardly feel his paw.

He stared up at Star Flower as she backed away, lifting her gaze to the others. "Rogues like to lame their enemies first, then attack. It's a sneaky trick, but it's effective. If I attacked Thunder now, he'd only be able to defend himself with three paws. And he'd be pretty confused about what had happened. It gives a rogue all the time they need to deliver a far more damaging blow." She glanced down at Thunder. "Are you okay?"

Sensation was flooding back into his leg. He pushed himself to his paws, staggering slightly. His shoulder felt weak. He blinked at Star Flower, impressed. Even play fighting with Lightning Tail he had never been overpowered so quickly.

"Don't worry," Star Flower reassured him. "It'll be fine in a moment."

He shook out his paw, relieved to feel strength flooding back into it. Dipping his head respectfully, he backed away.

A loud purr rumbled in Clear Sky's throat. "I'm sorry, Star Flower. I underestimated you."

Wind Runner padded closer to the golden she-cat, her eyes sparking with interest. "Can you show me exactly where you hit Thunder?" she asked. "That is a great move."

Jagged Peak, Lightning Tail, and River Ripple moved closer as Star Flower laid one paw on top of Wind Runner's shoulder and another on the side.

"Hit the top first," Star Flower instructed. "A short, sharp blow. Then follow it up with a hefty swipe to the side. You need to hit the right spot. It numbs the leg instantly."

Thunder padded toward Lightning Tail. "Can I try it on you?"

Lightning Tail nodded, bracing as Thunder lifted a paw. Focusing hard, Thunder slapped one forepaw down on Lightning Tail's shoulder and swung his other into his side.

Lightning Tail buckled, and Thunder felt satisfaction flood through his pelt, swiftly followed by guilt. "Did I hurt you?"

"You crippled me." Lightning Tail glanced up at him reproachfully. Then his eyes flashed with amusement. "But it *is* a good move."

Star Flower blinked at him. "You don't have to use it if you don't want to, but you'll know what to look out for." She circled Thunder. "Try it on me," she ordered.

Thunder stared at her. "I can't."

Star Flower rolled her eyes. "Just *try* it!"

Thunder lifted a forepaw. *I guess it won't really injure her.* As he aimed a blow at her shoulder, she spun and butted him away with her flank. Thunder wobbled. With one forepaw raised and the other preparing a second blow, he was unbalanced. As he struggled to stay on his paws, Star Flower grazed his muzzle with a swipe.

He steadied himself, blinking. "That's smart."

Star Flower whisked her tail. "If a rogue tries to start an attack by aiming for your shoulder, that's how you counter it."

River Ripple padded forward. "I know a fishing move that might work too."

Tall Shadow pricked her ears. "Try it on me."

River Ripple faced the black she-cat. "Use Star Flower's move," he told her.

Tall Shadow lifted a forepaw. Before she could touch the river cat, he'd dived beneath her belly. Arching his back, he thumped his spine against her chest. She reeled away, her eyes widening with surprise.

"You moved so fast!" she puffed. "You winded me!"

"It's a good way to stun a fish. It makes them easier to grab," River Ripple explained.

Jagged Peak's eyes shone with excitement. "I have an idea." He padded between the others, limping on his weak hind leg.

Thunder narrowed his eyes. Jagged Peak was a good fighter considering his lameness. But what could he teach cats with four good paws?

Jagged Peak caught his eye. "I know what you're thinking."

Thunder shifted self-consciously. "I was only—"

Jagged Peak cut him off. "What you don't realize is that I can use my lameness to my advantage. When a cat faces me in battle, the first thing they see is my limp. I can see their expression change as they realize I am fighting with three paws, not four. They suddenly look as though they've already won the fight. They don't realize that I've been fighting on three paws for as long as I can remember, and I'm good at it."

Clear Sky frowned. "How does that help *us*?" he asked. "We're not lame."

"No," Jagged Peak agreed. "Not now. But what if you're injured in battle?"

Shattered Ice chipped in. "Never let another cat see you're injured. They'll know you're vulnerable."

Jagged Peak shook his head. "Make *sure* they see you're injured. They'll underestimate you." His gaze flashed to Star Flower. "We've already seen how easy it is to beat a cat when they underestimate you."

Thunder felt his pelt grow hot. Was Jagged Peak referring

to how easily Star Flower had unbalanced him?

Jagged Peak went on. "You must all practice fighting on three paws so that you are as strong on three as you are on four. If you're wounded in battle, your enemy won't expect strength. You can take them by surprise."

Thunder lifted a hind paw, trying to imagine what it was like fighting without the steadiness of all four legs. He was looking forward to practicing. Jagged Peak was right. It would be a useful skill.

Clear Sky stepped into the middle. "We've taught one another a lot today." His thick pelt was smooth. He looked less worried than he had at the beginning of the meeting. "Let's go home and share what we've learned with our camp-mates. Trainers should share all these moves with the younger cats. The rogues may think they're winning, but they haven't seen us fight yet." He lifted his chin. "When they do, they will realize that we're not the easy prey they think we are."

"Come on!" Thunder veered onto the track that headed for Clear Sky's forest.

"Where are we going?" Lightning Tail raced behind him.

"To find the rogue camp."

"Why?" Lightning Tail sounded surprised. "I thought we were heading home to teach the others our new moves."

"We can do that later." Thunder leaped a fallen branch, his paws skimming the mossy bark. "I want to see this rogue camp for myself. I have to know what we're up against."

"But we don't know where the camp is," Lightning Tail

cleared the branch and thumped onto the track behind him.

"Gray Wing said it was in the marshland beyond Tall Shadow's pines," Thunder told him. "Near some willows. It can't be hard to find."

"What if we run into the rogues?"

Thunder slowed and stopped. His friend had a point. The marsh might be swarming with rogues. His ears twitched self-consciously. He should have thought of it first. "Let's find prey and take it with us," he suggested hastily. "If we're caught, we can say we came to give it to Slash."

Lightning Tail frowned. "What if they don't believe us? We've never offered them prey before. They've always had to steal it from us."

"We'll *make* them believe us," Thunder insisted. He was determined for this plan to work. "If we grovel to Slash, he'll enjoy our humiliation so much he won't bother wondering whether we're telling the truth."

Lightning Tail grunted. "You must really want to see the rogue camp if you're willing to grovel to Slash."

Thunder lifted his muzzle, sniffing for prey. "With any luck, we won't be seen, and we won't have to grovel to any cat." He stiffened as he smelled mouse. Perhaps the stars were on their side after all. In this long, hungry quarter moon, he had almost begun to think their ancestors had stopped watching over them. He pricked his ears as Lightning Tail followed his gaze. "It smells like there's a mouse nest under that bramble."

Lightning Tail dropped into a crouch and stalked toward the tangled bush.

Thunder dropped low and, belly brushing the leafy forest floor, began to make a wide circle around the bush. "You flush them out, and I'll catch what you miss." He stopped behind the bush and waited for Lightning Tail to make his move.

The brambles rustled. Squinting in the afternoon sunlight, Thunder could see Lightning Tail's black pelt squirming beneath the branches. The mouse scent was warm and strong. Thunder licked his lips. Leaves swished as Lightning Tail darted deeper into the bush.

Frightened squeaks pierced Thunder's ear fur. He scanned the ground for movement. Brown fur flashed to one side. Thunder leaped, thorns snagging his pelt, and slammed his paws down onto the soft body of a fleeing mouse. He hooked his claws around it and drew it close for a killing bite.

The musky scent made his mouth water. Should they take their catch home? Thistle and Clover were starting to look thin. *No. I have to see the rogues' camp. We'll take our catch home when we've seen it.* Thunder sat up as Lightning Tail padded toward him. A dead mouse dangled from his jaws.

Thunder purred. "Come on. Let's head for the pines." He scooped his mouse up and headed away.

Crossing the Thunderpath was easy. There was no sign of monsters. The pine forest beyond felt gloomy after the oaks. The trees here still had their thick needle pelts, and little sunlight filtered through the canopy. How could Tall Shadow and her cats bear to live in such gloom? The smell of pinesap filled his nose, drowning the warm scent of mouse. He was relieved as the trees thinned and he saw marshland ahead. He stopped at the edge of the forest. Behind him, the sun was sinking fast, throwing long shadows across the tussocks of grass.

Lightning Tail stopped behind him and dropped his mouse. He nodded toward a stretch of trees crowding a slope at one edge of the marshland. "Is that the willow copse?"

The bare branches looked like willow, and there were no other trees beyond the pines. It must be the right place. Nodding, he carried his mouse from the cover of the pines. He followed the trail as it grew muddy underpaw. Lightning Tail's paw steps squelched behind him. Scanning the marshland, Thunder saw a patch of thick grass and reeds.

He dropped his mouse. "That's it," he whispered. Gray Wing had described the camp. *A ring of grass near willows.*

"How are we going to spy on the rogues without being seen?" Lightning Tail stopped beside him and blinked over the tussocks.

Thunder nodded toward the camp. "There are plenty of reeds to hide in." He grabbed his mouse and slunk forward, ears pricked.

Lightning Tail crept behind him.

Thunder held his breath as they neared. Rogue smells mingled with the damp evening air. Relief prickled through his pelt as the sun dipped behind the pines and shadow swallowed the marsh. He ducked lower, moving like a snake over the earth until he reached a clump of reeds. He slipped past them and slid between two tussocks.

He stiffened as he heard voices from the marsh grass beyond. They were right outside the camp wall!

He laid his mouse on the ground and signaled to Lightning Tail with his muzzle to do the same.

Lightning Tail dropped his mouse on top of Thunder's and blinked at his friend. "What now?" he whispered.

"We wait." Thunder pressed his belly to the earth and flattened his ears. Stiff marsh grass surrounded them. Lightning Tail's flank felt warm against his as the black tom wriggled down beside him.

"Look!" Lightning Tail's mew was barely more than a whisper. He was staring at the grass wall of the camp. Narrow gaps showed near the roots, and as the sun disappeared and moonlight bathed the marshland, Thunder saw the rogues' clearing glowing beyond the stems. Heart pounding, he squirmed closer until he could see a wide stretch of earth in the middle of the camp. Cats moved at the edges, murmuring in soft voices. Paw steps scuffed the earth nearby, and sleek, dark gray fur blocked his view. He smelled the fragrant scent of a she-cat and peered closer.

"Here!" A tom's mew rang across the camp, and something thudded on the earth beside the she-cat. She hopped out of the way. Thunder could see a scrawny starling on the ground. The she-cat sniffed at it, and Thunder saw the delicate outline of her muzzle. Her amber gaze rested, dismayed, on the starling. Then she jerked her head toward a tom at the center of the clearing.

Slash!

Thunder recognized the white slash across the forelegs of the mangy brown rogue.

The she-cat curled her lip. "We've got better prey than this," she hissed.

Slash eyed her coldly. "You're lucky you're getting anything, Violet," he snarled. "You're the weakest hunter in the group."

"That's not true!" Violet snapped back. "And at least I *hunt*. You *steal*."

Slash's ears twitched. "I'm just taking what's mine."

"You wouldn't be like this if Rain were still alive!"

Thunder heard grief thicken the she-cat's mew.

Slash snorted. "What difference would Rain have made? He was so dumb he got killed on a Thunderpath."

Violet flinched. "He was never dumb!"

"Taking you as a mate was the only smart decision he ever made." Slash's mew grew suspiciously soft. Thunder narrowed his eyes. The rogue leader was gazing hungrily at the she-cat. "Why don't *you* get smart, Violet, and let me take his place? You would not go hungry if you were a leader's mate."

"Never!" Violet picked up the starling and stalked away.

Thunder's claws itched. How dare Slash try to bully this beautiful she-cat into becoming his mate? He felt Lightning Tail move beside him. "Why do they stay loyal to such a fox-heart?"

Thunder didn't answer. He was watching Violet. Her fur had the rich darkness of storm clouds. Her long tail was thick and sleek. Her ears were wide and soft, framing her pretty face perfectly. The fur prickled along his spine as she padded toward a group of cats who were crouching in the shadows at the far side of the clearing.

Movement caught Thunder's eye. Slash was heading toward

a large prey pile. Thunder's belly felt hollow with hunger as he saw pigeons stacked on top of rabbits. Mice and shrews were strewn around the edge. Slash plucked a skinny frog from the bottom of the pile and flung it toward one of the cats beside Violet. Then he tossed a dried shrew to another. One piece at a time, he flung the scrawniest prey to his campmates. Then he flicked his tail toward two toms, who had been silently watching the camp from the head of the clearing.

"Splinter! Come and choose your meal."

A black-and-white tom hurried toward the prey pile, licking his lips. "Go ahead, Splinter." Slash's mew was indulgent. "You've done well today. You deserve something good to eat."

As Splinter dragged a plump pigeon from the pile, Slash nodded toward the second tom. "Hurry up, Beetle. This one's still warm." He pawed a heavy rabbit from the pile, and the black-and-brown tom hurried to take it.

Thunder's gaze flitted around the camp once more. The other cats, hunched over their meager pieces of prey, were watching Slash through slitted eyes. "Why don't they object?" Thunder breathed to Lightning Tail. "He's giving all the best prey to his friends."

Lightning Tail's ears twitched. "I'm not sure. I'd claw his pelt off."

"Frog!" Slash called across the clearing.

A mottled gray tom jumped to his paws. "Yes?" Fear and hope flashed in his gaze.

Slash hauled a fat thrush from the prey pile and pushed it toward him.

Frog bounded eagerly across the clearing, slowing as

he neared Slash. Thunder could see his pelt clinging to his skinny frame. He suddenly realized that most of the rogues were thin. Only Slash, Beetle, and Splinter looked well fed. *But he's stolen enough prey from us to feed them all!* Frog stopped in front of Slash and glanced at the thrush.

Slash's eyes gleamed. "Are you hungry?"

Frog nodded.

Slash hooked up the thrush with a claw. "Hungry enough to eat this?"

Frog nodded again.

"What a shame." Slash tossed the thrush back onto the prey pile. "If you'd brought back more prey from the moor today, I'd have let you have it. But I can't reward laziness."

"It *wasn't* laziness!" Frog bristled.

Slash tipped his head. "What was it then? Stupidity?" His mew turned to a growl. "Because I don't tolerate stupidity. A kit could have brought back what you found."

"That's not true—"

Slash lashed out with his paw, slicing Frog's nose.

Frog backed away, pelt bristling. Blood welled on his muzzle.

Slash hooked a squashed wren from the bottom of the pile. It was no bigger than a shrew. He flung it at Frog's paws. "Be glad I'm letting you have that."

Frog held his gaze for a moment.

Thunder tensed. Was the skinny tom going to fight back? He hoped so. But his heart sank as Frog grabbed the wren between his teeth and padded slowly toward a campmate huddled beneath the arching reeds.

Fern. Thunder recognized the night-black she-cat as Frog settled beside her. Fern shifted closer to the mottled gray tom and licked the blood from his muzzle.

Slash picked a fat grouse from the prey pile and carried it across the clearing.

Thunder pulled his muzzle back sharply. "He's coming this way!" he warned Lightning Tail as the rogue leader padded closer. Splinter and Beetle followed, carrying their prey, and as Slash crouched to eat, they settled beside him.

Thunder felt his belly growl as the scent of grouse, rabbit, and pigeon wafted through the camp wall. *I hope it disguises our scent.* His heart pounded.

"Let's go," Lightning Tail breathed in his ear.

"Not yet." Thunder stilled his friend by laying his tail across his spine. "Let's listen." He couldn't leave now. He had to hear what Slash would say.

Slash took a bite from his grouse and gazed around the camp. "Keep them hungry and they do what you say," he told Splinter, chewing.

Beetle sniffed. "They're all spineless."

Splinter ripped a mouthful of flesh from his pigeon. "I don't know why you bother giving them anything at all."

"They have their uses," Slash muttered. "I need to give them enough to make them stay around. We won't be able to attack the moor cats by ourselves."

Thunder swallowed a gasp. Slash was planning to *attack?* He had to warn Gray Wing and Wind Runner. Every muscle twitched as he fought the urge to race for the moor. He might learn more by staying. He exchanged looks with Lightning Tail. Moonlight showed fear in his friend's gaze. "We'll leave as soon as they're asleep," he breathed.

Lightning Tail nodded.

A damp chill settled around them as they waited. The moon rose higher, turning the marshland silver. Thunder felt dizzy from the scent of Slash's feast. The mice at his paws were still warm, but he didn't dare take a bite. Any movement might set the grass rustling. Instead he waited, relieved as he saw Slash's head begin to droop. Splinter and Beetle were already asleep, their flanks bulging with their meal. As Slash's nose touched the ground, the rogue gave a satisfied burp and rolled onto his side. A few moments later, he was snoring.

Thunder shuddered, his pelt ruffling in disgust. "Come on," he hissed. Grabbing the mouse tails in his jaws, he crept slowly forward. His paws ached from crouching so long. Moving softly, he padded along the camp wall. Lightning Tail followed, making the grass swish behind them.

Suddenly a murmur sounded from the shadows ahead. "Why should we put up with it?"

Thunder froze.

Squinting to see through the darkness, he made out the shapes of four cats. They were crouched in the moon shade outside the camp wall.

He strained to hear what they were saying, but their mews softened to whispers. Lightning Tail stopped beside him and flashed him a look.

The huddled cats murmured, their voices quieter than the rustling of the reeds. They clearly didn't want anyone to hear what they were saying. Had they waited for Slash to fall asleep before they dared to talk? Could they be plotting against their leader?

Thunder jerked his muzzle toward the pines, the mice swaying beneath his chin. Lightning Tail nodded. Together they slipped silently away from the rogue camp.

As they neared the trees, he glanced back and saw a pair of eyes shining in the dark. He recognized the amber gaze of Violet at once. She must be one of the cats whispering outside the camp. Was she staring at him? He felt frozen by her gaze. His heart quickened. *She's beautiful.*

"Come on!" Lightning Tail's hiss jerked him from his thoughts. Quickly he darted after his friend into the shadows of the pines. Violet's gaze still burned in his mind. Then he remembered Slash's words. *Why don't you get smart and let me take his place? A leader's mate would never go hungry.* Rage surged beneath his pelt. He had to get her away from the vicious rogue. She wasn't safe here. He dropped the mice. "We'll take these back to camp," he told Lightning Tail. "Then tomorrow we'll leave at dawn and warn Wind Runner about the attack." *And somehow I'll find a way to help Violet escape.*

CHAPTER 11

Gray Wing narrowed his eyes against the fine rain as he scanned the moortop.

Slate pressed closer to his flank. "Are you sure you should be out in this weather?"

"Yes." Three days in his nest, struggling to breathe, had been enough for Gray Wing. When he'd woken this morning and found that the tightness in his chest had eased at last, he'd scrambled from his den and begged Wind Runner to let him join the hunting patrol.

She'd agreed, but not until Gorse Fur had shown him the battle moves they'd learned at the four trees hollow. The whole group had been practicing hard—harder after Thunder had visited to warn them that the rogues were planning to attack. The day before, Reed and Minnow had spent all afternoon drilling Moth Flight and Dust Muzzle on the new fighting techniques, and the kits had taken to the training so eagerly that they were still practicing long after the sun had dipped below the horizon. It had warmed Gray Wing's heart to see the young cats working so hard. Matching the cats with assigned trainers had brought out the best in all of them. *I knew they'd underestimated you, Moth Flight.*

Now he stood on the moortop and watched the rest of the patrol—Wind Runner, Gorse Fur, and Dust Muzzle—sniffing at the burrows that dotted the grass. Lifting his head, he relished the freshness of the wind and the rain whipping his whiskers. The chill that had gripped the moor had eased with the coming of cloud. He hoped the rough weather would keep the rogues in their camp.

He glanced down the slope, alert for unfamiliar pelts moving against the grass.

Slate was scanning the slope too. "I wish they'd just attack," she growled. "Waiting is making everyone anxious."

Gray Wing flicked his tail. "I'm just glad they haven't stolen prey for a while." Every rabbit, mouse, and bird his campmates had caught in the past few days had been brought back to the camp. Prey was still scarce, but at least they didn't have to share it with a bunch of mangy rogues.

Gray Wing glanced downslope, his pelt pricking uneasily. Were the rogues watching them now? He tried to ignore the queasy fear in his belly. Slate was right. Waiting for the attack was worse than fighting.

Movement caught his eye. He turned his gaze toward the moortop warren just as Dust Muzzle disappeared into a burrow. A few moments later, a rabbit burst from a hole farther along the slope. Wind Runner started forward, her gaze flashing with excitement, but Gorse Fur blocked her way. The gray tabby tom's eyes were fixed on the hole the rabbit had shot from. He lifted his tail as Dust Muzzle darted out. The young tom skimmed the grass, as fast as the wind, closing the gap on his quarry. With a leap, he soared and landed squarely on its back. Rolling over, he grasped it in his paws and bit down on its neck.

Gray Wing purred. "Dust Muzzle is a great hunter."

Slate swished her tail. "It's hard to believe he's only six moons old. He hunts as well as any of his campmates."

Wind Runner and Gorse Fur bounded toward them, Dust Muzzle running ahead. As they neared, Gray Wing heard the call of a grouse from beyond a swath of heather farther downslope.

Gorse Fur must have heard it too. He snapped his gaze toward the sound, his ears pricking.

Dust Muzzle slithered to a halt in front of Gray Wing. Pride glowed in his gaze as the rabbit swung from his jaws.

Its warm scent bathed Gray Wing's nose. "Well done," he purred.

As Wind Runner caught up, she nodded to Dust Muzzle. "Go and tuck it into the grass over there." She pointed to a tangled clump a few tail-lengths away. "We can pick it up on the way back to camp."

Gorse Fur was still staring downslope. "Did you hear the grouse?"

"Of course." Wind Runner headed toward the heather as Dust Muzzle slid the rabbit beneath the straggly grass. As she reached it, she lifted her forepaws off the ground and peered over the frost-browned bushes.

She turned and, with a flick of her tail, beckoned the others to join her. Gray Wing hurried eagerly toward her. Moth Flight, Minnow, Reed, and Spotted Fur would be pleased when they returned to camp with *two* fat pieces of prey.

"It's on the grass beyond this patch of heather," Wind Runner whispered. She nodded to Gray Wing. "I want you to sneak around it. Drive it toward the heather. The rest of us will be waiting in the bushes. Once you've chased it toward us, we can make the kill."

Gray Wing's pelt pricked irritably. Didn't she trust *him* to make the kill?

She spoke again, as though reading his thoughts. "We can't risk losing it," she told him. "Someone has to make sure it flies toward the heather."

But why me? Gray Wing wanted to argue, but he knew the answer she'd have to give, no matter how reluctantly. *Because you're not fit enough to hunt.* Even the short run downslope had left him breathless. How could he catch prey? He grunted and headed around the heather patch, tracing a wide circle as he reached the grass beyond. The grouse was pecking at the ground a few tail-lengths from the heather. Gray Wing dropped low and slowed his pace as he crept behind it. It lifted its head warily. Gray Wing froze. His heart quickened. Then the grouse began to peck at the ground once more. Moving even more cautiously, he scanned the heather. Wind Runner and the others must be in place by now. Fixing his gaze on the grouse, he crept toward it. He picked up speed. His paws hardly made a sound on the rain-soaked grass. The grouse kept pecking, oblivious to his approach. Perhaps he could make the kill himself after all. One leap and he'd be on it. He could pin it to the ground and kill it with a single bite.

Now!

He leaped, pelt bristling with excitement.

Yowls exploded behind him. Startled, he landed clumsily. Angry screeches split the air around him. The grouse fluttered upward, shedding feathers as it fled.

Gray Wing turned.

Eight rogues were streaming toward him, ranged across the hillside, teeth bared. Wind flattened their ears and their fur, blowing back their whiskers and stealing their scent so that he recognized none of them.

Shock flared beneath his pelt. "Wind Runner!"

Bushes rustled. Paw steps thrummed around him as, stiff with shock, Gray Wing watched the rogues pelt closer. Wind Runner, Gorse Fur, and Slate exploded from the heather. Gray Wing reared as an orange she-cat flew at him. Her weight hit him hard and sent him stumbling backward. As he thumped onto his back, he felt a paw press his throat. *I can't breathe!* He met the rogue's vicious stare as she pressed harder. Fighting panic, Gray Wing curled his hind legs in and tucked them beneath her belly. He felt his head throbbing as she choked him. Gurgling, he shoved out hard with his back paws. The orange tabby gripped with her claws. Pain spiked through his pelt as he flung her away. He felt his fur rip and saw clumps of it snagged in her claws as she flipped midair and landed nimbly on the grass.

Gray Wing jumped up, fear turning to energy as the rogue

she-cat raced toward him again. She lunged at him. Gray Wing saw her gaze flick to his shoulder. Star Flower's move flashed in his mind, the one Gorse Fur had shown him earlier. *She's going to try to lame me!* Quickly he slammed his forepaw on top of her shoulder before she could lift hers.

Surprise flashed in her amber gaze. Her paw buckled beneath her, and she tumbled to the ground.

Around him, shrieks and yowls filled the air. Slate reared as an orange tom and a tortoiseshell she-cat swiped blows at her head. Dust Muzzle wrestled on the grass with a black tom. Wind Runner was backing slowly away from three toms.

One of them was Slash. The rogue's eyes glinted with triumph as his campmates fanned out and began to circle her, cutting off her escape. "If we kill her," he snarled, "the others will give up." Eyes wild with panic, Wind Runner jerked one way then the other, spitting as she lashed out with her fore-paws.

"Go for her throat, Splinter." Slash nodded to a black-and-white tom.

Gray Wing raced to help, but as he neared, Gorse Fur streaked in front of him. His gaze was fixed on a gap between the toms. He raced through it, shoving Splinter aside. Gray Wing saw Gorse Fur catch Wind Runner's eye. She blinked back at him, as though words had silently passed between them, then ducked away from Slash and raked her claws along Splinter's flank. Streaking away, she glanced over her shoulder. Splinter hissed at her and gave chase. Gorse Fur tore after him, and Gray Wing stared in surprise as the two moor cats hared across the moorside, the rogue between them. *Who's chasing and who's being chased?* He looked back toward Slash. The rogue was staring after Gorse Fur, confusion darkening his gaze for a moment. Then he turned and narrowed his eyes.

Signaling to his companion with a nod, he lunged toward Slate. Gray Wing watched in horror as four rogues piled on top of her, hissing and spitting. Paws whirled. Tails lashed. From beneath the frenzied mass of squirming bodies, he heard Slate's terrified yowl.

He plunged into the fight, claws stretched. Pushing his way to the middle, he flipped over and began hitting out with every paw. He felt a soft body beneath him and smelled fear-scent. *Slate!* He fought harder, wincing as claws hooked into his pelt and scratched his cheek. Screwing up his eyes, he lashed out, desperate with fear. He felt Slate wriggle from underneath him. Suddenly she was on her paws, pressing against his flank as faces snarled around them.

"Tail to tail!" Slate hissed.

Gray Wing seemed to read her thoughts. As he reared, she reared, and he pressed his spine against hers. Back to back, they battered their attackers with a flurry of paws. Rain lashing his face, Gray Wing flung one hefty blow after another, bracing himself against Slate as she braced against him. Gradually, the blur of claws and faces grew clearer. Slash swung a paw at him, then turned to a black-and-brown tom. "Go for the legs, Beetle!" he hissed.

Gray Wing moved just in time as the rogue dived at his hind leg. Balancing on a single paw, he kicked out, slashing his hind claws against the rogue's cheek. The tom ducked away, yelping with pain, and reared, fury in his eyes.

Gray Wing felt his breath tighten. *No!* Panic gripped him. *Not now!* He had to keep fighting. Slate was fending off the other two rogues behind him. A black tom was on top of Dust Muzzle, who shrieked with pain as the orange she-cat jerked his hind leg between her jaws. *He's using all the right moves, but he's too young to fight off two grown cats.* Horror hollowed Gray Wing's belly. He wheezed, fighting for air.

"Wind Runner!" Hope sparked in Slate's mew.

The camp leader burst from the heather, Gorse Fur at her heels. She leaped toward Dust Muzzle and hooked her claws into one of the rogue tom's shoulders. With a grunt, she heaved him off and wrestled him to the ground.

Dust Muzzle struggled from beneath the black tom and turned on him, paws flailing.

Gorse Fur barged between Slash and his campmates. Rearing, he moved between Slate and Gray Wing and began swiping at the rogues. "We chased Splinter off!" he shouted, struggling to be heard over the sounds of battle. "He won't be coming back anytime soon."

That's one gone. Gray Wing thought grimly. *Only seven to go.* He raised a paw as Slash swung a blow toward his cheek. He blocked it and pressed harder against Gorse Fur and Slate. His hind paws felt weak as he struggled for breath. *I need air!* Claws raked his nose as his concentration slipped for a moment. How long could he keep this up? Gorse Fur lashed out at Beetle while Slate fended off the orange tom. Gray Wing glanced down as the tortoiseshell she-cat dived for his hind leg. He snatched it away, but too slowly. Her teeth sank into his flesh. Pain shot like lightning through his leg. With a grunt, he collapsed onto the grass. Paws slammed onto his flank. Rank breath billowed past his cheek. Slash was on top of him.

Help!

As he flailed desperately, a familiar yowl rang through the air.

Reed! Through a flurry of paws, he glimpsed his campmate's silver fur streaking from the heather. Minnow, Spotted Fur, and Moth Flight hurtled out after him. The air seemed to explode as they crashed into the attacking rogues.

Gray Wing dug his hind paws into Slash's belly and heaved. But Slash was clinging hard with thorn-sharp claws. Slash snarled in his ear as he sank his teeth into Gray Wing's neck and rolled him across the grass. Gray Wing thrashed in terror. He gulped for breath, but his chest was so tight he couldn't draw in air. The world seemed to shrink as darkness closed around him. *Breathe! I must breathe!* He struggled to stay conscious, hardly aware of Slash or the pain.

Suddenly the weight of the rogue was gone. Gray Wing lay as helpless as a fish hooked from the river. As he gasped for breath, his mind reeled. What if he couldn't get enough air? Around him, the yowl of battle ebbed away; darkness clouded his vision as rain soaked his pelt. *Am I dying?* Then, slowly, the stone jaws clasping his chest began to loosen. He drew in shallow breaths, which deepened one by one. His panic eased as he felt the world open around him once more. The grass beneath his cheek swam into vision. Lying limply on his side, he became aware of Slate.

"Gray Wing?" She was leaning over him, her warm breath on his muzzle. "Gray Wing!" Fear edged her mew.

He grunted, wanting desperately to reassure her.

Paws slithered to a halt beside him. "We chased them off." Wind Runner sounded pleased. "They won't come back in a hurry."

"Is Gray Wing okay?" Moth Flight's voice sounded beside him.

"I don't know!" Slate was trembling.

Gray Wing pulled in a shuddering breath and blinked at her. "I'll be fine," he whispered hoarsely.

Moth Flight was sniffing his pelt. "Slash has given him a nasty bite, but it will clean up nicely."

"It's a good thing you pulled Slash off him when you did, Slate." Wind Runner peered down at him, her eyes dark with concern.

Numb, Gray Wing rolled onto his paws and crouched, belly to the grass. He wanted to stand but didn't have the strength.

"Just rest there," Slate soothed.

"Thank you," Gray Wing wheezed. "For saving me."

"I had to," Slate purred. "I couldn't let anything happen to the father of my kits."

Gray Wing stiffened. "*Your* kits?" Confused, he stared at her. *Turtle Tail* was the mother of his kits. And they weren't really his kits. Hazily, he tried to understand.

"I'm going to have your kits," Slate explained softly.

Shock heated Gray Wing's pelt.

"Is it so surprising?" Slate purred.

Gray Wing lifted his chin and gazed at her in wonder. "My kits," he breathed. Joy flooded his heart like sunshine filling the sky. He was going to be a father. He purred a clumsy, wheezing purr. "My love," he murmured, burying his nose in Slate's thick, warm fur. "Thank you."

CHAPTER 12

❦

"*It will be safe if we* wait until dark," Lightning Tail muttered.

Thunder glanced at his friend as they padded between the pines. He knew Lightning Tail was right, but his paws itched to return to Slash's camp so much that he was willing to take the risk. "If we wait until dark, we might miss something."

"What's there to miss?" Thin shards of sunlight dappled Lightning Tail's pelt. "We know that Slash is planning to steal our prey and drive us out of the forest."

But I have to see Violet again! Thunder had hardly slept in the days following the attack on the moor cats. All he could think of was Violet. What if she'd been hurt in the struggle? When Gray Wing had visited the camp to share the news, his muzzle had been covered in scratches. He'd thanked Thunder for the warning—being prepared had helped them fend the rogues off—but even so, it must have been a vicious fight.

He avoided Lightning Tail's gaze. "If you don't want to come with me, that's fine." Why should he put his friend in danger?

"I'm not letting you go there alone. It's not safe." Lightning

Tail sniffed. "I just wish you'd admit why you really want to go there."

Thunder stopped walking. He flicked his ears self-consciously.

Lightning Tail turned and stared at him. "You want to see *her* again." His whiskers twitched.

Thunder's pelt grew hot.

"I don't mind." Lightning Tail shrugged and carried on toward the marsh. "Did you think I hadn't noticed you talking about Violet every chance you get? You're worried about her, aren't you?"

"Yes." Thunder hurried after him.

Lightning Tail quickened his pace. "Then let's see how she is."

Gratefully, Thunder followed the black tom through a narrow gap between the brambles. Light showed between the trunks ahead. They were nearing the marshland.

Lightning Tail lowered his voice. "I just hope we aren't spotted."

"Gray Wing said he rolled in rotting mushrooms to disguise his scent." Thunder scanned the tree roots for old fungi.

Lightning Tail wrinkled his nose. "Let's just stay downwind." He slowed as they reached the edge of the pine forest.

Thunder peered out from the trees. "I guess we can always run away if we're spotted. Most of the rogues are hopeless at running through woods. If we can get as far as the forest, we'll be safe—"

"Shh!" Lightning Tail cut him off.

Thunder followed his friend's alarmed gaze. Four rogues were filing between the marshy tussocks, heading for the woods. His heart lurched as he recognized Violet among them. "Hide!" Diving beneath a yew, he pressed his belly to the ground.

Lightning Tail shot in beside him. "They're coming this way!"

Thunder wriggled deeper beneath the bush as the rogue patrol headed toward them. As they pattered past, one of them spoke. Through the branches, Thunder could see a black tom. He looked anxious.

"Do you think Slash saw us leave?" the rogue mewed.

"Don't worry, Raven." Violet walked beside him. "He was too busy teaching battle moves."

A young tom followed her, his auburn pelt glossy. "Where are we going to hunt?"

A tortoiseshell she-cat hurried to catch up. "That's the third time you've asked, Red."

"He's just asking because he's nervous, Juniper," Violet told her. "You know how Slash feels about us hunting for ourselves."

"I'm not nervous." Red sounded indignant.

Violet ignored him. "Let's hunt near Twolegplace."

"What about the dogs?" Red gasped.

"We can run faster than dogs," Violet told him.

Juniper grunted. "We shouldn't *have* to go hunting when there's food rotting in camp."

"Why doesn't Slash share it?" Raven growled angrily. "He

gives the best pieces to Splinter and Beetle and leaves the rest to turn sour while we're eating scraps."

Fury surged through Thunder's pelt. Cats were going hungry because of Slash, and he was letting food rot!

"Slash is just mean." Violet's tail flicked against a yew branch. "Since Star Flower escaped, he has been worse than ever."

"I'm glad she got away," Juniper commented.

"I wonder how her kits are doing," Violet murmured. "Fern said she had three."

The rogues padded deeper into the forest. Thunder pricked his ears as their voices were swallowed by the pines. His heart was pounding. Rage bristled in every hair on his pelt. How *dare* Slash let food rot? He slid from beneath the yew. "Let's go and check the camp."

"Why?" Lightning Tail scrabbled after him. "You've seen that Violet's okay."

Thunder blinked at him "Didn't you hear? Slash is training his campmates to fight. We need to learn their new moves."

Lightning Tail's pelt rippled. "You're pushing your luck," he warned. "We've almost been spotted once. What if Violet had seen us?"

Thunder wished Violet *had* seen him. He couldn't believe the sleek gray she-cat would betray him, and he longed to meet her.

"*Thunder?*" Lightning Tail was staring at him.

He jerked his thoughts away from Violet. "If Slash is too busy to notice a hunting patrol leaving camp, he'll never see us." He ducked out from under the trees and headed onto the marsh.

Lightning Tail followed.

Keeping low, Thunder made for the patch of grass that walled the rogues' camp. He slowed as he neared and tasted the air, relieved to feel the wind ruffling his fur. It carried the smell of rogues and whisked his scent into the pines.

Weaving between the tussocks, he led the way to the hiding place they'd used last time. As he crouched low, Lightning Tail squeezed in beside him. He peered through the gaps between the stems.

Slash was pacing the edge of the clearing. Splinter was facing a brown, mottled she-cat in the middle. Fear shone in her eyes, and blood welled on her muzzle.

Slash padded closer. "This time, remember to block his first blow."

The mottled she-cat nodded stiffly, not taking her eyes from Splinter.

Splinter showed his teeth. "Should I go gentle on her this time, Slash?" he asked sarcastically.

"No!" Slash snapped his gaze toward the tom. He smirked as he saw amusement spark in Splinter's eye, then purred. "Beech has to learn that if she's slow, she gets hurt."

A pale tabby padded closer to the edge of the clearing. "Let me take her place."

"Go away, Willow." Slash gave her a warning look. "Your friend needs to learn."

Pity jabbed at Thunder's heart as he watched Willow

back reluctantly away and Beech brace herself for Splinter's attack.

The black-and-white tom crouched, his eyes slitted. Beech flattened her ears.

Slash stared at Beech mockingly. "Is that as scary as you can look?"

Beech fluffed out her fur and showed her teeth.

"That's better." Slash flicked his tail.

Splinter leaped. Paws flailing, he crashed into Beech. She ducked to one side to escape a swinging blow. Splinter's claws caught her ear tip, and Thunder saw pain flash in her eyes as she rolled away.

Splinter reared and slammed his paws down, but he was too slow. Beech leaped up and ducked behind him. Thunder's heart quickened. He found himself willing the brown she-cat to outwit the bullying tom. He held his breath as Splinter turned to face a flurry of blows. He backed away, wincing, but Beech kept lashing his muzzle.

Suddenly she stopped and glanced behind in surprise. Slash had pressed a paw onto her tail, pinning her to the spot. As she blinked at the rogue leader, Splinter leaped at her. Digging his claws into her pelt, he kicked her paws from beneath her and rolled her to the ground.

Willow started forward, her eyes wide with fear, but Slash hissed at her. "Stay back." The pale tabby looked on, anguish brimming in her gaze as Splinter battered Beech with merciless swipes.

Thunder trembled with rage, longing to barge through

the grass and defend the she-cat.

"Enough." At last Slash signaled with his tail, and Splinter backed away from Beech.

She staggered to her paws. Fur stuck out in clumps around her neck. Blood matted her pelt.

Willow hurried forward and guided her campmate toward the edge of the clearing.

"Is Beech okay?"

Thunder blinked as two kits scampered out from between the reeds and hurried to meet the injured she-cat.

The black tom-kit reached her first. "She looks hurt."

A gray-and-white she-kit scrambled to a halt beside him. "You fought really well, Beech!"

An orange-and-white she-cat hurried behind them. Her green eyes shone with worry as she saw Beech. "That's not training," she hissed under her breath. "That's cruelty."

"Dawn!" Willow gave her a pleading look, as though begging her to be quiet. "Don't frighten your kits."

Thunder pricked his ears as the orange-and-white queen replied. "I'm not going to hide the truth from them." Dawn glared at Slash. "Pine and Drizzle need to know what sort of group they belong to."

Thunder tensed as Slash met the queen's gaze. "If you don't like my group, you can leave and take your kits with you."

Dawn narrowed her eyes. "We might just do that."

A dark brown tom slid from the shadows. "Hush, Dawn," he murmured anxiously. "We *need* the safety of the group."

Dawn turned on him. "Do you call this safe?" She glanced

toward Beech. The battered she-cat was washing her wounds stiffly.

Slash's eyes glittered. "Perhaps *you* want to train next, Dawn?"

The dark brown tom moved in front of the queen. "She's still nursing," he growled.

Slash's ears twitched. "In that case, Moss, why don't *you* come and show us your moves."

The black tom-kit's eyes lit up with alarm.

His sister pressed herself against Moss. "Don't go. He'll hurt you."

Moss touched his nose to the she-kit's head. "No one's going to hurt me, Drizzle." He padded to the clearing and faced Slash. His gaze darted toward Splinter, then to Beetle, who was crouching at the edge of the clearing. "Which one of you am I going to train with?"

Thunder heard no fear in the tom's mew. Admiration warmed his pelt.

Lightning Tail fidgeted beside him. "I wish I could 'train' with one of those fox-hearts," he growled under his breath.

Slash motioned Beetle forward with a jerk of his muzzle.

Beetle got to his paws and crossed the clearing. His eyes shone with disdain as he looked at Moss.

Moss returned his gaze, unflinching.

Thunder tensed as he watched the two rogues face each other.

Moss threw Slash a look. "What move do you want me to practice?"

"Choose whatever you like," Slash sneered. "I'm sure Beetle can counter it."

Moss narrowed his eyes. Shifting his paws, he squared his shoulders.

Dawn watched anxiously while Pine and Drizzle huddled against her. Beech washed blood from her muzzle.

"Be carefu—"

Dawn's warning was cut off by a screech. It rang across the marshland like the desperate cry of an owl.

Thunder jerked his head up. The screech sounded again, followed by the howl of a dog.

Then Red shot from the pines, as fast as a hawk. He pelted across the marshland, his fur bushed with terror. As he hared for the camp, three dogs bounded after him. Their eyes glittered with excitement as they raced between the tussocks.

Thunder stiffened, fear surging beneath his pelt. "He's leading the dogs straight to the camp!"

"The kits!"

Before Thunder could stop him, Lightning Tail plunged through the camp wall. He raced across the clearing and bundled Pine and Drizzle toward the shadowy reeds beyond.

Dawn's eyes widened in in shock.

"Dogs!" Lightning Tail yowled. "They're heading this way."

As he spoke, Red streaked into the camp.

The heavy paw steps of the dogs pounded over the ground outside. A barrage of vicious barks seemed to shatter the air.

Blood roaring in his ears, Thunder leaped through the gap Lightning Tail had made and raced to his friend's side.

Lightning Tail had scooped up Drizzle by her scruff and was pushing her between the reed stems.

Dawn was nosing Pine after his sister. "Hide!" she hissed. "Don't come out, whatever happens."

"I'll defend them." Lightning Tail turned his back to the kits' makeshift hiding place and faced the clearing.

Dawn squared up beside him. "Who are you?"

"I'm Lightning Tail." He bushed out his pelt.

"I'm Thunder." Thunder scanned the camp. "We're forest cats." Moss was backing away from the clearing. Beetle and Splinter had leaped in front of Slash. An orange tom raced from the shadows. A mottled tabby followed.

As the dogs crashed through the grass wall, cats burst from their nests. Terror burned in their eyes. The dogs leaped and twisted in the clearing, their tails wagging as though they couldn't believe their luck. They snapped at the cats darting between their massive paws.

Thunder raced forward as a terrier thrust its sharp snout toward a striped she-cat. Rearing, he slashed its cheek. The dog turned on him, growling angrily. Fear scorched through Thunder as its foul, hot breath washed over him. He lashed out with both paws. It yelped, diving closer.

Fur brushed Thunder's flanks as Moss reared beside him. Fern dashed from the edge of the camp and ducked beneath the terrier's chin. Hissing, she rolled onto her back and scrabbled beneath the dog's belly. With a yowl, she began churning her hind paws. Thunder smelled the stone tang of blood and clawed the dog on the ear as it turned to bite at the hissing cat beneath him.

On the other side of the clearing, Slash, Splinter, and Beetle fought beside a yellow-eyed tabby, driving a russet-colored mongrel toward the camp entrance. They swiped at it, one after another, in a relentless barrage until the excited gleam in the dog's eyes turned to confusion.

Frog raced past Thunder, nearly unbalancing him as he fled a black dog. Slavering, it barged past Thunder, its greedy gaze fixed on the gray tabby tom. A burly brown tom leaped from the reeds, raking the dog's muzzle as he soared past. The dog scrabbled to a halt, yelping with rage. Frog reared and, while the brown tom found his footing, aimed a vicious blow at the dog's snout. Beech raced to help, blood still streaking her nose from her fight with Splinter. She ducked beneath the dog and fell in beside Frog. The brown tom joined them, and together they lashed out at the dog's snapping jaws.

"Thunder! Look out!" As Lightning Tail's cry sounded in his ear, paws shoved him aside. Teeth snapped beside his cheek. He turned. Fern had pushed him clear as the terrier had lunged for him. Fear surging through his muscles, he flung blow after blow at the dog's face. Moss was clinging like a tick to its back. Thunder flattened his ears as the camp rang with the shriek of battle.

Across the camp, the mongrel yelped with pain as Slash, Beetle, Splinter, and the tabby tom drove it away. Eyes blazing with hate, Slash swung his paw at the dog's nose. Blood sprayed his pelt as he sliced its muzzle open.

Yowling in agony, the mongrel turned and fled toward the pines.

Hope flared in Thunder's chest. He slashed at the terrier,

his eyes slitted. Fern pressed against him. She reared and sank her claws into the dog's cheek. It tried to bite her, but as it opened its jaws, she pulled hard on its flesh and it howled with pain. Ducking low, it tried to shake Moss from its back. Panic sparked in its gaze. Backing away, it stared in terror at the cats. Then it turned and leaped the grass wall. As it fled across the marsh, Moss jumped off its back and raced back to camp.

We're winning! Thunder turned to the black dog.

He froze.

A chill rippled along his spine. The burly tom lay unmoving at the edge of the clearing. Blood spattered the ground around him and oozed from his body, turning the earth red.

Frog batted desperately at the dog's muzzle. It snarled and snapped, drool bubbling at its lips. Limping on three paws, the gray tom lurched clumsily with each swipe. Beech stumbled beside him, her pelt scratched and matted. Pain gleaming in her eyes, she swung blow after blow at the dog.

It snapped its jaws around Frog's flanks. Thunder heard bone crunch. Beech swiped at its nose. The dog let go, its eyes blazing with rage. As Frog dropped to the ground, it turned on Beech.

"Frog!" Willow raced across the clearing. Grabbing his scruff, she pulled him clear of the dog's hefty paws.

Beech faced the dog alone.

Thunder and Lightning Tail raced to help.

Gray fur crossed Thunder's path. Slash was blocking his way.

"What are you doing?" Thunder stared at him. "She needs

help!" He glanced at Lightning Tail. Splinter and Beetle were holding him back, pinning him to the ground with their paws.

Slash snarled at Thunder. "Don't move, or I'll kill you."

Thunder's thoughts whirled. "Why?"

Slash stared at Beech, curling his lip. "It's time she proved she's not a burden."

"You can't!" Thunder tried to push past Slash, but the rogue reared and hooked his claws deep into his shoulder fur. Half blind with fury, Thunder scrabbled against the earth, but Slash held him back.

Beech stumbled, her gaze on Slash. Disbelief shone in her eyes as the black dog took her ribs in its huge jaws. She shrieked as it lifted her and shook her like prey. Screeching in terror, she flailed desperately, her eyes flashing with agony. Thunder heard a terrified yowl, and then Fern raced over. Spitting like a snake, she leaped onto the dog's shoulders and clawed at its eyes.

It yelped and dropped Beech, shaking Fern from its back.

Thunder ripped free of Slash's grip and flung himself toward the dog. But it was already fleeing, blood welling around its eyes. Howling, it ran from the camp and followed its pack mates to the pines.

"Beech?" Fern leaned over the she-cat as she lay, limp, on the ground.

Frog dragged himself toward her, his hind legs trailing along the ground behind him. "Is she breathing?" he whispered, staring at Beech.

Thunder hurried closer and sniffed her muzzle. No breath

touched his nose. Her flanks were still. "She's gone," he murmured.

A low moan sounded in Fern's throat.

Lightning Tail hauled himself to his paws, glaring angrily at Splinter and Beetle. "We could have saved her!"

"What for?" Slash snarled from the middle of the clearing. His campmates stared at him, shock sharpening their gaze.

Beetle shook out his pelt. "She couldn't fight or hunt."

Splinter padded to Slash's side. "She was a waste of prey."

Fern glared at Slash, her pelt pricking along her spine. Hatred filled her gaze. "You let her die."

Slash snorted. "Don't blame me," he huffed. "*I* didn't lead the dogs here."

Fern stiffened. "Red!" She jerked her muzzle around, scanning the clearing. "Where is he?"

"He ran away." Splinter's mew was thick with derision.

"Mouse-heart," Beetle snarled.

"Mouse-*brain*," Slash corrected. "Who would lead dogs back to his own camp?"

Splinter narrowed his eyes. "Perhaps he did it on purpose."

Beetle's eyes flashed with interest. "He *has* been complaining a lot. Perhaps he was hoping the dogs would kill you." He blinked at Slash. "It might have been a plot to destroy the group."

"No!" Fern stepped forward. "Red wouldn't hurt anyone!"

Willow narrowed her eyes. "Then why *did* he lead the dogs right into the camp?"

Splinter's ears twitched. "If *I* was being chased by dogs, I'd lead them away."

Thunder glanced around the camp. Blood spattered the ground and specked the grass wall. Cats stared, round-eyed with shock. Frog had collapsed, his eyes dull with pain. Blood welled above Moss's eye. Bloody gouges showed on Fern's flank. Clumps stuck out from Willow's pelt. These cats were in no state to look after themselves or each other.

An orange she-cat sniffed at the burly brown tom. "Stone's dead." She stared bleakly at his matted pelt.

Slash's eyes gleamed. "And it's all Red's fault."

Thunder growled. "Stop worrying about who to blame. You've got injured cats here. Two of your campmates are dead. It doesn't matter *why* it happened. You need to take care of your group." He glared at Slash.

Slash's hackles lifted. "How dare you tell me how to lead? What are you doing here anyway?" He bared his teeth.

Thunder shifted his paws uneasily as Splinter padded closer. "*I* think he's a spy."

CHAPTER 13

❧

Beetle flexed his claws. "He's trying to stir up trouble."

Slash flattened his ears. "I should claw your ears off for trespassing on my land."

Thunder faced the rogue leader, anger hardening his belly. Overhead, clouds darkened the sky. "Your campmates need help, not another fight."

"They brought the danger here themselves." Slash didn't even glance at the injured cats littering the clearing. "Anyway, they don't need help from a couple of cowardly group cats."

Thunder stared at him in disbelief. "We helped you fight the dogs off!"

Lightning Tail padded to Thunder's side. "Your cats are so starved, they couldn't defend themselves properly." He jerked his muzzle toward Beech. "And you clearly don't care whether they live or die."

"Why should I?" Slash's pelt rippled along his spine. "They're cowards. They fight like kits."

Thunder's paws trembled with fury. "They fight like foxes!" How could Slash despise the cats he was supposed to protect? Didn't he feel any responsibility for them at all?

Fern padded into the clearing, her eyes wide. She glared at Slash, her eyes blazing with anger. "You don't care about us at all. You never have!"

Dawn was lifting Pine and Drizzle from their hiding place among the reeds. She glanced at Fern, her expression somber.

Moss bristled beside her, his gaze on Slash. "Fern's right. You ordered us to steal, then kept the prey for yourself and your friends." His glanced at Splinter and Beetle. The vicious toms glared back at him and moved closer to Slash. "You've been treating us terribly for a long time! We practically starve, while you let food rot."

Dawn took a step toward Fern. "They're right," she said, looking nervously from the black she-cat to Slash. "You say you want to train us to fight, but you abuse your own cats."

Fern nodded at Dawn, then turned back to Slash, eyes narrowed. "We've put up with you for too long," she hissed. "You call the group cats weak, but look who fought alongside us. Maybe we'd be better off in a group! We'd definitely be better off without you."

Better off in a group? Thunder's pelt prickled with concern. Could the groups accommodate all these cats? *Would* they?

A tabby tom crossed the clearing and fell in beside Slash. "Why don't we just leave?" he hissed to Slash. "These mouse-hearts don't appreciate you, Slash. Let them try to make it on their own!"

Slash narrowed his eyes. "That's a good suggestion, Snake. I'm wasting my time here." He flicked his tail toward Splinter and Beetle. "Are you coming with me?"

"Why would we stay here?" Splinter lifted his chin.

Beetle shook out his pelt. "Let these vermin die alone."

Thunder stared at Slash. *I'd never let my group down like this!* "They're your campmates! They're injured—and they're right, you've let them down! How can you be so heartless?"

Slash shrugged. "If you're so worried about them, why don't *you* look after them?"

Thunder stiffened. Slash's words echoed the question he'd been turning over in his mind—a question he couldn't quite answer. *Can I care for these cats?* There was barely enough prey in his forest to feed his own group. But he couldn't just leave these battered cats here. They clearly needed help.

Moss's eyes lit with outrage. "No one needs to look after us!" he snarled.

"We'll take care of ourselves better than you ever did!" Fern squared her shoulders.

Dawn wrapped her tail around Pine and Drizzle, who were trembling, their fluffy fur spiked. "We shouldn't have put up with you for so long."

Thunder felt a rush of admiration for the rebelling rogues. And yet how would they recover from this? They were half-starved to begin with. And now they were wounded. They might say they wanted to look after themselves, but *could* they?

Whatever happened, at least they would be free from Slash. He met the rogue leader's gaze. "I don't think you'll be missed."

Slash glanced at Splinter. "Let's get out of here. It reeks

of fear." He glanced once more around his campmates, then headed for the entrance.

Splinter, Beetle, and Snake followed.

An orange she-cat hurried after them. "Can I come too?"

Slash turned and looked at her through narrowed eyes. "Don't you want to stay with these weaklings, Swallow?" he asked mockingly.

Swallow flattened her ears. "I don't want to live like prey," she growled. "I'm a hunter."

Slash blinked at her approvingly. "Then you'd better come with us."

He headed through the gap in the reeds. As Splinter, Beetle, Snake, and Swallow filed after him, Thunder's claws itched. He wanted to chase after the heartless cowards and claw their ears off. But there had been too much fighting already. Too many cats were hurt. He didn't want to drag them into another battle.

Fern's mew took him by surprise.

"We should fetch Pebble Heart."

He blinked at her.

"When I was with Tall Shadow's group, he helped heal his campmates," she went on. "And he tended to Quiet Rain when she was dying. He might be able to help here."

"You're right." Thunder dipped his head to Fern. "I don't know if he can help all these cats, but I know he'll try."

"I'll fetch him." Lightning Tail headed for the camp entrance.

Moss started after him. "Should I come too?"

Lightning Tail answered without stopping. "I know the forest," he called. "I'll travel faster alone."

Thunder watched his friend race out of the camp, impressed by his decisiveness. Even after the battle with the dogs, the black tom was still fired with courage and determination. *I'm lucky to have such strong support—and so is my group.* He padded toward Stone and sniffed his muzzle. Scenting death, he backed away, his pelt pricking. He glanced at Beech's body and shivered. These cats would still be alive if Slash had kept them well fed and had fought as their friend. Dogs were dangerous, but they were dumber than badgers. A loyal, united group could easily outthink and outfight them.

"Thunder?" Drizzle's small mew made him turn. The young kit was staring at him. "Will Slash come back?"

Thunder hesitated. The kit looked frightened. He wanted to promise her that everything was safe now, but how could he? Who knew what Slash would do next?

Dawn leaned down and licked the she-kit's head. "We don't know, dear," she murmured between laps. "But Moss and I will protect you, whatever happens."

Thunder felt responsibility weigh like a stone in his belly. He must help these cats. But how? As he wondered what to do, the reed entrance rustled. Was Lightning Tail back already? He looked up, his heart jumping as Violet hurried into camp. A pigeon dangled from her mouth, and her eyes were wide with fear.

She dropped her catch. "We smelled blood!" She stared around the camp, her ears flattening as she saw her wounded campmates. She raced to Frog, who was lying in the shadow of the camp wall. Blood stained the earth around him. "What happened?"

Before anyone could answer, Juniper and Raven followed her in. Each carried a mouse. They dropped their catch, their pelts bushing as they saw the ravaged camp.

Raven's nose twitched. "Dogs!"

Juniper stiffened. "Have you seen Red? He was hunting with us in Twolegplace. He wanted to explore an alley. We told him we'd meet up with him later, but he never turned up."

Willow narrowed her eyes. "He led the dogs here."

"Here?" Juniper's tail twitched fearfully. "Is he hurt?"

Fern glanced at Willow anxiously. "He ran away," she murmured.

Juniper and Violet exchanged glances.

"Mouse-heart," Willow hissed.

Violet looked past the pale tabby, her ears twitching as she saw Beech's body. "Is she dead?" She hurried to sniff the she-cat's matted fur.

"Stone was killed too." Moss limped toward the burly tom's body.

Juniper's eyes widened. "Are the kits okay?" She scanned the camp frantically until her gaze reached Pine and Drizzle, huddling beside Dawn.

Dawn scooped them closer with her tail. "They were safely hidden, thanks to Thunder and Lightning Tail."

"Who?" Juniper blinked at Thunder, but Thunder hardly noticed the tortoiseshell's green gaze. He was watching Violet.

The beautiful she-cat was staring at him, her warm amber eyes brimming with gratitude. "You saved the kits? Are you Thunder or Lightning Tail?"

Thunder shifted his paws, his pelt suddenly hot. "I'm Thunder. But, er . . . Lightning Tail helped." He dropped his gaze. Looking at Violet made his heart beat too fast.

Fern padded forward. "They helped us fight off the dogs."

Thunder stared at his paws. "I just wish we'd managed to save everyone." He lifted his gaze to meet Violet's, feeling suddenly shy.

She was watching him with soft eyes. "Thank you," she murmured.

A striped yellow she-cat hobbled forward. Blood matted the fur on her shoulder. "Slash has abandoned us."

An orange tom struggled to his paws at the edge of the clearing. "He called us mouse-hearts." He sounded hurt.

Violet lashed her tail. "What would you expect from that fool? We're not mouse-hearts, Ember."

The striped she-cat blinked at Violet uncertainly. "Perhaps we should have tried harder to fight off the dogs."

"Bee!" Violet padded toward the she-cat and sniffed her bleeding shoulder. "Look at you. Look at you *all*! You must have fought with the courage of eagles!"

Bee glanced at her anxiously. "But Slash is gone. What are we going to do now?"

Violet lifted her chin. "We're going to take care of our injuries and share this prey." She prodded the pigeon with her paw. "Tonight, no one will sleep with an empty belly."

As she spoke, paws sounded outside the camp. Lightning Tail charged in, Pebble Heart at his heels, holding a thick wad of cobweb between his jaws. He paused and surveyed the cats, his eyes glittering with apprehension. Then he hurried to Frog. The mottled gray tom was the only cat who hadn't struggled to his paws. Dropping his cobweb beside the rogue, Pebble Heart began sniffing his pelt. Then he ran his paw over his spine and down his legs. His gaze darkened.

Thunder hurried to Pebble Heart's side. "Is it bad?" The scent of blood filled his nose.

"I can clean his wounds and stop the bleeding." The gray tom lowered his voice. "But there's a jagged lump in his spine."

A chill crept into Thunder's fur. For the first time since the fight he was aware of the cold wind whipping across the marsh. "Is it broken?"

"I hope not," Pebble Heart whispered. "It may just be swollen. Only time will tell."

Violet joined them. "How can I help?" She blinked at Pebble Heart.

Pebble Heart ripped a pawful of cobwebs from his wad and placed it at her paws. "We must make sure every wound is cleaned before the bleeding is stanched. Make sure that—"

Violet didn't let him finish. "I understand." She hooked the cobweb between her mouth and one paw and padded toward Fern. "Where are you hurt?" she asked, sniffing the other she-cat's pelt.

Pebble Heart raised his voice. "Everyone who is hurt must wash their wounds thoroughly. If there's a scratch you can't reach, let your campmates wash it for you."

Dawn hurried toward Bee. Pine and Drizzle ran after her.

Moss began to sniff Ember's pelt. "There's a wound under your chin," he told the tom.

"Take care of your own wounds." Ember nodded toward the blood welling above Moss's eyes.

Violet turned toward Thunder. "Are *you* hurt?"

"No—" Thunder gasped suddenly as pain throbbed through his forepaw. He lifted it, surprised to find puncture wounds in his fur. Had the terrier managed to bite him? He hardly remembered.

Violet hurried toward him. "Dog bites can turn nasty." She sat down, lifted his forepaw between hers, and began to gently clean his wounds with long laps of her tongue.

Thunder snatched his paw away, his pelt burning.

Violet stared at him in surprise. "I'm sorry." Her ears twitched anxiously. "I was just trying to help."

Thunder's tongue seemed to twist into knots. "I can do it," he mumbled.

Violet shrugged. "If you like." She turned to Lightning Tail. "Are you hurt?"

Lightning Tail shook his head. "Not a scratch," he told her. "But I've always been lucky."

Pine and Drizzle huddled close to Dawn as the queen washed a wound behind Bee's ear. Pine was staring toward the camp entrance. Drizzle crouched so close to her mother, she was almost hidden beneath the queen's orange-and-white fur.

Rain was beginning to fall from the gray, heavy sky.

Thunder's heart twisted as he saw fear in the kits' eyes. What if Slash *did* come back? And what about the dogs? Now that they knew there was a rogue camp here, they might return. What if they were part of a bigger pack? He glanced around at the wounded, undernourished cats. They were in no state to defend themselves from another attack.

"You can't stay here," he murmured.

Violet jerked her muzzle toward him. "What?"

"This camp's not safe anymore," Thunder met her gaze solemnly. "You need to find a new home."

Violet blinked at him through the thickening rain. "And where exactly are we supposed to go?"

CHAPTER 14

Rain battered Gray Wing's face as he hurried after Lightning Tail.
The black tom had raced into the moor camp, breathless and
soaked to the skin. Gray Wing had tried to persuade him to
shelter until he'd dried off, but Lightning Tail had shaken out
his pelt and begged to see Wind Runner.

"She's hunting with Gorse Fur," Gray Wing had told him.

"Then *you* must come," Lightning Tail had puffed. "The
rogues need our help."

"The *rogues*?" Gray Wing had stared at him in disbelief.

His thoughts still whirled as he chased Lightning Tail into
the pines. The black tom was already racing down the slope
toward the Thunderpath. Gray Wing's chest tightened, and
he slowed, nodding reassuringly to Lightning Tail as the tom
looked back anxiously. *I must pace myself. I can't collapse now. Thunder needs me.*

How could the rogues need help? Only a few days ago
they'd attacked his patrol. Lightning Tail had babbled something about dogs and Slash and the camp being unsafe. Had
Slash abandoned his campmates and left the marsh?

Hope sparked beneath Gray Wing's pelt. If Slash was gone,

perhaps life on the moor could return to normal. No extra guards. Fewer hunting patrols. They could sleep soundly in their nests once more.

Lightning Tail stopped beside the Thunderpath and waited. As Gray Wing skidded to a halt on the wet grass beside him, a monster pounded toward them. When it shot past, Lightning Tail stepped in front of him, blocking the spray from its spinning paws. Gray Wing felt a prickle of irritation. *You don't need to protect me.* He padded around the tom and broke into a run, racing over the slick stone path. He kept running until he reached the shelter of the pines on the other side.

Gray Wing was relieved to be out of the rain. Only a few drops penetrated the thick needle canopy. Lightning Tail caught up to him and shook out his fur.

Gray Wing smoothed the rain from his whiskers, stiffening suddenly as a thought struck him. "Is Fern okay?"

"She's wounded. But not badly." Lightning Tail set off through the pines. "Pebble Heart's there. He'll take care of her."

Gray Wing leaped a ditch as they reached it. "Were many cats hurt?"

"Most of them," Lightning Tail told him. "Two are dead."

Dead! It must have been a horrific attack. "Where did Slash go?"

Lightning Tail shrugged. "I don't know."

"Why did he leave? Did the dogs drive him out?"

"No," Lightning Tail told him. "He abandoned his campmates after the attack."

Gray Wing's pelt prickled with shock. "*Abandoned* them?"

"They were glad to see him go."

At last! Satisfaction warmed Gray Wing's belly. Fern would be free now. "Is Slash alone?"

Lightning Tail shook his head. "Beetle, Splinter, Snake, and Swallow went with him."

Gray Wing's heart sank. Slash wasn't as isolated as he'd hoped. What if he returned to terrorize his campmates once more? "We need to get the others away from the marsh as soon as we can." But where could they take them?

The rain was easing by the time they reached the marsh camp. The dark, soggy afternoon was sliding quickly into evening. As Lightning Tail led Gray Wing through the entrance, Gray Wing stared at the gloomy clearing. His paws pricked with shock. Holes in the camp wall showed where the dogs had crashed through. The rain-soaked earth smelled of blood. Cats huddled in the shelter of the marsh grass at the edges. They gazed warily at Gray Wing as he entered.

He dipped his head. "My name is Gray Wing," he told them. "I've come to help."

Fern padded from a drooping clump of reeds. "Gray Wing." Her eyes were hollow with exhaustion. "Did Lightning Tail tell you? Slash is gone."

"I know." Gray Wing touched his nose to the young she-cat's head, relieved to find her well. "How are you?"

She drew away. "My sister is dead." She blinked at a mottled she-cat lying at the edge of the clearing.

"That was your sister?"

"She's why I had to come back."

Lightning Tail scanned the clearing. "Where's Thunder?"

"He's digging a grave with Juniper and Raven." Fern nodded toward a gap in the camp wall. "Out there."

A pretty gray she-cat crossed the clearing to meet them. Black fur edged her ears and paws, and her amber eyes were warm. "Are you Gray Wing?"

Gray Wing dipped his head in greeting. "Yes."

"Thank you for coming." She stopped in front of him. "I'm Violet. Thunder said you might be able to find us somewhere to stay." She glanced around at the battered camp. "I don't think we're safe here anymore."

Gray Wing's ears twitched uneasily. An orange tom was huddled beside a tortoiseshell she-cat. He recognized them from the attack on the moor. Only a few days ago, he and his campmates had fought these very cats. Violet was still staring at him expectantly. He fumbled for words. "I'll do what I can," he murmured. Turning his head, he gazed through the gap in the camp wall. "I must speak with Thunder first."

"Of course." Violet padded toward a tabby she-cat and crouched beside her. The tabby was trembling, her eyes glittering with grief as Violet leaned close and lapped her cheek softly.

Gray Wing was heading toward the grave when he recognized a gray pelt beneath a dropping clump of marsh grass. "Pebble Heart!"

The young tom was tending to another cat. He turned as he heard his name. A wad of cobweb hung from his jaws. He blinked a welcome at Gray Wing, then turned back to the wounded tom.

"He's treating injuries," Fern explained. "He's been busy since he arrived—cleaning cuts and bites and gathering cobweb to stop the bleeding."

"They are in safe paws." Gray Wing gave a purr. He wasn't surprised that Pebble Heart had helped the rogues eagerly and unquestioningly. He headed for the gap in the wall and hopped out of the camp. "Stay with the others," he called to Lightning Tail.

The black tom nodded. "I'll guard the entrance."

He followed a trail of crushed grass and churned mud until he saw Thunder's orange pelt, bright against the darkening sky. In a gap between the tussocks, the tom was leaning over a hole, hauling earth out with his paws. Another tom worked beside him. As Gray Wing reached the grave, he saw the tortoiseshell she-cat walk up to the edge and drop to the bottom, sinking paw-deep into the mud. She then scooped a pawful of mud up and dumped it on the rim.

Thunder pawed it away. The black tom next to him scraped peat from the side of the hole.

Gray Wing glanced sadly toward the two bodies lying nearby. Their bony frames showed through their bedraggled fur. Rain streamed down whiskers that would never twitch again.

Thunder looked up as Gray Wing reached him. "Thanks for coming." He straightened, wiping his muddy paws on his belly fur.

"Is Slash really gone?" Gray Wing asked.

"For now," Thunder told him. "But we need to bury these cats and get the others away. Who knows if he might come back?"

The rogue beside him sat up. "Or the dogs might return."

Thunder nodded toward the black tom. "This is Raven," he told Gray Wing. He glanced at the she-cat standing in the grave. "That's Juniper."

"Hi." Raven dipped his head.

"Hello." Juniper met Gray Wing's gaze, then blinked at Thunder. "Do you think this is deep enough?"

"It needs to be a bit deeper if it's to keep the bodies safe from foxes." Thunder stood up. Mud caked his paws. "Will you two be okay finishing here while I talk to Gray Wing?"

"We'll be fine." Juniper scooped out another pawful of wet dirt.

Thunder signaled to Gray Wing with a flick of his tail, then wove his way between the tussocks.

Gray Wing followed until they were clear of the others.

"What are we going to do with them?" Thunder whispered.

"They clearly can't stay here." Gray Wing stared across the empty marsh. "The camp's not safe anymore."

"We could take them to Tall Shadow's camp," Thunder suggested. "It's not too far."

Gray Wing frowned. "It might be too near. Now that the dogs have their scent, they might track these cats to Tall Shadow's camp if we take them there."

"The river?" Thunder wondered.

"It's a long trek for injured cats."

Thunder glanced toward the wrecked camp. "Frog's badly

injured. I'm not even sure he can walk. I don't know how we're going to get him over the Thunderpath."

"We'll deal with that when we come to it." Gray Wing shifted his paws. The moor would be the safest place for the rogues. The hollow had thick walls and was easy to defend. And every moor cat knew how to divert dogs away from the camp by leading them through swaths of heather and gorse and hiding in rabbit burrows until the dogs were exhausted and confused. But how would he convince Wind Runner to take the rogues in? Why would she welcome cats who had attacked her campmates and stolen their prey? Gray Wing frowned. He'd persuade her somehow. It would only be temporary: until the rogues recovered, or found new homes. "What about the moor?" he ventured.

"The hollow?" Thunder's eyes brightened. "They'd be safe there. I've seen how moor cats deal with dogs."

Gray Wing nodded. "Let's take them there for now. Tomorrow we'll decide where they can go next."

The grass rustled behind them. Gray Wing jerked his muzzle around to see Violet standing at their tails.

She blinked at him hopefully. "Can we join your group?"

Gray Wing froze. Wind Runner would never agree to that!

Violet must have sensed his hesitation. "We don't *all* have to join the same group. Perhaps a few could join yours, and some could live in the pines and some in the oak forest. There are cats by the river, too, aren't there? Maybe some could go there." Her gaze drifted to Thunder. "And perhaps I could join *your* group?"

Gray Wing's ears twitched. Thunder's eyes widened as Violet blinked at him hopefully. They seemed lost in each other's eyes.

Then Thunder spoke. "I'd have to speak with my camp-mates." His fur rippled self-consciously. "But I'd like you to join our group."

A burst of happiness spread over Violet's features before she dipped her head shyly. "Thank you."

"Thunder!" Juniper called from beyond the tussocks. "We're finished."

"I'm coming!" Thunder called back. He blinked at Gray Wing. "Is it decided? We take them back to the moor tonight. Then tomorrow we can see which groups will take the others."

"Yes." Gray Wing nodded. It seemed the only way. But would Wind Runner give the rogues shelter for the night? He pushed the worry away. The most important thing now was to get the rogues away from here.

"I'll fetch the others." Violet's mew cut into his thoughts. "They'll want to say good-bye to their campmates." She hesi-tated before she padded away, her mew turning wistful. "Slash used to make us take bodies to the carrion place and leave them for the crows and rats."

Gray Wing shuddered. Could rogues that had once treated their dead campmates as crow-food *ever* learn to live peace-fully among moor and forest cats?

By the time the rogues had said good-bye to Beech and Stone and buried their bodies so that no fox could dig them up, night had swallowed the marsh. The rain had eased, but clouds still covered the moon. Lightning Tail paced in the darkness, as though impatient to leave. Gray Wing gathered the rogues in the remains of the camp. "Are you well enough to walk as far as the moor?"

He glanced around the expectant faces.

Willow looked toward Frog, who was still lying at the edge of the clearing.

Pebble Heart was crouching beside the injured tom. "Frog will need to be carried."

Who was strong enough? Gray Wing scanned the rogues. Moss was hardly injured, and Raven looked fit. Juniper must be tired after the digging, but she met his gaze eagerly. If Lightning Tail helped, they should be able to carry the wounded rogue between them. "Moss, Raven, Juniper, and Lightning Tail. Will you carry Frog?"

"Of course." Moss padded toward his injured campmate at once, Juniper and Raven hurrying after him. As Lightning Tail followed, Moss tucked his nose beneath Frog's shoulder. The injured tom grunted as Raven grasped his scruff.

"Careful," Pebble Heart cautioned. His eyes glittered with worry. "He's injured his spine. Too much movement might make it worse."

Raven tugged Frog onto Moss's shoulders.

Frog screeched with pain.

Pebble Heart's fur bushed. "Stop!"

Gently, Moss moved away and Raven lowered Frog to the ground.

Thunder blinked at Pebble Heart. "What can we do? We can't leave him here."

Pebble Heart was gazing into the distance, his eyes clouded with a look that Gray Wing knew well. The young tom was thinking.

"Frog." Willow crouched beside the tom. "You'll be okay. We won't leave you behind."

"He needs to lie flat as we move him," Pebble Heart murmured.

Gray Wing frowned. "That's not possible."

Pebble Heart blinked at him, his eyes lighting up in the darkness. "Yes, it is!" He raced to the camp entrance. "We need to find the right sized piece of bark. I've seen plenty in the pine forest. It'll curve around his body but be flat enough to support him. We can use it to drag him to the moor."

Lightning Tail pricked his ears. "I'll help find some."

"I'll come too!" Moss hurried across the clearing.

"Where's Moss going?" Pine blinked anxiously at his father as he headed out of camp.

"He's not going far," Dawn soothed. "He'll be back soon."

Pine lifted his chin. "I'm going with him." He began to cross the clearing, following Moss's paw steps.

Violet darted forward and grabbed the tip of the kit's tail between her teeth. "You're staying here," she mewed through gritted teeth as she dragged Pine toward his mother. "Dawn has had enough to worry about today without you wandering off."

Pine struggled free and glared at the dark gray she-cat, but he didn't argue. Sticking his tail in the air, he stalked back to Dawn's side and sat down stiffly.

Gray Wing glanced toward the pine trees, no more than shadows against the cloudy night sky.

No one spoke as they waited for Pebble Heart, Moss, and Lightning Tail to return.

Gray Wing stiffened when, at last, paw steps sounded outside the camp. He hurried to the entrance, then hopped back as Lightning Tail burst, tail-first, into the clearing. He was dragging a piece of bark in his teeth while Moss and Pebble Heart pushed the other end with their paws. Gray Wing sniffed it as Lightning Tail let it drop beside Frog. The scent of sap was still fresh. It clearly had not been lying long on the forest floor. The bark would be strong.

Pebble Heart crouched beside Frog. "We need to move you onto the bark," he told the tom. "It will hurt, but not for long."

"I can bear it," Frog grunted.

Willow paced beside the injured rogue, her worried gaze on Pebble Heart. "You'll be careful, won't you?"

"Of course." Pebble Heart buried his muzzle into Frog's scruff and bit down. He blinked at Lightning Tail and Moss, and they hurried to help. Nosing Frog's hindquarters, they heaved him onto the piece of bark, while Pebble Heart guided his head.

Frog grunted, his eyes sparking with pain, then fell limp as they laid him into the curve of his bark nest.

Violet padded around him, looking worried. "Will we be able to drag it?"

Thunder puffed out his chest. "There's only one way to

find out." Leaning down, he grasped one corner of the bark between his teeth and tugged. The bark slid a little way over the ground. Juniper hurried to help, taking the other corner in her teeth. Between them, the two cats began to heave Frog toward the clearing.

Gray Wing watched them haul him through the entrance. The rogues limped behind them, a straggling trail of battered cats. His pelt prickled nervously. Could they really drag Frog all the way to the moor? And what would he tell Wind Runner when they arrived?

"Frog?" Willow's anxious mew sounded from the head of the group. Gray Wing hurried past the rogues and stopped beside her. Above, the clouds were thinning. Stars were glittering through the gaps. They had made it onto the moor. The hollow was visible in the weak starlight, no more than a shadow on the hillside.

Willow leaned over the bark nest. The rogue's body was slumped in its curve.

"He's not moving." Willow looked expectantly at Pebble Heart.

The young tom sniffed Frog's muzzle. "He's still breathing, but very weakly," he murmured.

"Do something to help him!" Willow's tail quivered.

Gray Wing's heart twisted as he heard horror in her mew.

Pebble Heart met her gaze. "I can clean wounds and stop them from bleeding, but Frog's injury is inside. There's nothing I can do."

Anger flared in Willow's gaze. "But you got him this far!"

She glanced toward the hollow. "We're so near. He *has* to make it."

Frog grunted softly.

Willow crouched beside him. "Frog. Hang on. We're nearly there. You're going to be okay."

Gray Wing saw Frog's tail slide limply onto the ground.

Willow hopped over the bark and tucked it in neatly beside him. "We're going to take care of you, Frog."

Frog made no sound.

"Frog?" Willow leaned into the nest and lapped at his shoulder urgently. "Say something. Wake up. Stay awake. You can sleep when we get to safety."

Pebble Heart placed his paw on Frog's flank.

Gray Wing's heart lurched as shock darkened the young tom's gaze. He looked at Frog and saw stillness beneath Pebble Heart's paw. Frog wasn't breathing.

"Frog!" Panic edged Willow's mew.

"I'm sorry." Pebble Heart's mew was husky. "He's dead."

"No!" Willow backed away, her eyes wide.

Violet hurried to her side, steadying Willow as she began to tremble. "So much death!"

Thunder padded forward. "This will be the last." He met Gray Wing's gaze. Was that doubt flickering in his starlit gaze?

Gray Wing dipped his head. "There's no point dragging Frog to the hollow now," he meowed softly. "We should bury him here and mark his grave so that he will not be forgotten."

As he spoke, he heard paws pounding across the hillside. He turned his head and saw, in the moonlight, Wind

Runner and Gorse Fur running toward them. He hurried to meet them. He didn't want Wind Runner stumbling into the rogues without warning.

"There you are, Gray Wing!" Wind Runner pulled up as she neared, her pelt rippling uneasily as she saw the rogues gathered behind him. Her mew hardened. "What are *they* doing here?"

Gorse Fur narrowed his eyes as he scanned the bedraggled cats.

Gray Wing shifted his paws. "Their camp was attacked by dogs. Slash deserted them with a few of his allies. Three of their campmates are dead and most of them are injured. I told them that we would give them shelter for the night." He held his leader's gaze unflinchingly. "Their camp is no longer safe. They need our help."

Wind Runner flattened her ears, her gaze flicking toward Juniper, Raven, and Ember. "They didn't need our help when they attacked our patrol a few days ago."

Gray Wing stood his ground. "They had no choice. Disobeying Slash would have cost them their lives." He glanced at Fern, remembering her terror of the cruel tom. "But Slash is gone now. These cats are no different from you and me." He hoped it was true.

"Really?" Wind Runner padded past Gray Wing and circled Juniper and Raven. She stared at them angrily. "Are we supposed to trust you now?"

"We won't hurt you," Raven told her quickly.

Wind Runner curled her lip. "If only you'd felt that way last time we met."

Gorse Fur padded to his mate's side. "They don't look in a fit state to harm anyone."

Wind Runner glared at him. "So we should take them into our camp?"

"Just until tomorrow," Gray Wing pleaded. The wind was turning cold and cutting through his damp pelt. He shivered. "They need shelter."

Dawn padded forward. She nosed Drizzle and Pine ahead of her. "Will you at least take my kits?"

"No!" Drizzle dug her paws into the grass.

"We want to stay with you!" Pine stared desperately at his mother.

Moss padded to his mate's side. "It's okay, Dawn. We can keep them safe."

Dawn ignored him. She kept her gaze fixed on Wind Runner. "They're so small, they'll freeze out here on the moor. Please give them shelter. They can't harm you."

Wind Runner eyed the kits, her gaze wavering with uncertainty.

Gray Wing hurried to her side. "We can't separate them from their mother. We have to take them all in. They're no threat to us now. They need our protection. What if the dogs follow their scent? Or Slash comes back?"

Wind Runner's pelt bristled. "If dogs are following them, we don't want them in our camp."

"We can drive off dogs." Gorse Fur's mew took Gray Wing by surprise. "*And* Slash if we need to." He glanced at the kits. "We can't turn them away."

Thunder stepped forward. "Lightning Tail and I will stay

in your camp too, if you'll let us. We can help if there's any trouble."

Gray Wing blinked hopefully at Wind Runner. "Let's prove that we're better than Slash," he begged. "He abandoned them. We can't."

Wind Runner's eyes flashed. "*We* don't need to prove anything."

Willow padded forward, her head low. "I understand why you don't want to take us in. But please let me bury my brother here before we move on. He deserves to rest in peace."

Wind Runner followed Willow's gaze toward the scrap of wet fur curled in the bark. "Did you drag him all the way here?"

"We thought we could save him," Willow told her bleakly.

Wind Runner blinked, her eyes clouding, as though suddenly overwhelmed by the tragic scene confronting her. "Very well." Her mew was husky. "You may all shelter in our camp for the night," Wind Runner told her. "We will post extra guards, and in the morning we'll decide what to do."

Above, a cloud drifted away from the moon. Silvery light bathed the rogues.

Gray Wing dipped his head. "Thank you, Wind Runner." Relief washed over him. The rogues would be safe for the night.

What would happen to them in the morning? He pushed the thought away and turned to Willow. "Let's find a sheltered spot to bury Frog."

CHAPTER 15

❧

Clear Sky glanced at the moon, not yet full in the indigo sky. Frost glittered on the branches as he padded through the dark woods.

Blossom walked beside him, her paws crunching leaves as they headed for the four trees hollow. "Do you think Wind Runner will ask you to take in some rogues again?" Her breath billowed in the cold night air.

"I hope not." Clear Sky fluffed out his pelt. Memories of One Eye pricked his conscience. He'd been a fool to trust *that* rogue, even if he was Star Flower's father. He was determined to protect his group better this time.

Blossom sniffed. "Then why did she call this meeting?"

"She wants to hear how the groups are getting on with their new campmates." It had been a quarter moon since Wind Runner had come to ask him to take in some of Slash's followers. She had seemed irritated by his refusal to take any rogues off her paws. But he'd pointed out that he'd taken in a loner the night before—a tom called Red who'd turned up at the border, ruffled and frightened, claiming he'd been attacked by dogs in Twolegplace. Clear Sky assumed they were the same dogs that had gone on to attack the rogue camp. He'd been ready to send Red back to Twolegplace, but Star Flower had insisted he let the skinny tom rest in their camp. Although Quick Water and Nettle had argued, still not ready to trust another rogue, the others had eventually voted them down based on Red's condition. He was clearly underfed, with lumps of fur missing where the dogs had snapped at him.

When Wind Runner had come to ask him to take in more rogues, he'd said simply, "I have enough mouths to feed already." It was true, after all. Clear Sky worried that Quick Water still nursed a lingering distrust of Star Flower and any other rogue cat. He sensed it best to limit the number of rogues he allowed into the group, lest Quick Water's wariness spread.

He slowed where a fallen branch blocked their path and let Blossom leap it first. He jumped after her, his paws sliding on the icy leaves beyond. Perhaps he *should* have offered to take one of the rogues. Now that Slash had stopped stealing their food, the prey pile was tall enough to feed all his cats. Red had proven himself a good hunter and fed more than his own belly.

The musty scent of the four trees hollow touched Clear Sky's nose. As they reached the rim, he paused and looked down.

Wind Runner was already pacing the clearing. Gray Wing sat and waited at the edge. River Ripple had brought Dappled Pelt with him. Tall Shadow sat beside them, while Pebble Heart sniffed curiously at the frost-wilted plants edging the slopes. Seeing Thunder's orange pelt, pale in the moonlight, Clear Sky was surprised once again how broad the younger cat's shoulders had grown. He still thought of his son as a young tom, feisty and argumentative. How mature he looked now.

Clear Sky shifted his paws guiltily. This past moon, Star Flower's kits had shown him how close the bond between father and kit could be. He knew he should have handled his firstborn son better. Instead of advising him, he'd reacted defensively to Thunder's challenges, and criticized where he should have guided. *Why did I waste my chance to be a father to him?*

But as he watched Thunder lead Leaf across the clearing, stopping to speak with Wind Runner, his chest swelled with pride. Thunder had grown into a fine leader even without his guidance.

Why worry about the past? He could only change the future.

Clear Sky plunged down the slope, Blossom at his heels, and crashed through the bracken into the clearing. The other leaders turned as he raced through the moonlight. "Good evening!" He greeted them warmly. For the first time in a moon, he felt optimistic. Slash was gone; the groups were growing; prey was starting to creep from its burrows so that, once more, bellies were full.

Wind Runner eyed him darkly. "You seem pleased with yourself."

Leaf snorted. "That's because *he* didn't take any of Slash's rogues into his group."

Clear Sky blinked in surprise. Why were they so resentful? Were the rogues causing trouble? "Is something wrong?"

Tall Shadow whisked her tail. "The groups are unsettled. *You* should try sleeping in a nest beside a cat who, half a moon ago, was stealing your prey."

"It must be hard," Clear Sky sympathized. "But they're hunting for us, not stealing, now."

River Ripple's eyes shone in the moonlight. "Actually, Dawn and Moss are *great* hunters," he reported. "They still haven't learned to swim, but they're trying. They'll be catching fish in another moon."

Gray Wing pricked his ears. "How are Pine and Drizzle?" he asked anxiously. "Have they settled in well?"

Dappled Pelt purred. "They're like a pair of ducklings. They can't wait to learn how to swim."

Thunder blinked. "Surely they're too young?"

River Ripple's whiskers twitched. "They're only allowed to paddle in the shallows for now. And there's always someone with them. They can learn to swim as soon as they're strong enough to ride the currents."

Wind Runner's tail twitched impatiently. "I'm pleased Dawn and Moss and their kits are adjusting to group life," she muttered. "I just wish I could say the same about Fern, Willow, and Bee."

Clear Sky noticed Gray Wing's pelt ripple irritably. Was he annoyed with Wind Runner?

"They're trying their best," Gray Wing meowed sharply.

Wind Runner flashed him a look. "Slate says that Fern

refuses to go into the warren."

"So does *Minnow*," Gray Wing reminded her. "Not *every* cat likes to hunt underground."

Wind Runner ignored him. "And Minnow tells me Willow keeps getting lost in the heather. Every time she goes missing, we have to stop the hunt and send someone to find her."

"Their trainers are working with them. Willow will learn the trails soon—"

Wind Runner cut him off. "Bee is the worst," she snapped. "At least Fern and Willow are trying. Reed tries to be nice, but I can see that Bee is lazy. She thinks being part of a group means having prey dropped at your paws. She doesn't realize that the group only works if it works *together*."

Tall Shadow nodded. "Juniper and Raven hunt, but only together. They won't work with Jagged Peak and Holly, who are meant to train them. Even when I send them on a patrol with others, they go off by themselves."

Clear Sky frowned. "They share their catch, though?" Worry wormed beneath his pelt. Were Slash's campmates going to undermine the hard-won unity of the groups?

"They add what they catch to the prey pile," Tall Shadow conceded. "But they eat by themselves, and they've made a nest as far from the others as they can."

"It's hardly surprising." Thunder whisked his tail. "I *saw* what it was like in Slash's camp. Slash starved his campmates. He ordered them to hurt one another. It will take a while for these rogues to trust that we are kinder."

Leaf narrowed his eyes. "Is that why Ember goes hunting by himself?"

Thunder glanced at his campmate. "He doesn't feel comfortable in a patrol yet," he mewed defensively. *And he won't work with Cloud Spots at all,* he added silently, remembering the tom's refusal to be trained in the ways of the group.

Leaf grunted. "And he eats what he catches outside camp. I've never seen him add anything to the prey pile."

Wind Runner shifted her paws. "These rogues live by a different code. They'll never learn to live by ours. We share what we catch and we take care of one another. They don't seem to understand that loyalty and sharing make us strong."

Gray Wing raised his gaze to the star-specked sky. "We must be patient," he murmured. "Remember how long it took us to learn to work together. It's only been a quarter moon since the rogues joined us. We must give them time."

Warmth surged beneath Clear Sky's pelt as he realized his brother was right. How kind and patient Gray Wing was.

Gray Wing went on. "Don't forget, we've taken in new cats before," he meowed. " You were a loner once, Wind Runner." He dipped his head respectfully to the moor cat. "And you, Blossom."

Clear Sky's gaze flicked to the tortoiseshell. Surely they must remember what it was like to adjust to group life?

Leaf's gaze glittered impatiently. "We may have been loners once, but we never hung out with cats like *Slash.* It's hard to trust any cat who chose someone like *that* as a leader."

Tall Shadow returned the forest cat's gaze grimly. "It's harder to trust cats who were thieves less than a moon ago."

"Cats can change." Clear Sky lifted his chin. Loving Star Flower and his kits had made him a different cat. She was

One Eye's daughter, and yet she was as good and loyal as any cat he knew. Where a cat came from did not have to define who they now were. Surely kindness would change the rogues? "We should not judge them on what they used to do, but on what they decide to do now."

Wind Runner snorted. "That's easy for you to say, Clear Sky. You didn't take in any of Slash's cats."

"I told you," Clear Sky said, defending himself, "we had too many mouths to feed already. Besides, it's not like I've *never* taken in rogues."

Leaf flattened an ear. "Like One Eye?" he muttered dryly.

Clear Sky fought back irritation. Would they ever let him forget his mistake? Would *they* have been able to predict how cruel and greedy One Eye would become? "Most of the time it turns out fine!" He nodded toward Blossom. "Blossom is a great campmate. Thorn, Nettle, Birch, and Alder are as loyal as any camp-born cat."

Blossom puffed out her chest. "Our new campmate, Red, is a good hunter. He catches far more than he eats, and I trust him as much as any cat."

Gray Wing blinked, surprise flashing in his eyes.

Thunder's ears pricked. "Did you say *Red*?"

Clear Sky's pelt pricked along his spine. "Yes," he answered uneasily. "Why?"

Gray Wing blinked at them. "Red was one of Slash's rogues."

Shock flashed through Clear Sky's pelt. He stared at Blossom. "Did you know that?"

She shook her head. "Red just said he'd been chased by dogs and needed somewhere safe to stay. I thought he was from Twolegplace."

Wind Runner's eyes sparked with interest. "He lied to you."

"He didn't lie." Clear Sky's hackles lifted. "He never *said* he was from Twolegplace. Just that the dogs had chased him from there. We *assumed* it was his home."

"And he didn't correct you." The moor cat padded closer. "Do you still trust him *now*?" Her gaze bored into Clear Sky's.

Clear Sky looked away, anxiety pricking in his paws. He understood why Red had misled him. The rogue must have guessed he'd be turned away if he confessed to being Slash's campmate. And yet Red *had* misled him. Was that trustworthy behavior?

River Ripple got to his paws. "It's not surprising we are wary of our new campmates," he meowed. "They have tried to hurt us in the past. But every cat makes mistakes. We all know how ruthless Slash is. He let Fern's sister *die*. Can any of you be sure that, faced with such cruelty, you'd refuse to do something you'd regret?"

Wind Runner curled her lip. "I'd *never* steal!"

"*Never*? Not even to protect your kits?" Tall Shadow narrowed her eyes.

Clear Sky saw Gray Wing's gaze flash toward him. "River Ripple is right," Clear Sky meowed. "When we're frightened or angry, we make mistakes. But among good friends, we find the best in ourselves. Just being in the groups will change these rogues. I'm sure of it."

But even as he spoke, his thoughts flicked to Red. He'd left the rogue in the camp. Fear prickled through his fur. A rogue was in the camp with his kits! He fought the urge to race home. He reminded himself of his own words: *Thorn, Nettle, Birch, and Alder are as loyal as any camp-born cat.* And yet panic sparked in his belly. What if Red was like One Eye? What if he turned the group against him? Would he drive him out? Would he harm Tiny Branch, Flower Foot, and Dew Petal?

"Clear Sky?" Gray Wing was staring at him anxiously. "Are you okay?"

Wind Runner interrupted before Clear Sky could answer. "He's suddenly realized what it feels like to live with your enemy."

Anger flared in Gray Wing's eyes. "These cats asked us for help!" He glared at Wind Runner. "So what if they hate rabbit burrows, or get lost in the heather." His glaze flashed to Leaf. "It might take a while before they feel like hunting in patrols or making nests beside cats they hardly know." He turned to Tall Shadow. "They asked us for help, and if we think we are so much better than they are, we should set an example and *help* them!"

River Ripple lifted his chin. "We can earn these cats' trust by trusting them. They came to us seeking safety, and we have given them that. Surely they will return our kindness with kindness of their own?"

Leaf huffed. "Do you think foxes would stop being foxes if we trusted them?"

"We're not talking about foxes," Clear Sky snapped. "We're

talking about cats." And yet he couldn't push from his mind the image of Red eyeing his kits as they played in the clearing. Could a rogue who'd concealed the truth ever be trusted?

River Ripple padded to the center of the clearing. "Clear Sky is right. If we want these rogues to live by our code, we must show them that our code makes life better. They must see that peace and sharing and honor are good for the group, and that what's good for the group is good for the individual. We find trust in trusting, and learn kindness by being kind."

Clear Sky steadied his breathing. *Find trust in trusting.* Red *would* be a good campmate, just like Blossom and Thorn and Nettle.

I only have to trust.

Thunder flicked his tail. "I know I can trust Violet. She's happy and grateful to be part of my group. And I'm sure Ember will feel part of the group before long."

Wind Runner frowned. "I hope you're right."

Pebble Heart lifted his tail. "No cat likes change, but change comes all the same. These cats may be a great gift to us." He glanced at the sky as though hoping for a sign.

Clear Sky followed his gaze. It had been a long time since their ancestors had shared with them. He wondered for a moment what Storm or Bright Stream thought of the rogues. Storm had visited him in a dream once and told him that she was glad he was with Star Flower. Her words had comforted him. Perhaps if she spoke to him now, she could tell him whether he could trust Red. But the stars glittered silently, and no ghostly figures flitted in the shadows of the clearing.

"Let's go home," he suggested. The frost was hardening. He could feel it in his pelt.

"We've said all we need to say," Gray Wing said, eyeing Wind Runner warily.

She fluffed out her fur. "I guess we might as well head for our nests. We'll only freeze standing here."

River Ripple licked his lips. "There's a trout waiting for me back at camp."

Dappled Pelt purred. "If the kits haven't eaten it. They like fish more than mouse now."

The cats began to head for the slopes. Clear Sky followed Blossom toward the edge of the clearing.

"Clear Sky?" Thunder called.

Clear Sky paused, puzzled, and looked over his shoulder.

Thunder was staring at him hopefully from the center while the others disappeared into the bracken.

"Go ahead without me." Clear Sky nodded to Blossom. "Check on Star Flower and the kits and tell them I won't be long." Leaf nodded and ran off, and Clear Sky headed toward Thunder, curiosity pricking in his pelt. "What is it?"

Thunder's eyes were dark. "I just wanted to warn you."

Clear Sky stiffened.

"Red brought the pack of dogs into the rogues' camp." Thunder blinked at him.

Clear Sky's heart quickened. *Were Quick Water and Nettle right?* "On purpose?"

"No. But it was a pretty dangerous mistake." Thunder glanced anxiously toward the forest at the top of the slope. "Just keep an eye on him."

Clear Sky shivered. "Thanks for letting me know."

Thunder glanced away. "I'm not trying to stir up trouble."

"Why would I think that?" Clear Sky blinked in surprise.

"We don't always trust the same cats." Thunder was avoiding his gaze.

Guilt jabbed Clear Sky's belly. Thunder had once warned him not to trust Star Flower—though he'd had good reason. Star Flower had broken the young tom's heart. Still, Clear Sky had lashed out at him. "We've had our differences," he admitted. "But that's been my fault. I should have been a better father to you." He waited for Thunder to meet his gaze before going on. "My new kits have made me realize how much I failed you."

"You didn't fail me," Thunder mumbled. "I guess I just wasn't the son you wanted."

"That's not true!" Clear Sky's mew thickened. He knew now with absolute clarity that Thunder had never been the problem. *I was the one who was difficult.* "I was just too thick-headed to realize how special you are. I'm proud of the cat you've become. I'm proud you're my son, and I'm sorry I missed the chance to be a proper father to you."

"Well, you can make up for that with your new family." There was bitterness in Thunder's mew.

"I love my new family," Clear Sly admitted. "But they have helped me realize how much I love you. I'm just sorry I couldn't show you that in the past." He leaned closer to Thunder. "But I hope you will always come to me if you need help. I hope you will share your joy and worries with me, whatever they are. It's too late for me to be the father you should have had. But I hope that one day I can become as important to you as Gray Wing."

Wariness glimmered in Thunder's gaze. For a moment, Clear Sky thought the young tom was going to tell him something meaningful. But Thunder just shrugged again.

"Thanks, Clear Sky," he murmured, and turned away.

Clear Sky watched him head for the slope and duck into the bracken. He realized that Thunder wasn't ready to confide in him. He might never be ready. Why should he be? Grief tugged at Clear Sky's heart. He'd let his firstborn son down, and no matter how hard he tried, he could never make up for the precious moons he'd wasted. He headed toward his forest. He had failed with Thunder, but he was determined he would never let his new family down. They would always know that he loved them more than he loved his own life.

CHAPTER 16

❧

Gray Wing dreamed.

Pine needles crunched beneath his paws. Smooth straight trunks loomed around him and disappeared into shadow on every side. The pungent scent of sap filled his nose. He glanced up. Darkness hid the treetops. His chest tightened. *What am I doing here?* The shadows closed in, pressing closer. *Where's the moor?* He tasted the air, anxiety sparking in his belly. *I need to get home.* Slate's kits were due any day. He began to wheeze as darkness enveloped him. He blinked, straining to see, struggling to breathe. Where was Slate? Where were his campmates? Why was he here alone?

Suddenly, light pierced the darkness. Starry figures were moving through the trees at the edge of his vision. He spun around, struggling for breath as he tried to see them properly. Were the ghost cats here? Had they come to share with him? "Turtle Tail?" he called through the darkness toward a distant shape shimmering with starlight. The shape flitted out of sight. "Jackdaw's Cry? Is that you?" A sparkling tom flashed in the distance then disappeared. "Are you hiding?" Frustration itched beneath Gray Wing's pelt. He heard murmuring mews and twisted each time he spotted a flash of starlight, always too late to see who it was. "What do you want?" His heart pounded as he gasped for breath. The murmuring faded, and the darkness eased. Light showed ahead, the soft rosy light of dawn.

"Gray Wing!" Slate's agonized cry echoed through the trees. "Help me."

"Where are you?" Gray Wing began to run, heading for the light. Wheezing, he zigzagged between the trees. "I'm coming, Slate!" If only he could get clear of this forest, he could find her. *I just hope my breath lasts.*

"Gray Wing!"

He jerked awake, pushing himself blearily onto his forepaws. Blinking, he saw his den walls, washed in the gray light of early morning. Relief washed over his pelt as his chest loosened and he drew in a deep breath.

Slate moved against him. "Gray Wing." Her mew was hard with pain. "The kits are coming."

He looked down. She lay panting beside him, her swollen belly resting against his flank. He stared at her, unsure what to do.

"Get Reed!" Slate growled. "Hurry!"

Gray Wing darted to the entrance and crossed the clearing in a few bounds. "Reed?" He poked his head into the tom's den.

Reed was curled around Minnow, his eyes closed.

"Reed!" Gray Wing called louder.

Reed lifted his head and blinked into the light. "What?"

"The kits are coming!" Gray Wing told him.

Minnow sat up sharply. "I'll fetch Wind Runner. She's had more experience."

Gray Wing blinked at her, remembering how their leader had helped at Star Flower's kitting. As Minnow slid past him, he stared at Reed. "Have *you* helped at a kitting before?"

"When I was a rogue." Reed's gaze darkened ominously.

Gray Wing stiffened. "What happened?"

"The kits were fine." Reed nosed past him, avoiding his gaze. "But the queen died."

Gray Wing's heart lurched as he hurried after the silver tabby "Why? How?"

"She was sick before she had the kits." Reed turned to meet Gray Wing's gaze. "Slate's as healthy as a hawk. She'll be fine." He raced across the clearing.

Gray Wing tried to calm his racing heart, remembering Turtle Tail's kitting. He'd arrived after the kits were born and still remembered his panic as though it was yesterday. He forced his fur flat. When he got anxious, his breathing got worse. He couldn't afford to be slowed down. Slate needed him. But what if he lost her? What if something happened to the kits? Suddenly he understood the desperation Clear Sky must have felt when Star Flower had been kidnapped.

Paws pounded across the clearing. Wind Runner whipped past him and disappeared into the den after Reed.

Gray Wing pushed his head inside. The two cats were crouching beside Slate, who lay on her side, her round flanks heaving.

"Everything will be fine," Wind Runner told her.

"We've both delivered kits before," Reed added.

"It's the simplest thing in the world," Wind Runner purred. "Countless queens have kitted for countless moons."

Gray Wing tensed as he saw pain cloud Slate's gaze. "She's suffering!" he gasped.

Wind Runner turned and blinked at him slowly. "Wait outside, Gray Wing."

"But—"

"You'll be little help here," she insisted.

"But I want to be with her." Gray Wing stared at the group leader.

"Go and pace the clearing," Reed told him. "Get as much fresh air into your chest as you can. Once it's over, you're going to need your breath to greet your new kits."

Slate groaned, her paws quivering.

"The first kit's on its way." Wind Runner jerked her nose toward Gray Wing. "Wait outside!"

Obediently, Gray Wing backed out of the den. Every instinct told him to barge inside and crouch beside Slate. But Reed was right. He needed fresh air and a chance to calm himself. Unable to stand still, he padded between the tussocks. The fresh moor wind lifted his fur. There was a chill in it, and he glanced toward the horizon. Pale blue sky shaded into pink where the sun was pushing up from beyond the trees. Cold weather was coming.

"Gray Wing?" Fern bounded toward him. "Minnow says the kits are coming." She glanced toward his den.

Gray Wing nodded. Cats were stirring around the camp. Gorse Fur blinked from his den. Dust Muzzle and Moth Flight stretched in a thin patch of sunlight beside the tall rock. Spotted Fur pawed through the remains of the prey pile while Bee watched him, her eyes narrowed. Was that scorn in the rogue she-cat's gaze?

Fern interrupted his thoughts. "Do you want toms or she-kits?" Her eyes were bright with excitement.

Gray Wing stared at her blankly. "I hadn't thought about it." *Any* kits would be wonderful.

"Willow says that kits born in leaf-bare are the strongest." Fern lifted her tail. "*I* was born in leaf-bare."

Gray Wing could hardly concentrate on her chatter, but it was good to see the young she-cat so cheerful. She'd been mourning Beech since her death, and though she'd eagerly joined in with camp duties, there had been slowness in her step and sadness in her eyes. This morning, she seemed truly happy for the first time since he'd known her. Her pelt was sleek, and lean muscle hid the bones that had once jutted out beneath her fur. "Life on the moor seems to suit you," he told her.

Fern purred. "I love living here. Being part of your group is so different from living in Slash's camp. Everyone is so kind, and Wind Runner is so wise." She paused. "But sometimes I see her looking at me like she doesn't trust me." Her gaze darkened. "Have I done something wrong?"

Gray Wing felt a prick of sympathy for Fern. "You've done nothing wrong. Wind Runner will take time to learn to trust you. But once she does, she'll be as loyal as your own mother."

Fern looked away. "My mother abandoned me and Beech."

"Is that how you ended up with Slash?"

Fern didn't answer, her tail drooping.

Gray Wing moved on, guilty that he'd awoken bad memories. "Well, you're here now. *We're* your new family."

"Willow's, too?" Fern glanced at the pale tabby she-cat as she emerged sleepily from her den. "And Bee's?"

"Of course." Gray Wing lowered his voice as he eyed the yellow-and-black-striped she-cat. She was still watching Spotted Fur disdainfully as he gnawed on a stale shrew. "But you need to persuade Bee to volunteer for more camp duties. We *all* have to help patrol and hunt."

Fern shifted her paws uneasily. "I'll try," she promised. "But Bee says she doesn't—"

"Gray Wing!" Wind Runner interrupted the young she-cat. "Come and see your kits."

"Already?" Excitement fizzed through his pelt. He hurried across the clearing and dived into his den.

Slate lay in her nest and blinked at him through the half-light. Her eyes glistened with joy. Gray Wing met her gaze, his heart swelling with love. Then he glanced along her flank. Three tiny kits suckled at her belly. He padded closer, sniffing them one by one. A dark gray tom-kit pushed against his pale gray tabby sister. Beside her, another tom-kit purred loudly, his black-and-white pelt fluffing as it dried.

"They're beautiful." A purr swelled in Gray Wing's throat. Love filled his heart. He was surprised how familiar it felt.

He'd expected to feel different about his own kits. With a jolt, he realized how much he'd loved Turtle Tail's kits, and his heart seemed to flood with joy. *I've known so much love!* He glanced fondly at Slate. "I promise to teach them how to hunt and keep them safe until they are as strong and brave as their mother."

Her eyes glowed as she returned his gaze. "They are lucky to have you as their father. You've raised so many kits, and they've all grown into fine cats."

Wind Runner dipped her head. "We should leave you in peace to get to know your new family." Leaning down, she lapped Slate's cheek. "You did well."

Reed nodded at Gray Wing. "I'll take a hunting patrol out. Slate will be hungry soon." The silver tabby padded from the den, Wind Runner at his tail.

Gray Wing settled behind Slate, curling himself around her as she nursed their kits. The air throbbed with their purring, and he joined in until the whole den seemed to resonate with joy.

"Gray Wing?" A soft mew woke him from his doze. He blinked open his eyes and saw Gorse Fur's face at the den entrance. "Jagged Peak and Tall Shadow have come to see the kits."

Gray Wing pushed himself to his paws, tucking the moss lining of the nest closer around Slate to keep her warm. The kits were sleeping at her belly while she snored softly. He crept past them and followed Gorse Fur out of the den.

Tiny flecks of snow whisked through the air, too small to settle. Tall Shadow and Jagged Peak stood outside, pine needles caught in their fur. A fat pigeon lay at their paws.

"We brought a gift." Jagged Peak dipped his head.

Gray Wing fluffed out his pelt, his nose aching in the icy chill. "Thank you."

"Congratulations!" Tall Shadow purred loudly. She glanced past him. "May I see them?"

"They're asleep," Gray Wing warned. "But I'm sure Slate would like to show them off."

"I'll try not to disturb them too much," Tall Shadow promised. She slid into the den.

Jagged Peak stayed beside the pigeon. "We met Reed on the border. He told us Slate had kitted. Tall Shadow says kits are a good omen. She wanted to see them for herself."

Gray Wing puffed out his chest. "There are three of them."

"They'll keep you busy," Jagged Peak warned him knowingly.

Gray Wing flicked his tail. "Don't forget I helped raise Pebble Heart, Owl Eyes, and Sparrow Fur. And Thunder."

"Of course." Jagged Peak's whiskers twitched. "You have kits in almost every group."

Pride warmed Gray Wing's pelt. He gazed happily at Jagged Peak, nostalgia sweeping over him. "It's hard to believe that I never wanted to leave the mountains." He gazed past the gorse camp wall, across the rugged moor, stark beneath the ice-blue sky. "Now I can't imagine any other home than here."

"You're glad you came?" There was worry in Jagged Peak's mew.

"Of course!" Gray Wing jerked his gaze back to his younger brother.

Jagged Peak looked at his paws. "I always felt guilty that Quiet Rain sent you to find me when I ran away. You wanted to stay with the Tribe. You only followed the others to find me."

Gray Wing blinked at the gray tom. "I'm *glad* you ran away," he meowed earnestly. "If you hadn't, I'd never have come here and realized how much I loved Turtle Tail . . . or met Slate." His heart pricked suddenly with regret. "I hope the Tribe is doing okay now. . . ."

"Quiet Water and Sun Shadow said they were still finding prey enough to survive."

Gray Wing tipped his head. "Life here is more than surviving." The wind rippled through his fur. "Even though prey has been scarce lately, we know newleaf will bring more than we ever had in the mountains, the moor and forest will grow lush once more, and the sun will warm our backs."

"It is good to be warm," Jagged Peak agreed. "And to raise kits knowing they won't starve."

Gray Wing purred, imagining his own kits racing through the heather, feeling warm wind in their fur and tasting their first mouthfuls of rabbit. "You were such a courageous kit," he told Jagged Peak. "It was your confidence that led me here. For that I will always be grateful."

"Really?" Jagged Peak's eyes glistened softly. "Weren't you

ever angry with me for dragging you into such a dangerous journey?"

"Not once I'd chased my first rabbit," Gray Wing reassured him. "And tasted my first grouse." He licked his lips, a sudden ache digging deep into his heart as he remembered sharing that grouse with Turtle Tail. His chest tightened, and a cough gripped him. He crouched, helpless, as it shook his body until he was gasping for breath.

"Gray Wing?" Jagged Peak crouched beside him.

Gray Wing wheezed, trembling as his coughing eased. Drawing in a shuddering breath, he lifted his chin. Why was his breath short? He hadn't been running. *Is it getting worse?* Worry nagged in his belly. He sat up, pushing it away. "It's been an exciting day," he rasped.

Jagged Peak was staring at him anxiously. "Right."

Gray Wing straightened, relieved as his chest loosened. *I'm not sick,* he told himself. *I just need to take it easy for a moon or two.*

"Wind Runner!" A shocked yowl rang from the moor. Gray Wing straightened. Alarm scorched through his pelt as he recognized Reed's horrified cry. "Help! Come quickly! Fern is hurt!"

CHAPTER 17

❧

Fern! *Gray Wing's heart lurched. Was* the camp under attack? "Guard the kits!" he told Jagged Peak. Dread gripped his belly. To his relief, his chest remained loose.

He raced across the clearing, glancing back toward his den. *Nothing must harm my kits.* Minnow and Spotted Fur were already haring for the camp entrance, their fur bushed. Moth Flight raced at their heels. She was carrying cobweb between her jaws. The young cat was already planning how to treat Fern's injuries!

Gray Wing burst from the camp after Minnow and Spotted Fur.

Wind Runner raced up the slope to meet them.

"Is the camp in danger?" Gray Wing skidded to a halt in front of her.

Wind Runner shook her head. "Something attacked Fern, but it's gone now. Reed's with her. He's trying to stop the bleeding."

Spotted Fur circled the group leader while Minnow dashed back and forth, scanning the heather. "Where is she?"

"Follow the blood-scent!" Moth Flight hurtled past, her

mew muffled by the cobweb.

As Spotted Fur and Minnow followed, Gray Wing held Wind Runner's gaze. "Was it a fox?"

"She hasn't said yet." Wind Runner bounded after the others, veering around a gorse patch. Gray Wing raced beside her as she went on. "Reed was hunting with me and Gorse Fur. We were tracking the scent of blood. We thought it must be an injured rabbit. Reed got to it first. Then he called out Fern's name. When we reached him, we saw her lying on the grass. She's badly hurt."

Gray Wing fought back panic. What had done this to her? Were dogs roaming the moor? *My kits!* His chest tightened. Forcing his fur flat, he slowed his breathing and followed Wind Runner to a dip beyond the gorse.

Fern lay on the grass. Blood matted her black pelt, glistening in the afternoon sun and welling on her ripped muzzle. Her ear tips were bleeding. Her eyes were clouded with pain and shock as she stared blindly at the cats crowding around her.

Gray Wing's heart ached for the brave cat who'd risked so much to save Star Flower.

Spotted Fur hung back, his eyes wide.

Gray Wing pushed between Minnow and Gorse Fur to where Reed was leaning over her. "Is she going to be okay?"

"We have to stop the bleeding," Reed told him.

Moth Flight nosed her way past Gray Wing and pressed her white paws over a gash in Fern's trembling flank. Blood seeped into her snowy fur.

Wind Runner lashed her tail angrily. "Stop getting in the way." She tried to nose Moth Flight away.

Moth Flight stiffened, holding her paws over the wound. "Didn't you hear? We have to stop the bleeding."

"Then go and find more cobwebs," Wind Runner ordered.

Reed flicked his tail. "Let her help," he snapped to Wind Runner. "Moth Flight knows what she's doing. Minnow can find cobwebs."

Gray Wing saw surprise flash in Wind Runner's gaze. She flicked her muzzle toward Minnow. "You heard him." But the gray-and-white she-cat was already racing downslope. She dived into the heather and disappeared.

Gorse Fur shifted his paws nervously. "What did this to her? Is there a dog loose?"

"These are cat scratches," Reed told him darkly.

Gray Wing scanned the moor for pelts. *Slash?* Had the rogue and his allies returned to wreak revenge?

Wind Runner lifted her tail. "Gorse Fur, take Spotted Fur and search for invaders."

"No." Fern's mew was no more than a breath. "Not invaders."

Gray Wing stiffened. She could speak! He dropped down beside her. Blood welled on her lip. He tried to catch her eye. "Can you tell us who did this to you?"

Her gaze flicked toward him, as though she was trying to focus.

Gray Wing leaned closer. "You're going to be okay." *I hope.* "Reed will take care of you. But we need to know what happened." Was the rest of the camp in danger?

Fern moved her head. Trembling, she dragged her gaze to meet Gray Wing's. "It was Bee."

"*Bee!*" Wind Runner gasped.

Gray Wing leaned closer, his thoughts whirling. "Why?"

Fern groaned. "She said I was a traitor for enjoying being a moor cat. She said Slash would call me a mouse-heart and she was going back to join him."

A low growl rumbled in Wind Runner's throat. "I knew we couldn't trust rogues!"

Fern flinched. "You can trust me," she croaked.

Gray Wing touched his muzzle to her cheek, the sour scent of blood filling his nose. "Wind Runner knows she can trust you." He ignored Wind Runner's grunt behind him. "You were a friend to us even before you joined our group. You just take it easy while Reed fixes you up."

"Where are those cobwebs?" Reed glanced over his shoulder, relief flickering in his gaze as he saw Minnow haring toward him.

She skidded to halt and dropped wads of cobweb at his paws.

Reed scooped them up at once and passed some to Moth Flight. "Press it into the wound, as gently as you can."

Moth Flight nodded and began to pad the gash in Fern's flank with the cobwebs while Reed pressed them across the scratches on her shoulder.

"Do you need more?" Spotted Fur asked.

"All you can find," Reed told her.

As Minnow raced away again, Wind Runner paced the grass. She signaled to Spotted Fur and Gorse Fur with a flick of her tail. "Hunt for Bee. Bring her back to camp."

Gray Wing straightened. "Is that a good idea?" He scanned the moor again. "What if she's already with Slash? It's too dangerous to send two cats alone."

Wind Runner narrowed her eyes. "We have to do *something!*"

Spotted Fur shifted his paws impatiently. "Perhaps Willow knows something about this."

Gorse Fur frowned. "She's hunting with Dust Muzzle."

Wind Runner's pelt spiked along her spine. "That's all the more reason to find her. What if she and Bee planned this together?"

"No!" Fern grunted. "Willow's not like Bee. She likes the group."

Gray Wing nodded. "Willow's always helped with hunting and collecting bedding and guarding the camp. I can't believe she'd wish us any harm."

Gorse Fur's ears twitched anxiously. "Let's find Dust Muzzle anyway."

As he spoke, pelts showed against the grass below.

"They're coming!" Relief swamped Gorse Fur's mew. He raced to meet them.

Wind Runner eyed Willow warily as the pale tabby stopped to greet Gorse Fur. "How can I trust any rogue now?"

Gray Wing glanced at Fern. *You can trust her.* But he understood Wind Runner's fear. Were any of the other rogues like

Bee? Should he warn the other groups? What if Slash's camp-mates had only joined the forest cats to cause trouble? As his thoughts quickened, Willow raced toward him.

As she stopped, she stared at Fern, her eyes blazing with rage. "Did Bee really do this?"

Gray Wing lowered his gaze. "She did."

Willow's pelt bushed. Pricking her ears, she scanned the moor. "I'm going to find her," she snarled. "How could she hurt Fern? How could she betray the cats that took her in?"

Wind Runner eyed the pale tabby suspiciously. "Don't *you* know?" she asked pointedly. "After all, you're a rogue like she is."

Willow stared at the camp leader. "Do you think I'd keep quiet if I'd known Bee was going to do something like this?" She flicked her nose toward Fern. "I'm going to make Bee sorry she was born." She started down the slope.

Gorse Fur blocked her way, Dust Muzzle at his heels. "It's too dangerous. We've already decided. She might have found Slash already, and they might be waiting for us to retaliate. It could be a trap."

Wind Runner narrowed her eyes. "Let her go, if she wants. Perhaps Slash is waiting for her to join him."

Willow turned on the moor leader, outrage flashing in her gaze. "How can I prove I'm loyal to you? If I stay, you won't trust me. If I leave, you think I'm betraying you—"

"Do you really think I'd trust you after this?" Wind Runner stared at Willow.

Willow's hackles lifted.

Gray Wing bristled. Why was Wind Runner being so harsh? Willow had hunted and patrolled as loyally as any cat. "Of course you can trust—"

Gorse Fur padded between the two she-cats. "We need to get Fern back to camp," he meowed firmly. "If this is the beginning of trouble, then she needs to be somewhere safe. We must post guards and be prepared for an attack. Willow and Spotted Fur can take the first watch."

Wind Runner opened her mouth to speak. Gray Wing guessed that she was about to complain about Willow being posted as camp guard. But Gorse Fur silenced her with a look. "Willow has done nothing wrong. We must trust her. Without trust, there is no group."

"Very well." Wind Runner agreed tersely. She glanced at Reed. "Can we move her?"

Reed inspected the gash Moth Flight had treated, then nodded. Gray Wing stood back as Minnow, Gorse Fur, Willow, and Spotted Fur lifted Fern onto their shoulders. Carrying her carefully, they headed back to camp.

Moth Flight lingered beside Gray Wing and Dust Muzzle. Her white pelt was stained with Fern's blood.

As Wind Runner followed the others, Gray Wing glanced at Moth Flight. "Are you okay?"

Moth Flight nodded.

Dust Muzzle sniffed his sister gingerly. "You look like you've been in a fight."

Moth Flight shook out her fur. "Poor Fern." She stared after the wounded she-cat, eyes round with worry. "I hope she's okay."

Gray Wing blinked at the young cat proudly. "You were very brave."

Dust Muzzle shuddered. "Didn't touching her wounds make you feel sick?"

"No." Moth Flight shrugged. "It seemed like the most natural thing to do. *Not* helping would have felt worse."

"Come on." Gray Wing shooed the two cats up the slope with a gentle flick of his tail. "If Slash is planning something, we shouldn't be caught out on the moor."

"I thought Slash would leave us alone now." Slate spoke in a whisper. White Tail, Silver Stripe, and Black Ear slept at her belly. The den was warm, but outside, the evening had brought a hard frost.

Gray Wing felt a twinge of pity for Gorse Fur and Minnow, who had replaced Willow and Spotted Fur as camp guards. They faced a long, cold vigil beside the heather entrance. He snuggled closer to Slate and the kits. "He might not be planning anything. Just because Bee decided to join him doesn't mean he'll attack."

Slate's eyes glittered in the darkness. "He has five allies now." She wrapped her tail around the dozing kits. "He might even have recruited *more*."

"We're safe here," he told Slate. "Gorse Fur and Minnow are guarding the camp." *It should be me.* But Wind Runner had refused his offer to help. Reed had backed her up when Gray Wing had argued.

"But I want to guard," he'd insisted.

"You should stay close to your kits," Wind Runner had told him.

Reed had nodded. "A warm den is better for your breathing than cold night air."

Gray Wing had glared angrily at the silver tom. But he hadn't argued. He knew it was true. Even here, cozy in his nest beside Slate and their kits, he felt invisible jaws tighten around his chest, as though some creature were trying to squeeze the breath from him. *It will pass,* he told himself as fear crept beneath his pelt. He leaned forward and sniffed White Tail's soft fur. The dark gray kit mewled in his sleep and rolled over. Silver Stripe stirred beside him, her tail sticking out.

Black Ear lifted his head and blinked sleepily at Gray Wing. "Is it time to wake up?"

Gray Wing lapped the black-and-white tom-kit's cheek softly. "No. Go back to sleep."

Black Ear rested his muzzle on his sister's back and closed his eyes.

Slate's gaze met Gray Wing. "Will they ever be safe?"

He pressed his cheek to hers. "Nothing bad will happen to our kits," he promised softly. "Not as long as I live."

CHAPTER 18

✧

Clear Sky settled down on the crooked bough that overhung the camp. The frosty bark felt cold against his belly. An icy chill had gripped the forest overnight and hadn't let go. Gazing down, he watched Tiny Branch, Dew Petal, and Flower Foot as they charged around the clearing. Each time they scampered past the yew, they peeked into the shadows, their eyes wide with gleeful terror.

Clear Sky's whiskers twitched with amusement. They'd been playing this game since sunhigh. Blossom was crouching deep beneath the yew.

As Dew Petal raced past, the tiny she-cat veered enticingly close to the bush. The yew trembled. Blossom darted out, grabbed the kit, and bundled her inside.

Dew Petal squealed with fear and delight as Flower Foot and Tiny Branch raced to rescue her. They dived beneath the branches, their fluffy tails sticking up.

"Let her go!"

Clear Sky heard Tiny Branch's defiant mew.

"You can't have her!" Flower Foot hissed.

Blossom's ominous growl sounded from the shadows.

"I'm going to eat her all up!"

"Nooooo!" Dew Petal half purred and half wailed.

The yew trembled again, and Tiny Branch backed out, pulling Dew Petal with him. Flower Foot scrambled clear, swiping at Blossom as the tortoiseshell stuck her nose from beneath the branches.

"I'll get you next time!" Blossom pretended to threaten the kits as they ran clear and skidded to a halt at the far side of the clearing.

Clear Sky purred with pride as he saw them bunch together, shooting glances at the yew. He guessed they were planning their revenge.

Sparrow Fur and Thorn glanced at the kits from the edge of the clearing, where they were sorting through the prey pile. Since Slash had stopped stealing from the group, no cat had gone hungry. Prey was still scarce, but Clear Sky was pleased to see that his campmates were growing ever more skillful at hunting. Red had brought a pigeon back yesterday. He'd climbed a tree to reach it, and promised to show the others how to hide in the crook of a branch and wait for birds.

Clear Sky had asked Red about Slash, of course. Red had confessed that he was from Slash's group, hanging his head with shame as he begged Clear Sky to believe that he'd only hidden the truth about being a rogue because he'd wanted to stay with Clear Sky's group so much. Clear Sky wanted to trust him, and yet Red *had* misled him. And he couldn't forget that Red had led dogs into Slash's camp. That was a dumb mistake. And dangerous. What if the rogue brought dogs here?

At the edge of the camp, Quick Water pushed her paw through the ice covering a puddle and lapped from it. "You must be thirsty," she called to the kits. "You've been running around all morning."

Their eyes lit up, and they raced to the she-cat's side and lapped eagerly from the puddle while Quick Water gingerly picked up a hunk of ice between her teeth and carried it across the clearing. She padded past Birch and Alder, who were sharing tongues at the bottom of the short slope that led to Clear Sky's den.

Birch shuddered as water dripped from the ice onto his tail. "Are you taking a drink to Star Flower?"

Quick Water nodded and hopped up the bank.

Nettle and Red padded into camp, their paws flecked with frost. A mouse hung from Red's jaws.

Nettle called to Clear Sky. "Gorse Fur is heading this way. We've just seen him crossing the border."

Clear Sky pushed himself to his paws and leaped down from the branch. Landing lightly beside Red, he glanced at the camp entrance.

Dew Petal, Tiny Branch, and Flower Foot hurried toward him.

"Can we go and meet him?" Tiny Branch asked excitedly.

Clear Sky flicked his tail. "You're not old enough to leave camp."

Dew Petal rolled her eyes. "You *always* say that!"

"We get older every day," Flower Foot argued. "When will we be old *enough?*"

Nettle nudged the kit's cheek with his muzzle. "When you can fight a fox."

"Or a rogue," Red added.

Tiny Branch squared up to Red. "Let me practice on you!" he begged. "You were a rogue once." He reared on his hind legs and threw a forepaw at Red's muzzle. Red pretended to stagger and collapsed to the ground. Dew Petal leaped onto his flank, squeaking with delight. Flower Foot grabbed the tom's tail. Wrapping her forepaws around it, she churned it with her hind legs. Tiny Branch flung himself onto the tom, and Red rolled over, purring as the kits swarmed over him.

Clear Sky shifted his paws uneasily. *Should I trust him?*

He shivered as he watched his kits pummeling Red. They squeaked with delight as, purring, Red begged for mercy. "No! Please let me go!" The kits were still so small, the glossy russet tom could shake them off any time he liked. A *dog* could snap them in two with a single bite.

Nettle interrupted Clear Sky's thoughts. "Should I escort Gorse Fur through the woods?"

"What?" Clear Sky blinked at the gray tom, only half hearing.

"I don't need an escort." Gorse Fur padded through the entrance. He dipped his head to Clear Sky. "I hope I am welcome."

"Of course." Clear Sky hurried to meet the moor cat, worry pricking in his paws as he saw the somber expression in the tom's eyes. "Is something wrong?"

Gorse Fur glanced at the kits and padded to the edge of the

clearing. He lowered his voice as Clear Sky followed. "One of our rogues has gone back to Slash," he murmured.

Clear Sky leaned close, alarm flashing through his fur. "Which one?"

"Bee."

So these rogues aren't trustworthy? Fear curled icy claws in his belly. "The others are still loyal?"

"They say they are. Fern's badly wounded. Bee attacked her before she ran away." Gorse Fur sat down and curled his tail across his paws. "Wind Runner is worried that the other rogues might do the same. I'm visiting the camps to warn all the leaders."

"Do you know why Bee went back to Slash?"

"She said we are mouse-hearts and she'd rather live with real cats like Slash."

Clear Sky glanced at Red.

Gorse Fur followed his gaze. "Do you trust him?"

Clear Sky's thoughts were whirling. "He's done nothing wrong."

"Does he help with camp duties?" Gorse Fur asked softly.

"Yes." Red was always first to volunteer for morning patrol. And he still caught far more prey than he ate.

Gorse Fur blinked at Clear Sky. "Wind Runner is worried that the rogues have infiltrated our groups to cause trouble. But I can't believe it. Willow is desperate to have her revenge on Bee. And why would Bee hurt Fern so badly if they were both part of the deception?" The wiry tom paused. "And yet it does no harm to be careful until we're sure where the rogues' real loyalties lie."

Clear Sky nodded and padded back to the clearing. "Tiny Branch! Dew Petal! Flower Foot! You've been playing all day. You must be tired. Go rest with Star Flower."

The kits stopped scrambling over Red and stared at their father, puzzled.

"But it's not even sunset," Tiny Branch complained.

"It soon will be," Clear Sky told him firmly. "Another frost is coming. You'll be warmer in your nest."

"But we were having fun," Flower Foot huffed.

Dew Petal lashed her stumpy tail. "It's not fair!"

Clear Sky frowned. "Go to your nest." Guilt pricked in his belly as the three kits clambered slowly off Red and padded toward the slope.

Tiny Branch glanced reproachfully over his shoulder. "It's not like we've done anything wrong."

"I know." Clear Sky's heart twisted in his chest. "Go and keep Star Flower company. I'll bring you something to eat soon."

As they scrambled up the slope, Nettle hurried toward Clear Sky. "Has something happened?" He nodded toward the kits as they disappeared through the bracken. "Why did you make them stop playing?"

Red jumped to his paws. He shook out his fur and headed for the fresh-kill pile.

Clear Sky watched him go. "Gorse Fur says one of their rogues has returned to Slash," he told Nettle quietly.

Nettle's gaze flashed toward Red. "Do you think he might do the same?"

Clear Sky's ears twitched. An idea was pushing at the edges

of his thoughts. "I don't know, but we need to find out."

Gorse Fur got to his paws and dipped his head. "I must go. I want to warn Thunder and River Ripple before dark."

As the moor cat headed for the entrance, Clear Sky called after him. "Will Fern be okay?"

"She's strong, and she's recovering quickly," Gorse Fur answered without stopping.

"I wish her the best." Clear Sky watched Gorse Fur disappear through the bramble barrier. "Thanks for coming."

Nettle's pelt was rippling along his spine. "How will you find out if Red can be trusted?"

Clear Sky narrowed his eyes. "I have a plan . . . but I need you to help me."

Rosy dawn light seeped between the bare branches. Clear Sky crouched lower beneath the arching root of an oak. Leaving the camp while the moon still shone, he'd tracked Nettle and Red's scent here. The two cats had been hunting all night.

"Why?" Red had asked when Clear Sky had drawn him aside and told him that he was to spend the night hunting.

"It's a test of your skills," Clear Sky told him. "And your courage. Nettle will go with you. You must hunt, but you cannot eat. Every piece of prey that you catch is for your campmates."

Red had blinked at him uncertainly, then nodded. "Okay."

Now he could see Red's pelt, fluffed out against the icy air. Clear Sky was downwind and hidden by the root. Neither cat would be able to see him.

He watched Nettle pad around the russet rogue. "Let's eat

one piece of prey," Nettle meowed pleadingly. "I'm starving. Clear Sky will never know."

"I promised him I'd take *everything* I caught back to camp," Red told him. "You can eat if you want, but I'm not going to."

Nettle rolled his eyes. "You're a mouse-brain." He pawed a dead mouse from beneath a pile of leaves and bit into it. "So delicious." Chewing, he looked at Red. "Are you sure you don't want some?"

Clear Sky leaned forward. The scent of fresh blood was making *his* mouth water. Red must be starving and frozen to the bone.

Red padded away from his campmate. "I promised Clear Sky, and I'm sticking to my promise."

Clear Sky frowned. Was Red being smart? Had he guessed that Nettle was spying for him? It was time to push the rogue a little harder. He slid from beneath the root and padded toward the toms.

He caught Nettle's eye as he neared. Red was scanning the trees distractedly, clearly looking for more prey. Quickly, Nettle swallowed his mouthful and kicked the remains of the mouse closer to the rogue.

Clear Sky padded toward them, his hackles high. "I thought I told you not to eat what you caught?"

Red swung around, shock rippling through his pelt. His gaze flashed guiltily to the remains of the mouse, then to Nettle.

Nettle blinked at Red calmly. "I told you we weren't supposed to eat."

Red stared at him in disbelief. "But—" He paused, then

faced Clear Sky. "I'm sorry," he meowed. "We were so hungry. We thought you wouldn't miss one mouse."

Clear Sky tipped his head in surprise. Red was taking the blame for his campmate. He forced himself to frown. "I need to be able to trust you," he growled.

"I promise, it will never happen again." Red began to haul away leaves from the pile, uncovering a heap of prey. A rabbit lay beside several shrews and another mouse. Two thrushes and a starling were draped over them. "We caught so much. No one will go hungry. And, if they do, *I'll* go without food."

This cat is too good to be true! Suspicion wormed beneath Clear Sky's pelt. Why was Red being so honorable? He narrowed his eyes. "That's not enough!" he snapped. "Catch more before you return to camp." Turning sharply, he stalked away. As he passed a clump of bracken, he ducked down and spied on Red once more.

Nettle scraped leaves back over the prey heap. "Why did you take the blame?"

Red shrugged. "It seemed like the right thing to do."

Nettle narrowed his eyes. "Clear Sky would never take the blame for *you.*"

"Wouldn't he?" Red blinked at Nettle in surprise.

"You know he's the meanest cat in all the groups, right?" Nettle didn't wait for an answer. "He was *spying* on us! After making us stay out all night hunting, he still doesn't trust us. He doesn't trust anyone. Not even me, and I've shown him nothing but loyalty." Nettle snorted. "Being loyal to Clear Sky is a waste of time. He's hardly better than Slash. Did you know he killed a cat once? *More* than one. His campmates only put up with him because they're scared of him."

"But he's so kind to Star Flower and his kits."

"Of course he is," Nettle snarled. "They belong to him. But he wasn't so kind to his *first* litter. Their mother ran away from him."

Clear Sky winced. He'd asked Nettle to test Red's loyalty, but he hadn't prepared himself to hear such harsh truths.

"Only one of them survived," Nettle went on.

"You mean Thunder?" Red's fur was prickling nervously now. "What happened to his littermates?"

Nettle slowly circled the rogue. "No one knows," he murmured darkly.

Red shifted his paws nervously. "Why are you telling me this?"

"Because you were a rogue once," Nettle told him. "Like me. Like most of the group. We thought you'd understand."

"*We?*" Red looked confused.

"A lot of us aren't happy with Clear Sky as leader," Nettle confessed. "When we found out you were one of the cats who drove Slash out, we started to hope."

"Hope for what?"

"That you'd help us do the same to Clear Sky." Nettle stopped and stared hard at Red.

Red backed away, hackles rising. "You want me to drive Clear Sky out?"

"You only have to help us." Nettle's mew grew enticing. "With Clear Sky gone, there'll be no more orders. No more night hunting. No more going hungry to feed your camp-mates."

"No." Red showed his teeth. "Clear Sky is a good leader. You're lucky to have him. If you think he's bad, then you've never met a cat like Slash." His tail whisked ominously as he thrust his muzzle closer to Nettle's. "I can't believe that you'd think I'd betray him!"

Nettle half closed his eyes. "What if we made *you* leader?"

With a hiss, Red lashed out at the gray tom.

Nettle yowled as the rogue slashed his nose. Jumping back, he lifted his paws defensively. "Okay! Forget I said anything."

A growl rolled in Red's throat. He dropped into an attack crouch. "You're a traitor."

Nettle backed away. "It was just an idea—"

Red leaped at him, snarling.

Heart lurching, Clear Sky sprang from his hiding place and raced for the two cats. Hooking his claws into Red's scruff, he dragged him away from Nettle.

Red twisted free, anger blazing in his eyes. "Why did you stop me?" he glared at Clear Sky. "He's a traitor! He wanted me to help drive you out! He—"

Clear Sky interrupted. "I told him to."

Red's eyes widened. "*You?*" Confusion clouded his gaze. "Why?"

Before Clear Sky could explain, Red's tail drooped. "You were testing me!" Disappointment filled his mew.

Clear Sky's pelt rippled guiltily. "Gorse Fur brought news that Bee has gone back to Slash. She attacked Fern before she left. I had to be sure you weren't going to do the same." The words tumbled out as he tried to justify himself.

Red blinked at him, and Clear Sky hesitated as he waited for the rogue to react. Had he pushed him too far? Would Red leave? Clear Sky's belly tightened. He didn't want to lose such a loyal and honest campmate.

"The kits." Red's mew was husky when he spoke at last. "You saw me playing with them, and you needed to know if you could trust me." Understanding flooded his gaze.

Clear Sky stared at the ground. "I can't risk anything happening to them."

Red seemed to relax. "I would protect your kits with my life," he promised.

Clear Sky looked up and saw honesty shining in the rogue's eyes. "I believe you would." He nodded to Nettle. "I think it's time we officially made Red part of the group."

CHAPTER 19

Thunder stretched up onto his hind legs. The branches of the hazel bush poked his belly as he reached high and threaded bracken between the twigs.

"This one is strong." Violet passed him another stem, and he hooked it with a claw and poked it in beside the first.

His legs ached with the effort, but it would be worth it. Snow was coming. He could smell it deep in the thick frost that had settled over the forest. The woven bracken would keep the cold wind out of the den that the cats had made inside the hazel. On the coldest nights, Milkweed, Clover, and Thistle could leave their bramble nursery and huddle for warmth with the rest of the group. Clover and Thistle were nearly old enough to move permanently into their own nests in the hazel den.

He dropped down onto four paws to rest for a moment. The stack of bracken beside Violet seemed to have grown. He blinked in surprise.

"Cloud Spots gathered more," Violet explained. She nodded toward the black tom's tail as it disappeared into the bracken patch beside the fallen tree. "He wants to keep us well supplied."

Thunder glanced at the hazel bush. "We'll need it." Gaps still showed between every branch. It was already past sun-high. By the end of the day he wanted every gap filled. His cats were going to sleep in warm nests tonight. He turned to Milkweed. "Have you found much moss?" Extra moss lining would keep out the cold.

Milkweed hopped down from the fallen tree where she'd been peeling moss and dropped a shred onto the pile she'd already gathered. "I've stripped the trunk. I'd better head up the ravine to search for more."

Thunder glanced toward the top of the hollow. "Be careful up there by yourself." Since Gorse Fur had brought news of Bee's betrayal, he'd been wary of fresh attacks. Lightning Tail and Leaf were training Clover and Thistle in the clearing below the high rock. They'd abandoned hunting moves and were practicing battle moves once more.

Owl Eyes padded from the tangle of branches jutting from the fallen tree. "I'll keep an eye on Milkweed," he promised. "I'm going to show Pink Eyes the new route I found up the cliff."

Pink Eyes followed Owl Eyes into the leaf-bare sunshine. "I can still manage the old route."

"Your eyesight is getting worse, Pink Eyes," Owl Eyes told him. "One wrong leap and you could fall. This new route is safer. The ledges are closer together."

Pink Eyes snorted as he followed Owl Eyes through the gorse barrier. "I can see well enough to jump down a few ledges."

Milkweed hurried after them. "I'll stay close to the top of the ravine and call down if I see Sl—" She paused as her eyes met Violet's.

"Slash." Violet guessed her next word. "It's okay to say his name. I don't like him any more than you do." She hooked up a fresh stalk of bracken. "When will you realize I'm not a rogue anymore?"

Milkweed dipped her head. "Of course," she purred. "And we're glad to have you."

Thunder glanced at Violet as Milkweed headed out of camp. He was pleased that his campmates had accepted her, but he wasn't surprised. She was kind to everyone. She picked stale moss from Pink Eyes's nest each morning. She joined every hunting patrol. And she made sure Clover and Thistle got the juiciest prey from the prey pile.

If only Ember fit into the group as easily. But the orange tom still chose to hunt alone. He left camp at dawn each morning and returned, fed and silent, with nothing for the prey pile. Last night he hadn't come home at all.

"So?" Violet's mew interrupted his thoughts. "Are we finishing this or are you going to stare at me all day?" There was a purr in her mew.

Heat flashed through Thunder's pelt, and he looked away quickly. He'd forgotten he'd been gazing at her pretty face.

Violet reached up beside him and began to thread a piece of bracken through the hazel branches. "It's okay," she murmured. "I like looking at you, too." She didn't meet his gaze but poked the bracken deeper into the bush.

Thunder fumbled for something to say. Excitement fizzed through his fur. He'd spent sleepless nights wondering if Violet felt the same way about him as he did about her. On first sight, Thunder had been amazed by her beauty. But after sharing a camp with her, he thought she was the most warm, kind, helpful cat he'd ever known. Somehow he'd never found the courage to tell her. Perhaps this was his chance.

"Violet?" He glanced at her as she stooped to grab another stem.

She paused and met his gaze. "Yes?" Interest sparkled in her amber eyes.

"Do you think we could . . ." Thunder's pelt prickled nervously. What should he say next? His tongue lay like dead prey in his mouth. "Perhaps . . ." He started again but found himself staring at her, fear tying knots in his belly.

Clover's call made him jump. "Thunder! Look at this."

He spun around and saw the young cat crouching beside her brother. Lightning Tail faced them, his hackles up, while Leaf prowled behind them.

Thistle blinked at Thunder. "Lightning Tail taught us how to fight together."

Leaf narrowed his eyes. "Ready?" he asked the kits.

Clover nodded. Thistle flicked his tail.

Leaf swapped glances with Lightning Tail; then both toms lunged at the kits.

In a moment, Clover and Thistle had reared up. Turning on their hind legs, they pressed their backs to each other and swiped at Lightning Tail and Leaf with their forepaws.

Lightning Tail and Leaf darted around them, but each time they moved, Clover and Thistle turned to meet their snapping jaws with well-aimed blows. Working together, the littermates defended themselves like experienced fighters.

Thunder purred loudly. "That's great!" He padded toward them, his heart swelling with pride.

Leaf and Lightning Tail backed away, and the kits dropped back onto all fours.

"It's really easy once we've found our footing," Clover panted.

"We could fight off a whole patrol!" Thistle boasted.

Violet padded after Thunder and blinked at the young cats. "Even rogues wouldn't be able to counter a move like that."

Clover lifted her chin. "If Slash attacks us again, we'll be able to defend the whole camp."

Thistle's gaze darkened. "Will he attack again?"

Thunder met his gaze solemnly. "I don't know." Thunder's cats could defend the ravine if they had to, but he was uneasy about having Ember sleep alongside them. Since Bee's attack on Fern, a dark fear had haunted his dreams. What if Ember was staying with the group for a reason? What if he, too, was planning to betray his new campmates?

Violet nudged him. "We'd better get back to work." She glanced toward the hazel bush. Cloud Spots was carrying a fresh bundle of bracken toward the pile.

"We can help!" Thistle ran past Thunder and raced toward the hazel.

Clover chased after him. "I can thread bracken quicker than you."

Cloud Spots blinked at them warmly as they barged in front of him. "You two had better start on the lower branches," he suggested. "I'll reach up to the top."

As they began work, padding the bush against the cold, Thunder blinked at Lightning Tail. "You've taught them well."

Lightning Tail shrugged. "That move was Leaf's idea."

Thunder dipped his head to Leaf. "Since you've been training them, they've improved so much."

"I've enjoyed it," Leaf answered. His glance flicked past Thunder toward the young cats. They were both tugging the same piece of bracken.

"I picked it up first!" Clover growled.

"You only want it because *I* said it looked like a strong piece," Thistle retorted.

Leaf rolled his eyes. "We've trained them to fight rogues," he huffed. "Now we must train them not to *behave* like rogues." He headed toward them, whisking his tail. "Clover! Let your brother have the bracken. There are plenty of other stems."

Lightning Tail gazed toward the trees. "Ember's still not back," he mewed thoughtfully. His gaze flashed toward Violet. "Can't you explain to him that he needs to try to fit in to the group?"

Violet dropped her gaze. "I've told him," she sighed. "He just says he prefers to travel alone."

"Then why does he stay at all?" Lightning Tail snapped.

Thunder guessed his friend was anxious about the independent rogue too. "Perhaps we should suggest he leave the group."

Violet's eyes glittered with worry. "Give him another moon," she suggested. "He may change. He's got a good heart. He's just not used to living in this sort of group. Life with Slash was different. We shared a camp and did as Slash told us, but we knew that no one would look after us but ourselves. It's hard getting used to looking after one another."

Thunder's paws pricked as she turned her imploring gaze on him. Lightning Tail was staring at him too. He guessed by the black tom's solemn look that his friend wasn't as keen as Violet on giving Ember another chance. Feeling torn, Thunder changed the subject. "I wonder how River Ripple is getting on with *his* rogues." He was worried about the river cats. They were a small group—River Ripple, Night, Dappled Pelt, and Shattered Ice. Having four extra mouths to feed would prove no problem with a river full of fish. But what if Dawn and Moss decided to betray them as Bee had done? River Ripple and his cats might be badly hurt.

Violet surprised him. "Why don't we go and find out?"

"Good idea." Lightning Tail agreed. "We can go together."

Violet flashed a look at the black tom. "I thought Thunder and I could go *alone*."

Amusement shone in Lightning Tail's eyes. "I suppose I should stay and help the others." His whiskers twitched knowingly.

Thunder shifted his paws self-consciously. What would he say all the way to the river? Talking to Violet while he was on patrol or in camp with the others was easy. "Are you sure we should go alone?"

Lightning Tail headed for the hazel bush. "Don't worry, Thunder. I'm sure Violet will keep you safe from rogue attacks."

"I'm not scared of rogue attacks," Thunder answered without thinking.

Lighting Tail's whiskers twitched. "Why are you looking so worried, then? Violet doesn't bite."

"Don't be too sure." Violet sniffed and padded toward the gorse entrance. "Are you coming?" she called to Thunder.

Lightning Tail flashed Thunder a teasing look. "You'd better hurry up."

Thunder glared at his friend and followed Violet out of camp.

They climbed the ravine in silence, only breaking it as they met Owl Eyes and Pink Eyes at the top. The two cats were staring down the steep cliff.

"What does it matter if I can't see the bottom?" Pink Eyes mewed to Owl Eyes. "I only have to see the next ledge, don't I?"

"Just follow me and remember which route I use," Owl Eyes told him.

Pink Eyes nodded to Thunder as he reached the top. "Are you going hunting?"

"We're going to visit River Ripple to see how he's managing with the new rogues."

Violet scrambled over the rim and shook out her pelt. "It'll be great to see Dawn and Moss again."

Pink Eyes tipped his head, his rosy gaze gleaming in the cold afternoon sunlight. "They were the rogues with kits, weren't they?"

Thunder nodded. "I can't imagine they'll be any trouble," he told Pink Eyes. "They seemed happier than anyone to be leaving Slash's camp. And I'm sure River Ripple will have made them welcome."

Owl Eyes's neck fur rippled. "We've tried to make Ember feel welcome," he meowed pointedly. "But he's determined to act like an outsider."

Violet lifted her chin defiantly and headed toward the river. "Ember just needs time, that's all."

Thunder trotted after her, nodding to Milkweed as he passed her stripping moss from the roots of a beech. Tasting the air warily, he was relieved to scent only the musty smell of leaf-bare. He caught up with Violet as she headed down the wooded slope that led to the shore.

"Nice weather," he meowed awkwardly.

She glanced at him and didn't reply.

He tried again, wishing he could think of something to say that wasn't mouse-brained. "Are you enjoying life in the forest?"

"I guess trees are okay." Violet wove between patches of frost-wilted nettles.

"Yeah, I guess." Thunder felt a prickle of irritation. It was Violet who'd suggested they go alone. Couldn't she help make conversation? He tried again. "Have you been to the river before?"

"Yes." She jumped down a steep bank and crunched through the leaves beyond.

Thunder could see water glittering between the trees. He quickened his pace. The sooner they reached the river camp, the better.

"You're in a hurry," Violet commented as he passed her.

"I want to get there before sundown." *I want to stop feeling as awkward as a rabbit up a tree.*

Violet halted.

Thunder turned and stared at her. "What are you waiting for?"

Violet's eyes shone playfully. "For you to finish what you started to say while we were weaving bracken into the den walls." She padded closer until her sweet breath touched his nose. "You said, 'Do you think we could . . .' I was wondering what you thought we could do."

Thunder's pelt burned. "I just wanted us to be friends."

Violet looked hurt. "I thought we were already friends."

Thunder stared at his paws. "We are." *This is harder than facing a camp full of rogues and dogs.* "But I think you're special. I thought it the first time I saw you." He lifted his head and forced himself to go on. "I love you, and when we know each other a little better, I hope that you'll be my mate."

Violet gazed at him for a moment.

Thunder thought his chest would burst. "Well?"

Violet purred. "I would love that more than anything." She reached out and touched her muzzle to his. Its softness made him shiver with happiness.

"It's just that I thought—"

She cut him off. "Let's visit River Ripple. Then we can talk about our future." Padding away, she headed for the river.

Thunder hurried after her, his heart pounding. His paws felt as light as feathers as they skimmed over the forest floor. He reached her as she padded onto the shore and headed for the stepping-stones.

Violet brushed against him as he fell in beside her. "I was beginning to think that Lightning Tail would have to ask *for* you."

Thunder purred, and they walked for a while in silence. This time it felt comfortable, and Thunder's thoughts strayed to Lightning Tail. *I was beginning to think that Lightning Tail would have to ask* for *you.* Lightning Tail probably would have. He was a good, kind friend, and Thunder hoped Violet would come to value his friendship as much as he did.

"Do you like Lightning Tail?" he asked tentatively.

"Of course," she answered. "He's so loyal to you. And he's turned Clover into a great hunter and fighter."

"He'll be a leader one day," Thunder murmured.

Violet halted. "Is he going to start his own group?" Alarm glittered in her gaze.

"No." Thunder reassured her. "But if something happens to me, he'll be the next leader. He's the only one who would be able keep the group together. He always knows what to do in a crisis, and he puts his campmates before himself."

Violet stared at him. "Why should something happen to you?" Fear edged her mew.

"It won't," Thunder promised quickly. "But just in case—"

"I won't let *anything* happen to you!" Violet snapped. "You're going to be father to my kits one day. I need you." She held his gaze.

Thunder saw love in her eyes. His heart seemed to flutter like a bird in his chest. "I need you, too," he whispered.

As he leaned forward to touch her cheek with his nose,

water splashed beside them. He jerked his head around as River Ripple waded from the river, holding a gleaming fish between his jaws.

"Hungry?" The river cat dropped the fish at their paws.

Thunder wrinkled his nose. "I prefer mouse, thanks."

River Ripple shrugged. "Is the prey running better in the forest?"

Thunder nodded. "And Clover and Thistle are growing into fine hunters. They help fill the prey pile."

"Milkweed must be proud," River Ripple purred.

"We all are." Thunder's gaze drifted across the water, toward the river camp. "How are the rogues settling in?"

River Ripple followed his gaze. "Dawn and Moss are enjoying it here," he meowed warmly. "Come. I'll show you."

He picked up the fish between his jaws and hurried to the stepping-stones. Hopping over them, he crossed the river easily.

Thunder followed, Violet at his heels. He shivered as icy water splashed his paws. How did River Ripple *swim* in there? He followed the river cat along the winding trail that led through the reed beds until the rushes opened onto the camp.

Pine and Drizzle were wading in the shallows where the clearing dipped into the river. Shattered Ice stood beside them, watching them pick their way between the tufts of grass sticking out of the water.

As River Ripple crossed the clearing toward them, Drizzle blinked at him happily. "Look!" She flicked her tail toward the water. Three heads bobbed above the surface. "Moss and Dawn are swimming!"

Thunder felt Violet's fur prickle against his as he followed River Ripple to the water's edge.

Shattered Ice nodded toward the swimming cats.

Dappled Pelt darted between Dawn and Moss. "Keep your paws churning!" she called.

Moss was moving frantically through the water, panic shining in his eyes.

Dawn glided more easily among the ripples. Water dripped from her ears, and her back showed above the surface, as slick as an otter's.

River Ripple purred. "They'll be diving for fish soon."

Violet stopped beside Thunder. "Won't they freeze in there?" she asked, wonder in her mew.

"Not if they keep moving," River Ripple told her.

"But how do they dry off?" Thunder asked, shivering at the thought of being so wet.

"A quick shake and a run through the reed beds," River Ripple told him. He poked the fish he had dropped. "*And* a good meal."

Dappled Pelt began to head for the shore.

Dawn followed, Moss trailing after. Relief showed in the rogue tom's gaze as he padded from the water, his pelt dripping.

Pine raced to meet him. "You did really well!" he mewed excitedly. "You didn't sink like last time."

Drizzle splashed around her mother. "Shake out your pelt!" she pleaded, eyes shining with excitement.

Dawn shook out her fur, spraying the kit with drops of water. Drizzle squealed with delight.

River Ripple purred. "They're natural river cats."

Drizzle blinked at Thunder. "*I'm* going to learn to swim next."

Shattered Ice frowned. "Not until you're bigger. The currents are strong."

Moss shook himself, his pelt dripping.

Pine lifted his tail. "I'll race you through the reeds!" Before Moss could answer, the black tom-kit hared away. Drizzle chased after him, Moss at her heels.

"Wait for me!" Dawn followed, her wet paws pattering the ground. Dappled Pelt raced after them.

As they disappeared into the reeds, Thunder blinked at River Ripple. "They seem happy here."

River Ripple shrugged. "Why wouldn't they be? They have the river and fish and warm, dry nests at night."

Thunder gazed across the water. *If only Ember felt the same way about living in the forest.*

River Ripple flicked his tail. "You look worried," he mewed.

"I suppose you've heard Gorse Fur's news." Shattered Ice twitched his ears. "Is that why you came? To see if we were having trouble with our rogues?"

"Yes," Thunder confessed.

River Ripple glanced at Violet. "You look happy to be a forest cat."

Violet moved closer to Thunder. "I've never been happier," she purred.

"What about Ember?" Shattered Ice's gaze stayed on Thunder. "Has he settled in?"

Thunder's pelt pricked uneasily. "He still hunts alone."

He felt Violet stiffen beside him. "He'll be okay," she mewed quickly. But even she didn't sound convinced.

Shattered Ice snorted. "I wouldn't trust any cat who wouldn't hunt with me."

River Ripple met Thunder's gaze solemnly. "If Ember can't hunt beside his campmates, perhaps he shouldn't be part of a group."

"Don't say that!" Violet sounded startled.

Thunder swallowed, his mouth suddenly dry. He didn't want to upset Violet, but he saw sense in River Ripple's words. *If I ask him to leave, where will he go? Would I be giving Slash another ally?*

CHAPTER 20

❧

Thunder fluffed out his pelt against the cold. Snow drifted at the edges of the camp. It sparkled in the moonlight, crusted by a thick frost.

Thistle and Clover bounded across the clearing, their pelts bristling with excitement.

Thistle slid to a halt in front of Thunder and stared at him eagerly. "Are *all* the cats going to be there?"

"From *every* group?" Clover thumped into her brother's side, her paws slithering on the snowy ground.

"Most of them." Thunder purred. The young cats' training had made them great hunters, always eager to share the duties of their campmates. That morning they had gathered fresh bracken for Pink Eyes's nest and returned to the clearing, their pelts dusted with snow and a bundle of stems between their jaws. But tonight they were as excited as kits on their first time out of their den.

Milkweed hopped over the snow that drifted beside the bramble, and hurried across the clearing. She began lapping Thistle's tufted fur.

He ducked away, scowling.

"You must look neat," she scolded.

Thistle glared at her indignantly. "We've already washed."

"Twice," Clover added pointedly.

Violet shifted closer to Thunder, and his heart quickened as it always did when he felt the warmth of her pelt against his. "They'll be the handsomest kits there," she assured Milkweed.

As Milkweed puffed out her chest, Clover's eyes widened excitedly. "Will Tiny Branch, Dew Petal, and Flower Foot be there?"

Thunder shook his head. "They're too young," he told them. "They'll be staying in their nest with Star Flower. It's too cold for very young kits to be out."

Clover looked crestfallen. "Does that mean we won't get to meet Silver Stripe, Black Ear, and White Tail?"

Milkweed whisked a tuft of fur on Clover's back smooth with her tail. "They will be staying with Slate in their den. They're not even a moon old."

Thistle frowned. "Drizzle and Pine will be coming, won't they?"

"They have to!" Clover lifted her chin. "They're rogues! And the four trees meeting is to welcome all the rogues into our groups."

"They'll be there," Thunder promised. "They're old enough to weather the cold. River Ripple says they've been looking forward to it for days."

River Ripple had suggested the full-moon gathering. Thunder hoped that the river cat's plan would work—a formal ceremony to welcome the rogues into the groups would help worries over their loyalty be forgotten. He glanced across the clearing to where Ember sat. The tom's eyes were narrowed, and his orange pelt showed starkly against the white snow. Would a ceremony be enough to change him from a rogue to a campmate? Would he stop hunting alone and join patrols from now on? Thunder's ears twitched nervously. *At least he's coming to the gathering. Surely that has to be a good sign?*

Cloud Spots slid from the fern tunnel. "Are we ready to leave?" he called across the clearing.

Lightning Tail and Leaf paced beside the entrance. Pink Eyes huddled beside Owl Eyes, his milky gaze bright in the moonlight.

Thunder nodded at Cloud Spots. "Let's go."

Lightning Tail and Leaf moved to let him pass. Violet stayed close to his side as he padded out of the camp. Thunder unsheathed his claws when he reached the edge of the ravine. The rocky ledges would be icy. He leaped onto the first wide boulder and waited while the others passed. They scrambled ahead of him and he followed, keeping close.

As he looked up to check if any cat had slipped, snow showered his face. Clover and Thistle were pushing past each other, each determined to reach the top first. Thistle lost his grip, slithering from a frosty ledge, and Thunder's heart lurched. He braced himself to catch the falling kit, but Lightning Tail grabbed the young cat's scruff as he tumbled past and hooked him onto a rock, holding on to him until he found his footing.

"It's pointless to rush if you don't get there at all," Lightning Tail told the young cat sternly.

Thistle dipped his head. "Sorry." Slowly he clambered onto the next ledge.

Thunder hopped up behind, shaking snow from his whiskers. His claws scraped the icy rock as he fought to keep from sliding. He reached the top with a sigh of relief and hopped onto the snowy rim.

Pink Eyes blinked into the forest as though straining to see through the shadows.

Thunder padded past him and led the way between the trees. "Stay close together." Snow had drifted around the roots of the trees, but it was easy to find the familiar path that led toward the four trees hollow. Thunder glanced up at the snow-spattered trunks, recognizing each one easily, as though seeing old friends. This wood was his home now, and he knew it as well as he'd ever known the rabbit runs and heather trails of the moor.

Ice crunched beneath his paws as he headed deeper into the woods. As he neared the hollow, he saw fresh tracks churning the snow. Opening his mouth, he tasted the air and smelled River Ripple's scent. The river cats had passed this way. Their scent was still fresh.

He quickened his pace, wondering if he'd catch up to them before they reached the rim of the hollow.

River Ripple was already leading his group down the slope by the time Thunder reached the edge. Thunder could see Night threading between the stems. Shattered Ice and

Dappled Pelt followed her, Moss and Dawn at their heels. The bracken hid Pine and Drizzle, but he could hear their excited mewing.

"Can we stay up till dawn?" Drizzle's question echoed through the stone-cold air.

"Let's not go to sleep at all!" Pine squeaked. "When we get home we can go out on the ice."

Thunder blinked. Had the river frozen?

River Ripple's mew rumbled from the head of the group. "No kits on the ice. If it cracks, you'll be swept under."

Milkweed shivered as she stopped beside Thunder. "I'm glad we don't live by the river. I'd never have let Thistle and Clover out of my sight."

Leaf brushed past her and touched his nose to her cheek. "If they'd been raised beside a river, they'd be swimming like ducks by now. They're fast learners."

Clover pushed between Leaf and her mother. "Stop talking and hurry up." She stared into the hollow.

Cats moved at the bottom, throwing moon shadows across the snowy ground.

"Everyone's here!" Thistle hurried to the edge.

Thunder followed the young cats' gazes. Clear Sky was weaving between his cats, his tail fluffed out. Wind Runner sat near the edge, watching the others through slitted eyes while Gorse Fur paced up and down. Thunder was pleased to see Gray Wing beside them, though the gray tom looked thin. Moth Flight padded around Fern, sniffing anxiously at her tattered pelt. Tall Shadow sat between Mouse Ear and

Pebble Heart, while Sun Shadow leaned close to Juniper and Raven. Ears pricked and fur sleek, the mountain cat seemed comfortable beside the rogues. As River Ripple emerged from the bracken, eyes flashed in the moonlight, and heads turned to watch the river cats arrive.

"Come on." Thunder plunged over the edge and pushed through the bracken. Snow thumped onto his back as he shook the stems. Breaking into a run, he lifted his tail as he heard the others swishing through the undergrowth behind him.

He burst into the clearing and tilted his chin.

Tall Shadow padded to meet him. "Did they come?" Her gaze flitted past him, showing relief as Ember and Violet slid from the bracken.

"*Everyone's* here," Thunder reassured her.

She glanced toward Juniper and Raven. "They like the plan."

River Ripple joined them. "Drizzle and Pine are excited."

Thunder gazed around the gathered cats. His heart lifted as he saw excitement shining in their eyes. A breeze whipped over the snowy clearing, sending flecks swirling in the air. Above, the black sky shimmered with stars. Moonlight sliced between the bare branches of the oak.

"Let's begin." Tall Shadow padded to the center. She blinked at Wind Runner, who lingered at the edge of the clearing. "Are you ready?"

Wind Runner padded across the snow and stopped beside the black she-cat. "Do you really think a few words will turn *them* into one of us?" She meowed loudly, eyeing Fern and Willow.

They bristled, moving closer together.

Thunder blinked in surprise at Wind Runner. "Don't you trust her, even after what she suffered?" Fern's pelt still showed wounds, the fur clumped along her flanks; her eye was swollen and her nose stained with dried blood.

Moth Flight stared at her mother. "Why are you so stubborn? Bee hurt Fern because Fern refused to go with her."

Willow lifted her chin. "We will earn your trust."

Gray Wing padded forward. "Trust takes time, Wind Runner. But you will never feel it unless you open your heart." His mew was rasping, hardly more than a whisper.

Thunder searched his gaze and saw weariness there. Anxiety pricked through his pelt. Gray Wing was sicker than he'd ever seen him.

Wind Runner flicked her tail. "Let's begin the ceremony," she mewed briskly.

Thunder saw irritation rippling through Moth Flight's pelt. He understood the young cat's frustration, but Gray Wing was right. Trust came with time. He glanced toward Violet. Even though he'd felt a deep connection with Violet the moment he'd seen her, Star Flower's betrayal had taught him to be wary. As she stepped forward with the other rogues, Violet met his gaze, her amber eyes lighting with affection. Thunder nodded to her, swallowing a purr as he slid between Lightning Tail and Leaf.

Warm breath billowed in the air as the cats formed a circle around the rogues. Wind Runner padded to Gorse Fur's side. Gray Wing nestled between Spotted Fur and Minnow. Clear Sky stood beside Nettle, his gaze fixed on Red.

The russet tom shifted his paws nervously. Thunder noticed Willow glaring at the rogue tom with undisguised contempt.

Juniper and Raven stood, heads high, while Moss and Dawn huddled close to Drizzle and Pine, shielding their kits from the icy wind.

River Ripple stood at the center. He gazed around the rogues as peace fell over the hollow. The breeze dropped, and only the sound of snow crunching beneath paws stirred the chilly air.

"Do you promise loyalty to your new campmates?" River Ripple glanced around the rogues.

"Yes." Willow was the first to answer. The others murmured their agreement.

Thunder narrowed his eyes, watching Ember. Had the orange tom spoken along with the others? He pricked his ears as River Ripple went on.

"Will you hunt for them and fight for them? Protect them when they are weak and stand by them when they are strong?"

"Yes!" Raven fluffed out his fur, his gaze flashing toward Tall Shadow.

Drizzle's mew piped up. "I'm not allowed to hunt yet." She sounded worried. "Does that mean I can't be part of the group?"

River Ripple purred, fixing his gaze on the kit. "Will you promise to fight and hunt for us when you're old enough?"

"Yes!" Drizzle nodded her head eagerly.

"Then you are part of our group." He lifted his gaze to

the stars. "Our ancestors have watched us tonight. They have heard the promise you have made to your new campmates. May you keep it always, for their sake and all of ours."

Thunder purred loudly. Beside him, Lighting Tail's eyes shone with satisfaction. Murmurs of approval rippled among the watching cats, while the rogues blinked at one another proudly.

Dawn lifted her tail. "I want to change my name so that I sound more like a forest cat."

River Ripple blinked at her. "What would you like to be called?"

"Dawn Mist." The orange-and-white queen puffed out her chest.

"I want to be called Willow Tail!" Willow called.

"Fern Leaf!" Fern's mew sounded beside her friend.

Clear Sky padded to River Ripple's side. "Taking a new name is a great idea!" He looked expectantly at Red. "Will you change yours?"

Red purred. "Call me Red Claw from now on."

Clear Sky dipped his head. "A good name for a fine hunter."

River Ripple turned to Moss. "Would you like to change your name?"

"Yes." Moss's whiskers twitched happily. "I'd like to be known as Moss Tail."

"And I want to be Pine Needle!" Pine mewed beside his father.

River Ripple glanced expectantly at Drizzle.

She was staring thoughtfully at her paws. As silence fell

around her, she lifted her head. "Do I *have* to change my name?" Worry sparkled in her eyes. "I *like* being Drizzle."

River Ripple purred. "You can be Drizzle for as long as you like."

Drizzle gazed at him gratefully with round, blue eyes. "Thank you."

Tall Shadow nodded toward Juniper and Raven. "Do you want new names?"

Juniper nodded. "Will you choose them for us?"

Tall Shadow frowned, her eyes clouding with thought.

Sun Shadow blinked at her. "What about Juniper Branch?"

"And Raven Pelt!" Pebble Heart chimed in.

Tall Shadow faced her new campmates. "Do you like those names?"

Juniper purred loudly. "Yes."

Raven dipped his head. "May I join the first patrol tomorrow?" he asked. "As Raven *Pelt*?"

Tall Shadow's eyes shone. "You can lead it, if you like." She glanced toward Sun Shadow, Mud Paws, and Mouse Ear as though searching for approval. As they nodded, Jagged Peak stepped forward. "You can show us new places to hunt."

Holly whisked her tail. "You said there was a great place to hunt frogs near the Thunderpath."

Thunder wrinkled his nose. Did the pine cats eat *frogs*?

Reed padded forward. "I've been a moor cat for many moons, and I think my name should reflect that."

"Mine too!" Minnow hurried to join him. "I'd like to be Swift Minnow."

Wind Runner blinked at them in surprise. "But—"

Reed interrupted her. "I know you don't like change, Wind Runner. But I'd appreciate it if you'd call me Reed Tail from now on."

"Reed Tail." Wind Runner echoed the words, her pelt rippling uncomfortably along her spine. "Okay."

River Ripple nodded to Thunder. "Are your cats going to take new names?"

Thunder glanced at Violet. "You'll have to ask them."

Violet gazed at him warmly, as though there were no other cats in the hollow. "I'd like to be Violet Dawn," she mewed huskily.

"Violet Dawn." Thunder repeated her new name dreamily. "That's beautiful."

He jerked from his thoughts as River Ripple turned to Ember. "And what about you? Do you want a new name now that you're part of Thunder's group?"

Ember stared at him. "Just because I sleep in the same camp doesn't mean I want to change who I am."

Tall Shadow's tail quivered. "I guess he doesn't *have* to change his name," she meowed cautiously. "Drizzle kept *her* old name."

River Ripple ignored her. His gaze was fixed on Ember. "Are you part of Thunder's group or not?" he asked softly but firmly.

Ember eyed him challengingly. "Thunder lets me sleep in his camp. Does that mean I have to act like we're kin?"

Thunder shivered. Ember sounded hostile. Was it safe to let him stay in the ravine?

River Ripple hadn't moved. "You've just promised to hunt

for your campmates and protect them when they are weak and stand beside them when they are strong. Isn't that a little like being kin?"

Ember snorted. "Slash never expected anything of us. Our lives were our own."

Anger surged beneath Thunder's pelt. He darted forward and faced the orange rogue. "Your lives were *never* your own with Slash. You had to obey every word he said!"

A vicious snarl sounded from the high rock.

Thunder spun, his eyes widening as he saw the thin, muscly outline of Slash. The rogue was glaring down at them, lit by moonlight at the top of the boulder. Thunder's fur lifted along his spine. Had the rogue come here to fight?

"No one ever had to obey me," Slash hissed. "They could have left if they wanted."

"That's not true." Fern limped forward and glared at Slash. "You said you'd hurt Beech if I didn't come back."

"So?" Slash curled his lip. "Beech died anyway." As he spoke, Bee padded from behind Slash.

Fern recoiled, hissing.

More shapes moved at the bottom of the rock. Splinter, Beetle, and Snake emerged from the shadows and faced the gathered cats.

Thunder pushed his way through his campmates and glared at Slash. Anger churned in his belly. "How dare you come here!"

Slash looked past him, his gaze flicking over his old campmates. Moss Tail and Dawn Mist moved closer to their kits.

Willow Tail shifted her paws. Fear showed in Red Claw's eyes. "Thank you for looking after the weakest members of my group," Slash hissed. "But it's time for them to come home now."

Thunder stiffened. These rogues had just pledged loyalty to their new campmates. Surely they wouldn't leave now? Could Slash bully them into returning to their old group?

Wind Runner backed away, her pelt spiking. Her distrustful gaze flicked over Willow Tail and Fern Leaf.

She thinks they will betray us! Thunder's heart pounded in his ears. *Prove her wrong!* He stiffened as Ember barged his way through the gathered cats and padded toward the high rock. "I want to come back," he told Slash.

Slash's eyes lit up with triumph. "Of course you do. Bee's told me what a bunch of simpering mouse-hearts these cats are." He glared at Thunder. "Perhaps *you'd* like to join us. Your skills are wasted on these chattering pigeons!"

Thunder growled. "Never!" He braced himself, ready to defend his campmates. His thoughts quickened. Violet Dawn would fight beside him. Lightning Tail too. Every cat he'd grown up beside would face these rogues at his side.

But what about the others? He glanced toward Juniper Branch and Raven Pelt. He hardly knew them. What if they joined Slash? Gray Wing was clearly not as strong as he used to be. If a fight broke out, protecting him would be tricky. Suddenly Thunder felt vulnerable. The wind moaned through the branches overhead as the cats glared at one another.

"I will never share a camp with you again." Moss Tail's hiss cut through the icy air.

"Nor me!" Dawn Mist stiffened beside her mate.

"I belong to Clear Sky's group now!" Red Claw padded forward and stopped at Clear Sky's side. "I am loyal to him."

Thunder glanced at Juniper Branch, Raven Pelt, Willow Tail, and Fern Leaf as they lined up beside their new campmates, hackles high.

Relief swept through his fur. He stared at Slash. "Take Ember and go," he snarled. "We didn't take your weakest cats. We took your strongest." Pride swelled in his chest.

Slash glared at him angrily. "You can keep them," he hissed. "But don't think you've won. Go back to your camps, you mouse-brains. You'll learn quickly enough the price you've paid for defying me."

CHAPTER 21

At *Slash's words, Gray Wing's heart* lurched. He blinked at Clear Sky. Where was Star Flower? And the kits? Was Slash planning to kidnap her again?

Fear sparked in Clear Sky's eyes. "Star Flower!" He raced for the slope. Acorn Fur, Nettle, and Birch tore after him, pelts bristling.

Breath tightening, Gray Wing looked up at Slash, who was watching the shocked cats, his whiskers twitching with delight. "If you've hurt Star Flower or her kits—"

Slash cut Gray Wing off. "Why should I bother with *them*? I've had enough of making Clear Sky suffer. It was *you* who led my cats away." Hatred gleamed in the rogue's slitted gaze.

Fear slipped icy claws beneath Gray Wing's pelt. "What do you mean?"

Slash didn't answer. Instead he signaled to his rogues with a flick of his tail and leaped from the great rock. Slinking into the shadows, they disappeared.

Gray Wing began to tremble. Slash was blaming *him*.

"Slate and the kits!" Wind Runner's panicked mew shook Gray Wing from his thoughts.

He stared at her across the snowy clearing. "Spotted Fur's with her." Even as he spoke, he knew that Spotted Fur couldn't fight a band of rogues single-pawed. "We have to get home!" He turned for the slope. Invisible jaws clamped his chest. He could hardly breathe.

Wind Runner raced to his side. She glanced at River Ripple. "Get back to your camp. Take shelter in your strongest den and protect Drizzle and Pine Needle until we know what Slash has planned next." As River Ripple nodded, she turned to Thunder. "Take your cats home too. We'll all be safest in our camps."

Clear Sky's cats had already disappeared into the forest. Only Sparrow Fur lingered, her pelt pricking along her spine.

Thunder lifted his chin. "If Slate and the kits are in danger, I'm staying with Gray Wing." He nodded to Lightning Tail. "Take our campmates home. You're in charge until I get back."

Leaf's eyes widened. "You can't leave us now, Thunder! Slash is back and wants revenge."

"Lightning Tail is in charge for now," Thunder told the black-and-white tom. "He's the strongest cat in the group, and I trust him completely. Do whatever he tells you." Thunder leaned closer to Lightning Tail, lowering his voice until Gray Wing had to prick his ears to hear. "If I don't return, *you* must be leader. I trust you to take care of our campmates. Keep the group together. The future lies in your paws."

Lightning Tail blinked in surprise at his friend. "You're coming back, aren't you?"

Before he could answer, Violet Dawn pushed past Lightning Tail and pressed her nose to Thunder's cheek. "You *must* come back!"

Thunder let her cheek rest against his for a moment, then pulled away. He whisked his tail. "I'll be home as soon as I can," he promised.

Gray Wing stared desperately up the slope. "We have to go!" Slash could be in the camp right now. Struggling for breath, he stumbled toward the bracken.

"Let me come." Pebble Heart crossed the clearing and pushed his shoulder beneath Gray Wing's. He looked back to Tall Shadow. "I'll be back in camp as soon as I can."

Tall Shadow dipped her head to the young tom. "Take Sun Shadow with you," she ordered. "He can help."

"I'll do what I can." Sun Shadow nodded quickly and rushed to join the moor cats.

"I'll help too!" Owl Eyes hurried forward and pressed against Gray Wing's other side.

Gray Wing was surprised at the young tom's strength. He remembered him as a kit, clambering over his flank while Turtle Tail looked on fondly. Now he felt Owl Eyes's powerful muscles press against his own bony frame.

Wind Runner had already crashed through the bracken, her campmates at her side. Dust Muzzle and Moth Flight kicked snow up as they followed.

"Let me come!" Sparrow Fur's mew startled Gray Wing. Gratitude swamped him as the tortoiseshell she-cat streaked after the others. All of Turtle Tail's kits wanted to help.

Willow Tail lashed her tail. "If Slash has harmed a hair on their pelts, I'll hunt him down and kill him!"

Fern Leaf showed her teeth. "I'll help you," she hissed.

As they disappeared between the orange fronds, Owl Eyes and Pebble Heart guided Gray Wing up the slope. At the top, he blinked into the icy wind that flayed the snow-covered moor. Flecks of snow stung his eyes.

The camp hollow showed in the distance, a shadow on the moonlit hillside. Wind Runner and the others raced toward it.

Gray Wing stumbled, desperate to keep up. Pebble Heart and Owl Eyes pressed closer against him, supporting him as he struggled through the deep snow. His chest burned. Darkness pressed at the edge of his vision as he struggled for breath. His thoughts focused on the camp. *Please let Slate be okay! And the kits!* Perhaps Slash had been bluffing, just to scare him.

His campmates streaked ahead, their dark shapes showing against the snow as they pelted uphill. They disappeared into heather, then broke from the far side.

Frustration pulsed through Gray Wing. "Faster!" he gasped.

Pebble Heart's shoulder pressed harder against his. Owl Eyes leaned closer on his other side. Lifting him between them, they carried him over the snow. Gray Wing's paws churned helplessly beneath him as they whisked him toward the camp.

By the time they reached the gorse entrance, the others had disappeared inside.

Gray Wing smelled blood. Heart quickening, he pricked his ears and listened for the sound of fighting. But he heard no battle cries. Only the eerie moaning of the wind over the moonlit moor.

He shook free of Pebble Heart and Owl Eyes and staggered through the entrance. Stumbling over the tussocks, he saw blood staining the snow.

Wind Runner and the others were circling around two shapes on the ground.

Hardly breathing, Gray Wing barged past his campmates and stopped.

Spotted Fur and Slate were lying like abandoned prey in the snow, their pelts glistening with blood.

Are they dead? Gray Wing's heart seemed to stop as he stared.

Then Spotted Fur groaned and pushed himself heavily to his paws. "I tried to save them," he croaked. With a gasp, he began to collapse as his hind legs buckled beneath him.

Pebble Heart dashed to the golden tom's side and began sniffing his pelt anxiously.

Gray Wing hardly noticed. His gaze was fixed on Slate.

She lay unmoving while her campmates stared in horror.

Reed Tail crouched beside her and was lapping her bloody neck with urgent strokes.

Gray Wing stumbled closer. "Slate—" Her name seemed to stick in his throat. Above, the silent stars glittered. *Don't take her,* he silently begged his ancestors. Were they watching? The ground swayed beneath him. Grief spread barbed claws around his heart. *Not again.* Wasn't it enough he'd lost Turtle Tail?

Slate stirred. "Gray Wing?" Her mew was barely a whisper.

Gray Wing dropped to his belly beside her. As he struggled for breath, Slate opened her eyes. She stared at him blankly for a moment; then terror shot through her amber gaze. "The kits!" Fighting to stand up, she yowled across the clearing. "Silver Stripe! Black Ear! White Tail!"

Gray Wing jerked his muzzle around. Where were they?

Slate's gaze was frantic. "We fought for them!" she gasped. "Slash came with his cats after you'd all left. We tried to drive them out of the camp. But there were too many of them." She darted forward, scrambling this way and that across the clearing, her pelt bristling. "White Tail! Black Ear!"

"Slate?" A frightened mew sounded from the gorse wall of the camp. The branches trembled and snow showered down as a tiny dark gray tom-kit slid out. A pale gray tabby she-kit followed him, sprigs of gorse sticking out of her fur.

"Silver Stripe!" Slate ran toward them, her bloody paws staining the snow. "White Tail!"

Relief washed Gray Wing's pelt. Two of his kits were safe.

Silver Stripe blinked at her mother as Slate stopped beside them. "We hid like you told us."

"We hardly breathed," White Tail whispered. Trembling, he dived beneath Slate's belly and crouched there.

"We thought they'd killed you," Silver Stripe wailed.

White Tail shrank deeper under his mother's fur as Slate scooped Silver Stripe close. "You were very brave to hide when we told you to."

"Black Ear wasn't quick enough," White Tail sobbed. "They saw him and grabbed him."

Slate swung her gaze toward Gray Wing. Horror froze her face. "Black Ear!"

"I'll find him." Gray Wing tried to straighten, but his breath was so shallow, darkness threatened to overwhelm him.

Thunder padded to his side. "Stay here, Gray Wing. I'll find him for you." Determination hardened his mew.

Gray Wing gazed at him helplessly, frustration throbbing in his paws. "But they're *my* kits!" he wheezed.

Thunder gazed at him solemnly. "You have done so much for me, Gray Wing. Let me do this for you."

Gray Wing held his gaze for a moment, touched by Thunder's warmth. "Thank you."

Wind Runner lashed her tail. "We don't know which way they're headed. Thunder, Sparrow Fur, and Owl Eyes! Head toward the pines. Slash might be taking Black Ear to his old camp. Swift Minnow, you take Reed Tail and Dust Muzzle toward the river. Check the gorge and the reed beds. I'll take Sun Shadow, Gorse Fur, and Moth Flight to the oak forest. We'll search the woods."

Willow Tail lifted her chin. "I'm coming with you," she told Wind Runner.

"And me." Fern Leaf stood next to her friend.

Wind Runner eyed them doubtfully.

Gray Wing tensed. Surely she couldn't reject their help?

Wind Runner flicked her tail. "You're still recovering from your wounds, Fern Leaf," she meowed briskly. "Stay here in camp and help Pebble Heart. Willow Tail." She dipped her head to the pale tabby. "You can join my patrol. You know the routes the rogues use. And you're smart and strong. We'll need you."

Willow Tail puffed out her chest. "I won't let you down."

Gray Wing tried to stand again, but his paws buckled. Rage flared through him. *I can't even save my own kit!*

Pebble Heart pressed against him and nodded to Fern Leaf. "Do you know what coltsfoot looks like?" he asked the young she-cat.

Fern Leaf nodded.

"It'll be wilted by the cold," Pebble Heart warned her. "But you should be able to find stems. Frost-burned ones will do. Bring them here. They'll help Gray Wing's breathing." He turned to Slate. "Get the kits into your den and keep them warm. I'll check on your wounds when I've seen to Spotted Fur."

The world swam around Gray Wing. Paws thrummed on every side. His campmates were heading for the entrance.

Thunder's mew sounded fiercely in his ear. "I'm going to find Black Ear," he promised. "And I'll bring him home safe."

Darkness closed in as Gray Wing felt the last of his strength seep into the snowy earth.

CHAPTER 22

Thunder's thoughts whirled as he watched Gray Wing collapse. *He's so ill! Black Ear's missing! Everything's gone wrong!* Above, the moon shone bright in the midnight sky. It was the same moon that had shone on the naming ceremony not long before. How had so much changed so fast?

His gaze darted to the entrance. Wind Runner, Moth Flight, Gorse Fur, and Willow Tail were already haring after Reed Tail and Dust Muzzle. Sparrow Fur and Owl Eyes were waiting for him, their tails flicking impatiently.

"Go!" Pebble Heart nudged Thunder with his muzzle. "I'll make sure Gray Wing's okay. Just find Black Ear."

Thunder blinked at the young tom, then bounded across the tussocks. Racing past Owl Eyes and Sparrow Fur, he led the way out of camp. Wind Runner's brown tabby pelt showed against the snow as she headed for the oak forest. Swift Minnow charged toward the gorge.

"Can you see any tracks?" Thunder called to Sparrow Fur as the tortoiseshell caught up to him. Had the rogues left a trail?

"Here!" Owl Eyes's yowl sounded behind him.

Thunder spun, skidding to a halt.

Owl Eyes was sniffing churned-up snow. Tracks led over a ridge and down into a dip. Thunder hurried to Owl Eyes's side. Sniffing the tracks, he smelled rogue stench. He scrambled clumsily to the bottom of the dip.

Sparrow Fur landed beside him. Owl Eyes tumbled after. Thunder sniffed the flattened snow. "They stopped here," he guessed. Paw prints circled and crossed. "Perhaps they were wondering where to go next."

Sparrow Fur frowned. "Wouldn't Slash have already planned where they were taking Black Ear?"

"Look!" Owl Eyes was following a trail up the far side of the dip. "They must have gone this way."

"But there's a trail here as well!" Sparrow Fur was sniffing a single track of paw prints.

Thunder frowned. "Did they split up?"

Owl Eyes looked confused. "Why?"

Thunder frowned, trying to understand. "Slash and his campmates were at the gathering. They didn't have Black Ear with them." He stared at Sparrow Fur. "But they must have snatched him pretty soon after we all left our camps. There wasn't enough time for them to attack *after* the meeting."

Sparrow Fur pricked her ears. "They must have taken Black Ear and hidden him somewhere."

Owl Eyes's tail twitched. "He'd have needed a guard."

Thunder began to pace. "There was one rogue missing from the gathering." He suddenly remembered the orange she-cat who had begged to go with Slash as he abandoned the marsh camp. He had not seen her among Slash's allies at the four trees. "*Swallow* wasn't there!" His thoughts quickened, but Sparrow Fur was faster.

"Swallow guarded Black Ear while Slash was at the meeting!" The tortoiseshell's eyes widened.

"So they *did* split up." Owl Eyes nodded from one set of tracks to the other. "Slash and the others went to the clearing while Swallow took Black Ear somewhere else."

Hope flickered in Thunder's belly. "We have to find where they hid him."

"He won't be there anymore," Owl Eyes pointed out.

"But Slash and the others must have come back to fetch him," Thunder reasoned. "That would have taken time."

Sparrow Fur's tail swished over the snow. "We can't be far behind them."

Owl Eyes shifted his paws impatiently. "Which trail do we follow?"

"This one will lead us to the hiding place." Thunder jerked his muzzle toward the single set of tracks.

"Come on!" Sparrow Fur bounded out of the dip.

Thunder was hard on her heels as the tortoiseshell followed the trail through the snow toward the high moor. Freezing wind streamed through Thunder's fur, blowing from Highstones and carrying the chilly scent of the mountains. Thunder quickened his pace. Black Ear was too small to be exposed to such cold. He could freeze to death out here.

The trail sliced through the smooth snow ahead. Thunder saw it was leading to a rocky outcrop jutting from the hillside. He raced past Sparrow Fur, relieved as he saw a gap between the wind-smoothed boulders. At least Swallow had had the sense to find shelter for Black Ear while she waited for Slash to return.

He spotted more tracks veering to meet the single trail. Slowing, he sniffed them and growled softly as he smelled Slash's scent. It was fresh. They'd guessed right. Slash and his campmates *had* come to fetch Swallow and Black Ear after the meeting.

Sparrow Fur hared past him and dived through the gap between the boulders.

Owl Eyes raced after his sister, disappearing into the shadowy cave.

"How recently were they there?" Thunder called, following them in. Rocks closed overhead as darkness swallowed him. Fear-stench hit his nose. Swallow must have crouched here nervously. He brushed past Sparrow Fur, who was sniffing the ground.

"Black Ear was definitely here," the tortoiseshell meowed. "I can smell his scent."

Thunder shoved his muzzle close and smelled warm kit scent. Relief pricked though his fur. *No blood-scent.* The kit wasn't injured.

Owl Eyes slid past him, his pelt brushing rock. "They're not long gone," he mewed excitedly. "We can catch them easily. Carrying a kit must be slowing them down."

Thunder raised his head as fear jabbed his belly. He'd seen Slash let a campmate be mauled to death by a dog. What pity would he show a kit? "How do we get Black Ear away from them without him getting hurt?"

"We'll cross that river when we come to it." Sparrow Fur's eyes glinted in the shadows.

Thunder nodded. First they had to find them.

He headed for the cave entrance.

A growl sounded outside.

Thunder froze. A familiar stench touched his nose as a shadow blocked the moonlight filtering through the gap. "Fox!"

Owl Eyes stiffened beside him. Sparrow Fur's pelt bristled.

"It must have followed the scents," Thunder whispered. "It's waiting for us outside." As he spoke, a muzzle poked through the gap. The snarling face of a fox appeared, its eyes gleaming with delight as it saw them.

Thunder retreated slowly, pressing Sparrow Fur and Owl Eyes backward.

The fox whined as it tried to push farther into the cave.

"It's too big," Owl Eyes breathed.

"But we have to get out!" Sparrow Fur hissed.

"We'll drive it back," Thunder decided. "Then make a run for it."

"It'll chase us." Owl Eyes's mew trembled.

"We might lead it to Black Ear," Sparrow Fur pointed out.

Thunder hesitated. Rage pulsed through his paws. There wasn't time to fight a fox. Slash and his campmates would be getting farther away with each moment they wasted. But what else could they do? "I'll drive it away from the entrance." He unsheathed his claws. "You slide out behind me. Owl Eyes, go for its tail. Sparrow Fur, get on its back." They were taking a huge risk. Leaf-bare foxes were more vicious than badgers. But they had to do it. For Gray Wing. He nodded to Owl Eyes and Sparrow Fur. "Ready?"

"Ready," Sparrow Fur growled.

Owl Eyes lashed his tail. "Ready."

Diving forward, Thunder slashed at the fox's muzzle.

It shrank backward, snarling.

Thunder felt Sparrow Fur and Owl Eyes barge past. Moonlit snow flashed before his eyes as the entrance cleared. He dashed outside.

The fox lunged at him, its teeth catching the fur on his shoulder and ripping it from his flesh. Screeching with pain, Thunder whipped around and swung a blow at the fox's nose. His claws whisked over its black snout, and he threw a second blow at its cheek.

The fox's eyes shone with rage. Thrusting its snout closer, it snapped at Thunder. Thunder backed away. It drove him against the boulder, looming so close that there was no room to swing his paws. Fear surged through his pelt. He glimpsed Owl Eyes tugging desperately at the fox's tail. Sparrow Fur clung to its shoulders, shredding its pelt with her hind paws so that red fur fluttered over the glittering snow.

The fox didn't seem to feel the blows. Excitement shone in its eyes as it paused and showed its glistening teeth.

It's going to kill me! Terror raged through Thunder. He thought of Violet Dawn, waiting for him in camp. And Lightning Tail. *You must be their next leader.* Silently he begged his friend to take care of the cats he'd brought together.

A battle cry split the air.

The fox jerked its muzzle around, fear sparking in its gaze.

A broad-shouldered gray tom was racing toward it.

Clear Sky!

With a yowl, Clear Sky leaped, slamming his paws into the fox's neck. The fox staggered, slithering on the snow. Sparrow Fur growled and dragged at its pelt, unbalancing the fox. Owl Eyes yanked its tail to one side, and the fox fell.

Thunder leaped on it, his flank pressing against his father's as, side by side, they battered the fox with merciless blows.

The fox screeched, fear sharpening its cry. It struggled beneath the spitting cats and wriggled free.

Thunder backed away as it scrambled to its paws. Flashing a terrified glance at the cats, it turned and fled across the hillside.

"Clear Sky!" Catching his breath, Thunder stared at his father. "Why did you come?"

Clear Sly was panting, his thick gray pelt ruffled. Starlight glittered in his eyes. "When I reached camp and found Star Flower safe, I guessed." He blinked at Thunder. "Slash attacked Gray Wing's camp, didn't he?"

Thunder nodded. "He's taken Black Ear."

"Are the others okay?" Clear Sky didn't flinch, his gaze sharp.

"Silver Stripe and White Tail are safe. Slate and Spotted Fur were wounded trying to protect them, but Pebble Heart's with them."

"Good." Clear Sky turned his head, scanning the moor. "Do you know which way Slash went?"

Sparrow Fur shook out her ruffled pelt. "We were following their tracks."

Owl Eyes darted toward the churned snow leading away from the outcrop. "Swallow hid Black Ear here while Slash went to the gathering," he explained. "Slash and the others came to fetch them afterward."

Clear Sky hurried to the trail and sniffed it. "It's still fresh."

"They can't be far ahead. We were—"

Before Thunder could finish, Clear Sky bounded away, kicking up snow. Thunder leaped after him. They chased across the moonlit hillside, following the rogues' trail. Owl Eyes veered downslope, his gaze flicking one way, then the other. Sparrow Fur raced fast over the snow, hardly denting it.

The moor sloped out of the moonlight and into shadow. Heather and pine stretched ahead. The trail veered around it. Sparrow Fur headed between the bushes, chasing her brother as Owl Eyes plunged through them. Thunder stayed at Clear Sky's heels, the cold air burning his chest. Heat pulsed from his pelt. As they rounded the heather, Owl Eyes burst from the bushes ahead of them.

The gray tom stopped. His gaze followed the trail as it straightened and led toward Tall Shadow's territory. "They're heading for the pines."

Thunder scrambled to a halt.

The heather trembled as Sparrow Fur darted out. She followed her brother's gaze toward the dark wood below. "They must be trying to get to their old camp."

"They'll have to cross the Thunderpath." Thunder's pelt prickled with fear as he saw it cutting between the moor and the pines. The snow there had been churned into filthy sludge by monster paws. He scanned the trail, searching for the rogues. But shadow hid the verges. He flattened his ears as a monster screamed past, spraying slush from its paws.

"They might *not* cross the Thunderpath," Sparrow Fur mewed hopefully. "Perhaps they'll just follow it as far as the oak forest. The woods there are thick. It would make a good place to hide."

"Let's find out." Clear Sky leaped down the slope.

Thunder bounded after him, his paws sinking into the snow as he reached the bottom. The rogues' trail turned and followed the verge. The scents were fresh. Even as the stench of the Thunderpath soured his nostrils, Thunder could smell warmth in the rogues' tracks. They'd passed here very recently. He narrowed his eyes, straining to see through the darkness. *Where are they?*

Monster eyes flashed toward him, dazzling him for a moment. Frowning, he made out dark shapes on the verge a few tree-lengths away, silhouetted against the blinding light. The rogues were beside the Thunderpath. A small shape dangled from the jaws of one.

"Black Ear!" Thunder gasped.

Clear Sky halted and followed his gaze, flinching as the monster pounded past. "I see him!"

Thunder flattened his ears against the monster's deafening

roar. Squinting, Sparrow Fur and Owl Eyes pushed between them and stared along the verge.

The rogues clustered at the edge, clearly waiting to cross, their pelts dripping from the monster's spray. Slash circled them, tail lashing, then halted as his gaze fixed on Thunder.

"He's seen us." Thunder shuddered.

Light flashed in the distance. Another monster was bearing down the Thunderpath.

"We can't attack here," Sparrow Fur growled. "It's too dangerous."

"We can let them cross, then follow them into the pines," Owl Eyes suggested.

Clear Sky frowned. "There'll be no snow under the pines. It'll be harder to follow their trail. We might lose them."

Thunder agreed. "We have to stop them from getting to the trees." He began to pad along the verge. Dread hollowed his belly. They were outnumbered. Snake, Slash, Splinter, Ember, and Beetle were facing them now, hackles high. Swallow padded closer to the edge of the road. Black Ear dangled from her jaws, his legs churning as he twisted in the air. The monster rolled toward them, its eyes lighting its path.

"Wait." Sparrow Fur's mew was sharp with fear. "Wait for the monster to pass."

"Then what?" Owl Eyes asked.

"We attack," Clear Sky growled.

Thunder met Slash's gaze. The rogue's eyes glittered with delight for a moment; then, with a wild yowl, he hared across the Thunderpath. His campmates followed, streaming across the wet stone. Their pelts lit up in the flaming gaze of the monster as it thundered toward them.

Thunder's heart seemed to burst in his chest. "They're getting away!"

As he spoke, Swallow stumbled. Her paws slipped in the slush and she dropped to her belly. Her gaze jerked toward the monster. It hurtled closer, letting out a scream. Scrambling to her paws, Swallow fled, chasing her campmates to the verge at the far side. In a moment they'd disappeared into the trees.

"Black Ear!" Sparrow Fur's terrified yowl drowned the roar of the monster.

Thunder followed her horrified gaze.

The kit stood in the middle of the Thunderpath as the blazing light of the monster raced toward him. Like a terrified rabbit, he stared, his pelt bushed.

Owl Eyes opened his mouth, gasping in disbelief. "The monster's going to kill him!"

CHAPTER 23

❧

Clear Sky stared at Black Ear, half dazzled by the glare of the monster's eyes as it bore down on the tiny kit. The world grew silent. Time slowed. Bounding forward, Clear Sky moved as though invisible paws carried him. The verge blurred as he raced onto the Thunderpath. Slush splashed beneath his pads, but he hardly felt its wet chill. His gaze was fixed on Black Ear, blind to the monster thundering closer with every moment. Skimming the filthy snow, he grabbed Black Ear's scruff without stopping.

Wind slammed him like stone. It sent him tumbling toward the far edge of the Thunderpath. The monster screamed past, its paws whisking so close that grit strafed his flank. Pain shrilled through his tail and scorched his fur. Rolling onto the sludge-covered grass, he felt the tug of Black Ear's scruff between his jaws. *I got him.* Clear Sky hardly dared open his eyes. The kit wasn't moving. Clear Sky gently let go and curled himself around the tiny kit.

"Clear Sky!" Thunder's mew sounded in his ear.

Paws squelched around him. Teeth dug into his scruff, and he felt himself being dragged clear of the verge. He wrapped his paws around Black Ear, holding him close to his belly, and opened his eyes as they reached the shadow of the pines.

"Clear Sky?" Thunder's frightened mew sounded again.

The teeth let go of his scruff. Blinking, he looked up to see Thunder, Owl Eyes, and Sparrow Fur crowding around him.

"We thought you'd been killed!" Owl Eyes stared at him, pelt bristling.

"The monster missed you by a whisker!" Sparrow Fur croaked.

Clear Sky loosened his grip on Black Ear. "Is the kit alive?" He hardly dared ask. The wind from the monster had hit them hard. Pain throbbed in his tail. His flanks were numb.

Thunder leaned down and sniffed the wet scrap of fur beside Clear Sky's belly.

Black Ear mewled softly. "I want to go home."

Relief washed Clear Sky's aching body. He struggled to sit up, wincing at the pain in his tail, and sniffed the kit. Rogue stench bathed the tiny tom's scruff, and his pelt reeked of Thunderpath fumes. "Did the rogues hurt you?"

"They wouldn't let me go home." Black Ear looked up at Clear Sky, eyes glistening with fear. "Is Slate okay? I saw them hurt her. Then they took me away."

Clear Sky's throat tightened. "Slate's fine," he promised the kit. "She just has a few scratches. Pebble Heart is taking care of her."

"Are Silver Stripe and White Tail all right too?" Black Ear asked.

Clear Sky pressed his muzzle to Black Ear's cheek. "They're

safe and sound." He was trembling, his pelt soaked with freezing water. But he'd saved Black Ear. As the kit scrambled shakily to his paws, he thought of Tiny Branch, safe in his nest at home. "We need to get you back to your mother."

"First we need to get him warm and dry. Let's head for Tall Shadow's camp. It's closest." Sparrow Fur plucked Black Ear up by his scruff.

"Ow!" The kit struggled, churning his paws. "My scruff hurts!"

"Here." Thunder crouched in front of him. "You can ride on my back."

Sparrow Fur laid Black Ear gently between Thunder's shoulder blades and lifted a paw to pat Thunder's thick fur around the kit. "Just make sure you hang on."

Black Ear snuggled deeper in, curling his claws into Thunder's pelt.

Clear Sky glanced at Thunder.

Thunder looked worried. "Are you well enough to travel?"

Clear Sky ached in every limb. But he wasn't staying here. "I'm fine." He pushed himself onto his paws and tested his legs. They seemed to hold, though he couldn't stop them shaking. The worst pain was in his tail. He hardly dared look. It felt as though the monster had shredded it. "My tail," he croaked softly.

Sparrow Fur sniffed it. "It's injured," she meowed. "Can you move it?"

Clear Sky tried to lift it. Pain blazed though him, but his tail remained limp. He glanced at it nervously. It drooped behind him like a dead snake, slick with filth from the Thunderpath.

Sparrow Fur shook out her pelt. "While you go to Tall Shadow's camp, I'll fetch Pebble Heart and tell Slate and Gray Wing that Black Ear is safe. Pebble Heart might know how to fix Clear Sky's tail."

Black Ear lifted his muzzle. "I want to go back to the moor!"

Sparrow Fur met the kit's gaze. "You need shelter and warmth. You've had a nasty shock. If Slate is well enough, I'll bring her back with Pebble Heart."

"Will you bring Gray Wing, too?" Black Ear eyed the tortoiseshell hopefully.

Clear Sky frowned as he saw Sparrow Fur and Thunder exchange an anxious look. "What's wrong with Gray Wing?"

Thunder's ear twitched. "Nothing," he mewed quickly. "He's probably still out looking for Black Ear."

Clear Sky narrowed his eyes. Thunder was lying. He glanced at Black Ear. There was something Thunder didn't want the kit to know. He touched his nose to Black Ear's head, changing the subject. "You're lucky," he meowed. "Not many kits get to visit another camp before they're a moon old." He tried to ignore the pain in his tail. His pads stung, scratched by the Thunderpath.

Sparrow Fur turned toward the moor. "I'll be as quick as I can." Nodding a farewell, she hurried away through the pines.

Owl Eyes slid in beside Clear Sky and pressed his shoulder against him. "Lean on me."

Clear Sky stiffened, resisting help, but another spike of

pain made him gasp. Reluctantly, he let his weight rest against the young tom and limped slowly toward Tall Shadow's camp.

As they neared the bramble wall of the camp, flecks of snow drifted down from the pines. The forest floor was lightly dusted, but the trees held a heavy weight of snow. The sounds of the forest were muffled beneath them, and shadow pressed on every side. Clear Sky felt as though he were walking in a strange dream. Cold seemed to reach through his pelt and his flesh, reaching his bones until he felt himself shivering.

"Clear Sky?" Jagged Peak's surprised mew rang between the trees.

Clear Sky blinked through the darkness and made out the gray tom's shape.

Jagged Peak hurried toward them. "What happened?" He pulled up and stared, first at Clear Sky, then at the bedraggled kit on Thunder's back.

Owl Eyes pressed harder against Clear Sky. "Slash attacked Wind Runner's camp while we were at the meeting. They took Black Ear. But we got him back."

Jagged Peak's eyes flashed with outrage. "Will we ever see the back of that fox-heart?"

Thunder growled. "I think he knows that he'd be a fool to show his pelt anywhere near us after this." He nodded toward the camp. "We need to get Black Ear somewhere warm, and Clear Sky needs rest. He was hit by a monster."

"It didn't hit me," Clear Sky croaked.

"Just your tail," Thunder grunted. He padded past Jagged Peak, heading toward camp.

Black Ear stared up into the branches from between Thunder's shoulder blades. "Is it always this dark?"

"It's not yet dawn." Jagged Peak hurried to catch up with Thunder.

"Then why are you awake?" Black Ear asked.

"We've been waiting for news."

"Jagged Peak?" Tall Shadow's mew sounded from the entrance. Her eyes widened as she stuck out her head and saw the party. Her gaze flicked over them quickly; then she withdrew and called across her camp. "Mouse Ear! We need your den! Clear Sky is injured. Holly! Black Ear is with them. He looks frozen to the bone."

By the time Clear Sky had trailed through the entrance after Thunder, cats were moving around the camp. He could hardly see them, shadows against the bramble walls.

"This way." Mouse Ear's reassuring mew beckoned them toward the edge of the clearing.

A gap opened in the thick bramble wall. Thunder ducked in first and Clear Sky stumbled after, leaving Jagged Peak and Owl Eyes outside. He smelled the warmth of Mouse Ear's nest. The tom had clearly been sleeping in it until only a few moments ago. Clear Sky padded toward it and collapsed gratefully into the softness of the moss-lined pine brush.

Thunder tipped Black Ear next to him, and the kit snuggled close for warmth as Holly slid into the den.

Holly crouched beside them and began lapping the wet kit.

Black Ear began to purr at once. "You smell like Slate, only different," he told Holly.

Thunder shifted beside the nest. "Slate is surely on her way here," he insisted, "with Pebble Heart." He hoped he was right.

Holly lifted her head, her nose twitching. She glanced at Clear Sky's tail.

Clear Sky saw her wince, and his heart quickened. "Is it bad?"

"I've seen worse," Holly meowed briskly, and returned to watching Black Ear. "This kit is freezing. Can you fetch more moss, Thunder?"

"Of course." Thunder nodded and disappeared from the den.

Weariness swept over Clear Sky. "Will Black Ear be okay?" he asked thickly.

"He'll be fine once he's warm." She blinked at Clear Sky. "Why don't you close your eyes and get some sleep while we wait for Pebble Heart."

Clear Sky didn't argue. His pelt felt as heavy as dead prey. His paws stung, and the throbbing in his tail possessed every thought. Head swimming, he rested his muzzle against the side of the nest and closed his eyes.

Warm breath bathed Clear Sky's muzzle. He smelled mouse on it and wrinkled his nose. Blinking open his eyes, he saw Thunder, hazy in the half-light.

"Is the sun up?" he asked blearily.

"It's starting to set." Thunder shifted his paws stiffly, as though he'd not moved in a while.

"Have you been here long?" Clear Sky lifted his muzzle.

"Long enough."

"Don't your campmates need you?"

"Lightning Tail's in charge. They'll manage without me for a while. I wanted to make sure you were okay."

Clear Sky pricked his ears. Was Thunder worried about him? He glanced at his tail. The pain had eased. Thick gobs of chewed herbs were smeared along it.

"Pebble Heart made a poultice," Thunder explained, following his father's gaze. "How does it feel?"

"Better."

"He says it's snapped in three places. The monster must have run right over it. But it will mend."

Clear Sky gazed into Thunder's eyes, amazed by the warmth shining in their amber depths. "You're staring at me like you think I'm dying." He looked away, self-consciously.

"You saved Black Ear," Thunder breathed. "One moment you were beside me; the next you were running into the path of a monster. You could have been killed."

"I couldn't let Black Ear die." Clear Sky lifted his gaze. "Gray Wing saved my kits. It was my duty to save his."

"It wasn't your duty to die trying," Thunder murmured.

"But I didn't die." Clear Sky moved in his nest, suddenly aware that Black Ear was gone. "Where is he?" Fear jabbed his belly.

"Holly took him to her nest," Thunder told him. "She said the best thing for him was to have Storm Pelt, Dew Nose, and Eagle Feather fidgeting around him. They'd warm him up and help him forget his ordeal quicker than anything."

Clear Sky tried to purr, but his throat was too dry.

Thunder pawed a clump of wet moss toward him.

Gratefully, Clear Sky stretched his nose toward it and pressed his tongue into the damp wad. Water streamed into his mouth. Closing his eyes, he relished the coolness on his throat. Without opening them, he spoke. "I said Gray Wing saved my kits. But I didn't mean just Tiny Branch, Dew Petal, and Flower Foot. I meant you, too." Emotion thickened his mew, but he forced himself to go on. "I didn't look after you when you needed me. Gray Wing did. He was more of a father to you than I ever was, and I'm grateful to him for that."

He tensed, waiting for Thunder to speak. But Thunder remained silent.

Clear Sky opened his eyes and looked at his son.

Thunder's eyes glistened with emotion. "You did the best you could," he mewed huskily.

Sharp voices suddenly sounded outside the den.

"I *have* to take Black Ear home." It was Slate's anxious mew.

Holly answered her fretfully. "He's not well enough to travel yet."

"He'll be fine now that he's warm and fed," Pebble Heart reassured her.

"He must see Gray Wing." Slate's mew tightened. "It might be his last chance before . . ." Her mew trailed away.

Clear Sky stiffened. "Before what?" He remembered Thunder's lie to Black Ear. "Gray Wing's sick, isn't he?"

Thunder blinked at him sadly. "I don't think he's going to recover this time."

"He's *dying?*" Clear Sky struggled to his paws as shock pulsed through him. "I have to see him."

Thunder narrowed his eyes. "Can you travel as far as the moor?"

"I *have* to see him," Clear Sky growled. Pushing past Thunder, he slid from the den. Bright sunshine made him wince as it reflected off the snow-powdered camp. He stared at Slate. Black Ear was tucked beneath her belly. "I'm coming with you."

Slate dipped her head.

"So am I." Thunder padded from the den and stood close to Clear Sky.

Pain throbbed through Clear Sky's tail. He staggered and fell against Thunder.

"Don't worry, Clear Sky." Thunder pushed against him, tucking his shoulder in hard as Slate picked up Black Ear and headed out of camp. "I'll make sure you get there in time."

CHAPTER 24

Pain stabbed in Gray Wing's chest with every gasp. Exhausted by the battle for breath, he longed to give up. But he couldn't. Not now. Not until Black Ear was safely back in camp.

Wind Runner shifted beside him. "You should be in your den. It's freezing here."

Gray Wing shook his head, too breathless to speak. He stared stubbornly toward the camp entrance from where he lay between the tussocks. Snowflakes drifted onto his fur. The heavy clouds were dusting the moor once again.

"Have some more coltsfoot." Reed Tail pawed leaves close to his muzzle. "It'll help."

Gray Wing blinked up at the gentle tom. The coltsfoot had stopped working long ago. He was beyond help now. He could only wait and fight for a last glimpse of his beloved Slate and Black Ear.

"Gray Wing?" Silver Stripe huddled next to him. "Slate's been gone for ages. She *is* coming back, isn't she?"

"Of course she is," Gray Wing rasped.

White Tail nuzzled closer. "And Black Ear?"

"Gorse Fur said they found him." Gray Wing coughed

weakly. "Slate's fetching him right now."

"Save your breath." Swift Minnow padded closer and sat beside Gray Wing, pressing the kits between her flank and his. She wrapped her tail over their tiny bodies, protecting them from the thickening snow. "Wind Runner's right. You should all be inside."

Gray Wing didn't answer. He didn't dare take his gaze from the gorse entrance. For a moment his thoughts drifted into the past, moons ago, when he'd waited for Turtle Tail to return from Twolegplace. She'd never come home. *Let Slate come home.* His heart ached with the need to see her and Black Ear.

Moth Flight padded from Spotted Fur's den.

Reed Tail glanced at her. "How is he?"

Moth Flight fluffed out her fur. "He's asleep."

"Any sign of fever?"

"No," Moth Flight told him. "I felt his muzzle. It was cool. His wounds are all clean, and the dressing Pebble Heart made will keep them from turning sour."

White Tail fidgeted beside Gray Wing. "I want Slate. I'm hungry."

"She'll be home soon," Gray Wing murmured weakly.

Swift Minnow glanced toward the snow-capped prey pile. "You could try some mouse."

"He's too young," Wind Runner mewed.

"Perhaps I could chew it for him first—"

"Hush." Gray Wing pricked his ears. Paw steps were crunching through the snow outside the camp. He struggled to push himself up, but his paws buckled beneath him. *Slate can't see me so helpless!* Panic surged through him, stealing the small breath he had left. He began to cough.

"It's okay." Swift Minnow lapped his pelt with long smooth strokes. "She's coming. Everything will be all right."

Gray Wing's heart quickened as the gorse trembled and Slate padded into camp. Black Ear was clinging to her back.

He slithered down as soon as he saw Gray Wing. "Why are you lying there in the snow?" He raced toward his father and flung himself against Gray Wing's chest, huddling in the soft fur. "Slash stole me, but I escaped!" he mewed. "Now I'm home! I missed you so much."

Gray Wing's throat tightened as White Tail and Silver Stripe scrambled out from beneath Swift Minnow's tail and greeted their brother.

"White Tail said Slash ate you!" Silver Stripe squeaked.

"I did not!" White Tail pushed his sister out of the way and nuzzled Black Ear, purring.

Gray Wing breathed their scent as they huddled beneath his chin.

Then his gaze met Slate's.

She had stopped a tail-length away. Her eyes glistened with grief as she stared at him.

I'm sorry. Guilt washed over Gray Wing's pelt. He'd promised to help her raise their kits, but he knew that with each desperate breath, he was coming closer to his end. She'd have to raise them alone.

Slate blinked her sadness away. "Give your father some

space." Padding forward, she scooped White Tail away by his scruff.

"Is Black Ear okay?" Gray Wing searched Slate's gaze.

"He's fine," she told him. "But he's had quite an adventure. He can tell you about it once we've got you into your den, where it's warm."

As she spoke, Gray Wing realized that Thunder, Pebble Heart, Jagged Peak, and Clear Sky had followed her into camp. Clear Sky was leaning against Thunder, his battered tail slick with sticky herbs. Gray Wing blinked at his brother. "What happened?"

But Slate was already nudging him to his paws. "Let's get you out of the snow," she mewed briskly. He wobbled, and she pressed against him. Wind Runner ducked around his other side, and they steered him toward his den.

After helping him inside, they let him drop into his nest. It felt soft and warm beneath him. The roomy gorse cave was dark. Evening light filtered through the entrance. He lay still for a moment while he struggled for breath. Then Silver Stripe, Black Ear, and White Tail charged in.

"Thunder says Black Ear was nearly killed by a monster," White Tail told him as he scrambled into the nest beside him.

"But Clear Sky saved him," Silver Stripe added, hopping in after him.

"One of the rogues dropped me right in the middle of the Thunderpath," Black Ear announced dramatically.

Gray Wing's heart lurched.

Slate bustled past him. "But you're safe now," she told Black

Ear. "That's all that matters." She scooped him up and placed him beside the others.

Happy to feel the kits warm against his flank, Gray Wing tried to purr. But he wasn't strong enough and started coughing.

"Is Gray Wing sick?" Black Ear asked Slate.

White Tail lifted his nose knowledgeably. "He's got the *sniffles*. Reed Tail's been giving him herbs just like the ones he gave me when I had the sniffles."

Gray Wing didn't dare look at Slate. Grief clawed his heart.

Wind Runner padded forward and met Gray Wing's gaze. "I'm glad you got Black Ear back." Sorrow clouded her eyes. "We'll never lose him again. I promise that your kits will always be safe here." Suddenly she thrust her nose forward and touched it to Gray Wing's head. "Good-bye, old friend."

Silver Stripe frowned, puzzled. "Why's Wind Runner acting soppy?"

Gray Wing's throat tightened. "It's been a long day, that's all." He held Wind Runner's gaze for a moment. Then she turned away, and he watched her pad from the den. Gray Wing pulled Black Ear closer. He trusted Wind Runner to keep her word. She was a brave and honorable leader, and he felt fortunate to have been trusted by her. Whatever happened, his kits would be safe.

As she disappeared into the evening light, Thunder stuck his head in. "Can I come in?"

Gray Wing blinked at him. "Yes," he rasped. "Pebble Heart, Jagged Peak, and Clear Sky must come too." He wanted to see the faces that had meant so much to him.

Jagged Peak entered first. Gray Wing blinked warmly at the reckless younger brother whose fearlessness had led him here. Was there still a spark of spirit in his solemn blue eyes? Gray Wing searched them through the half-light and saw only grief.

Pebble Heart followed, and Gray Wing tried to purr as he saw him, warmth flooding his heart. Sparrow Fur and Owl Eyes should be here too. They'd helped rescue Black Ear. Turtle Tail would have been proud of them. Sparrow Fur and Owl Eyes had matured over the moons from feisty kits into brave, trustworthy cats. But Pebble Heart had not changed. Turtle Tail's quietest kit had always been so serious, and yet in his seriousness there had always been kindness and wisdom. "Look," Gray Wing whispered to Black Ear as he held him close.

Black Ear stopped wriggling and followed his gaze. "Why? It's only Pebble Heart."

"Pebble Heart is the gentlest cat I know," Gray Wing breathed. "Go to him if you're ever in trouble. He will always know what to do."

Thunder padded into the den, his huge white paws bright in the fading light. Gray Wing gazed at him proudly. The hot-headed young tom had become a strong leader. His cats looked up to him. Gray Wing had seen the warmth and respect with which his campmates looked at him.

White Tail put his paws on the side of the nest and stared at the forest cat. "Why is everyone visiting you, Gray Wing?"

They've come to say good-bye. Gray Wing lapped White Tail's head. "They've come to make sure Black Ear's okay."

"But why *them*?" White Tail pressed. "Are they kin?"

"Yes," Gray Wing told him gently.

He frowned. "Then why don't they live in our group?"

"They have their own groups."

Groups. Suddenly the word didn't seem enough to describe the closeness he felt for his campmates. Wind Runner, Gorse Fur, Slate, Swift Minnow, Reed Tail, and Spotted Fur—he suddenly realized that he felt as close to them as he felt to his own kin. His thoughts quickened, searching for a word that meant *more* than *groups*. A word that reflected the kinship he felt for those he hunted and fought beside. "They have their own *Clans*," he meowed suddenly.

Pebble Heart blinked. *"Clans!"* Satisfaction sparked in his gaze. "The five Clans, like the five petals of the Blazing Star."

Black Ear pricked his ears. "What's our Clan called?"

Gray Wing paused. What name would reflect all they had come from and how they lived? He thought of the high, wide moor, the breeze forever streaming through his pelt. "We are WindClan," he whispered at last.

Silver Stripe clambered onto Gray Wing's flank. "Then Thunder's group must be ThunderClan."

White Tail hopped up beside his sister. "And Tall Shadow's Clan can be ShadowClan!"

Black Ear squirmed free of Gray Wing. "River Ripple's group must be RiverClan!"

Slate slid into the nest beside him and pressed her flank to his. Warmth flowed through his fur, reaching his bones.

"What should Clear Sky's group be called?" White Tail asked.

Gray Wing gazed at Clear Sky. His brother's fur was matted. His cheek was swollen, his eyes dull with pain. And yet Gray Wing recognized the determined gaze he'd known as a kit when they'd shared a nest in the mountains and explored the cave together. It had been Clear Sky who had cajoled and bullied him into taking his first peek at the snow beyond the waterfall. Whatever had happened in Gray Wing's life, Clear Sky had been part of it, and whatever troubles they had faced, Clear Sky had always had his gaze fixed bravely on the distant horizon. "SkyClan," Gray Wing breathed, reaching for his brother's gaze with the dark knowledge that soon he'd see it no more.

Clear Sky's whiskers twitched. "SkyClan," he murmured. "Trust you to name my Clan for something beyond my reach."

Gray Wing held his gaze. "The sky is all around you," he mewed softly. "You walk through it every day. It's just that you don't realize it." He went on before Clear Sky could speak. "Did you really save my kit?"

Thunder butted in. "He risked his life to grab him from the paws of a monster."

"Thank you." Gray Wing's mew was hoarse.

Movement caught his eye. In the shadows behind Clear Sky, stars seemed to sparkle. The walls of the gorse den shifted as a new face appeared, a face Gray Wing recognized at once. "Bright Stream!" He could see her as she stopped beside Clear

Sky. Two kits stood at her paws, one tabby and one pale gray.

She blinked at him, then touched her nose to the kits' heads. "They are the kits I was carrying when I died," she whispered.

Gray Wing's gaze darted to Clear Sky. "Did you hear that?"

"Hear what?" Clear Sky tipped his head.

"Bright Stream! She's beside you. With your kits."

"My kits?" Clear Sky shifted his paws uneasily. "Can you see them now?"

"Yes! She was carrying them when she died." Joy filled Gray Wing's heart. "They're . . . beautiful."

Bright Stream purred, stars twinkling in her whiskers. "They will be with me always."

Another cat stepped from the shadowy depths of the den. *Shaded Moss!* Gray Wing recognized him with joy. *And Rain-swept Flower!* More dead cats from his past gathered around the living, making the den walls sparkle with their starry pelts. Storm, whom both he and Clear Sky had once loved, stood with her kits. And Stoneteller, her eyes softly welcoming as she met Gray Wing's gaze. Quiet Rain, too, and his tiny sister, Fluttering Bird. Moon Shadow dipped his head, his pelt lustrous, with no sign of the pain that had tortured him in his final moments.

Turtle Tail!

She blinked at him, her eyes sparkling with sadness as her gaze flitted to White Tail, Black Ear, and Silver Stripe. "I wish you could stay with them, Gray Wing," she whispered. "But it's their destiny to know you only as a memory."

Pain gripped Gray Wing's chest. His breath was so shallow

that he could hardly breathe at all. And still, familiar pelts glimmered from the shadows—Hawk Swoop and Jackdaw's Cry, their tails entwined. And Wind Runner's tiny kits, pressing close to Turtle Tail. Every cat he'd known was here. All the friends he'd lost—on the journey, in the Great Battle, from illness or from accident. They were all here, waiting for him to join them.

"Gray Wing?" Slate's mew ruffled his ear fur. "What are you looking at?"

Gray Wing took a shuddering breath. "They've come for me. They're not dead. They're just waiting for me to go with them." He nuzzled Slate's cheek. "Never forget how much I love you." Then he touched the heads of his kits one by one. "Silver Stripe, be brave and take care of your mother. White Tail, learn all that you can so that one day you will make your Clan proud. Black Ear, forgive any harm you've been done and show kindness to your Clanmates. For we are all fighting a hard battle, and sometimes kindness is all we need."

Black Ear blinked at him, his eyes clouding with confusion. "You sound like you're saying good-bye."

"I am." Gray Wing lapped his cheek.

"No!" Black Ear scrambled over his flank and began pummeling his shoulder.

"Don't go!" White Tail's cry faded as Gray Wing felt his last breath leave his body. The tightness in his chest eased as the invisible jaws finally let go.

Drawing in a deep breath, Gray Wing got to his paws. Lightly he stepped from his nest. He glanced back and saw

Slate, Silver Stripe, White Tail, and Black Ear clinging to the body he no longer needed. "I will always be watching you," he whispered.

He turned toward the starry cats, and they moved aside and let him pass. Padding into the shadows of the den, he felt their pelts brush his and heard their welcoming purrs.

He walked at their side, deeper into the darkness, until the gorse walls opened onto a vast horizon of rolling hills. In the distance, the sun was rising, sending dazzling streams of light spilling over the earth.

I have traveled so far and loved so much, and yet I am still following the Sun Trail, heading for my new hunting grounds.

A new adventure begins for the warrior Clans.
Read on for a sneak peek at

BOOK ONE:
THE APPRENTICE'S
QUEST

For many moons, the warrior cats have lived in peace in their territories around the lake. But a dark shadow looms on the horizon, and the time has come for Alderpaw—son of the ThunderClan leader, Bramblestar, and his deputy, Squirrelflight—to shape his destiny . . . and the fate of all the warrior Clans.

CHAPTER 1

Alderkit stood in front of the nursery, nervously shifting his weight. He unsheathed his claws, digging them into the beaten earth of the stone hollow, then sheathed them again and shook dust from his paws.

Now what happens? he asked himself, his belly churning as he thought about his apprentice ceremony that was only moments away. *What if there's some sort of an assessment before I can be an apprentice?*

Alderkit thought he had heard something about an assessment once. Perhaps it had been a few moons ago when Hollytuft, Fernsong, and Sorrelstripe were made warriors. *But I can't really remember . . . I was so little then.*

His heart started to pound faster and faster. He tried to convince himself that some cat would have told him if he was supposed to prove that he was ready. *Because I'm not sure that I am ready to become an apprentice. Not sure at all. What if I can't do it?*

Deep in his own thoughts, Alderkit jumped in surprise as some cat nudged him hard from behind. Spinning around, he saw his sister Sparkkit, her orange tabby fur bushing out in all directions.

"Aren't you excited?" she asked with an enthusiastic bounce. "Don't you want to know who your mentor will be? I hope I get someone *fun*! Not a bossy cat like Berrynose, or one like Whitewing. She sticks so close to the rules I think she must recite the warrior code in her sleep!"

"That's enough." The kits' mother, Squirrelflight, emerged from the nursery in time to hear Sparkkit's last words. "You're not supposed to *have fun* with your mentor," she added, licking one paw and smoothing it over Sparkkit's pelt. "You're supposed to *learn* from them. Berrynose and Whitewing are both fine warriors. You'd be very lucky to have either of them as your mentor."

Though Squirrelflight's voice was sharp, her green gaze shone with love for her kits. Alderkit knew how much his mother adored him and his sister. He was only a kit, but he knew that Squirrelflight was old to have her first litter, and he remembered their shared grief for his lost littermates: Juniperkit, who had barely taken a breath before he died, and Dandelionkit, who had never been strong and who had slowly weakened until she also died two moons later.

Sparkkit and I have to be the best cats we can be for Squirrelflight and Bramblestar.

Sparkkit, meanwhile, wasn't at all cowed by her mother's scolding. She twitched her tail and cheerfully shook her pelt until her fur fluffed up again.

Alderkit wished he had her confidence. He hadn't wondered until now who his mentor would be, and he gazed around the clearing at the other cats with new and curious eyes. *Ivypool would be an okay mentor,* he thought, spotting the silver-and-white tabby she-cat returning from a hunting patrol with Lionblaze and Blossomfall. *She's friendly and a good hunter. Lionblaze is a bit scary, though.* Alderkit suppressed a shiver at the sight of the muscles rippling beneath the golden warrior's pelt. *And it won't be Blossomfall, because she was just mentor for Hollytuft. Or Brackenfur or Rosepetal, because they mentored Sorrelstripe and Fernsong.*

Lost in thought, Alderkit watched Thornclaw, who had paused in the middle of the clearing to give himself a good scratch behind one ear. *He'd probably be okay, though he's sort of short-tempered....*

"Hey, wake up!" Sparkkit trod down hard on Alderkit's paw. "It's starting!"

Alderkit realized that Bramblestar had appeared on the Highledge outside his den, way above their heads on the wall of the stone hollow.

"Let every cat old enough to catch their own prey join here beneath the Highledge for a Clan meeting!" Bramblestar yowled.

Alderkit gazed at his father admiringly as all the cats in the clearing turned their attention to him and began to gather together. *He's so confident and strong. I'm so lucky to be the son of such an amazing cat.*

Bramblestar ran lightly down the tumbled rocks and took his place in the center of the ragged circle of cats that was forming at the foot of the rock wall. Squirrelflight gently nudged her two kits forward until they too stood in the circle.

Alderkit's belly began to churn even harder, and he tightened all his muscles to stop himself from trembling. *I can't do this!* he thought, struggling not to panic.

Then he caught sight of his father's gaze on him: such a warm, proud look that Alderkit instantly felt comforted. He took a few deep breaths, forcing himself to relax.

"Cats of ThunderClan," Bramblestar began, "this is a good day for us, because it's time to make two new apprentices. Sparkkit, come here, please."

Instantly Sparkkit bounced into the center of the circle, her tail standing straight up and her fur bristling with excitement. She gazed confidently at her leader.

"From this day forward," Bramblestar meowed, touching Sparkkit on her shoulder with his tail-tip, "this apprentice will be known as Sparkpaw. Cherryfall, you will be her mentor. I trust that you will pass on to her your dedication to your Clan, your quick mind, and your excellent hunting skills."

Sparkpaw dashed across the circle to Cherryfall, bouncing with happiness, and the ginger she-cat bent her head to touch noses with her.

"Sparkpaw! Sparkpaw!" the Clan began to yowl.

Sparkpaw gave a pleased little hop as her Clanmates chanted her new name, her eyes shining as she stood beside her mentor.

Alderkit joined in the acclamation, pleased to see how happy his sister looked. *Thank StarClan! There wasn't any kind of test to prove that she was ready.*

As the yowling died away, Bramblestar beckoned to Alderkit with his tail. "Your turn," he meowed, his gaze encouraging Alderkit on.

Alderkit's legs suddenly felt wobbly as he staggered into the center of the circle. His chest felt tight, as if he couldn't breathe properly. But as he halted in front of Bramblestar, his father gave him a slight nod to steady him, and he stood with his head raised as Bramblestar rested the tip of his tail on his shoulder.

"From this day forward, this apprentice will be known as Alderpaw," Bramblestar announced. "Molewhisker, you will be his mentor. You are loyal, determined, and brave, and I know that you will do your best to pass on these qualities to your apprentice."

As he padded across the clearing to join his mentor, Alderpaw wasn't sure how he felt. He knew that Molewhisker was Cherryfall's littermate, but the big cream-and-brown tom was much quieter than his sister, and had never shown much interest in the kits. His gaze was solemn as he bent to touch noses with Alderpaw.

I hope I can make you proud of me, Alderpaw thought. *I'm going to try my hardest!*

"Alderpaw! Alderpaw!"

Alderpaw ducked his head and gave his chest fur a few embarrassed licks as he heard his Clan caterwauling his name. At the same time, he thought he would burst with happiness.

At last the chanting died away and the crowd of cats began to disperse, heading toward their dens or the fresh-kill pile. Squirrelflight and Bramblestar padded over to join their kits.

"Well done," Bramblestar meowed. "It wasn't so scary, was it?"

"It was great!" Sparkpaw responded, her tail waving in the air. "I can't wait to go hunting!"

"We're so proud of both of you," Squirrelflight purred, giving Sparkpaw and then Alderpaw a lick around their ears. "I'm sure you'll both be wonderful warriors one day."

Bramblestar dipped his head in agreement. "I know you both have so much to give your Clan." He stepped back as he finished speaking, and waved his tail to draw Molewhisker and Cherryfall closer. "Listen to your mentors," he told the two new apprentices. "I'm looking forward to hearing good things about your progress."

With an affectionate nuzzle he turned away and headed toward his den. Squirrelflight too gave her kits a quick cuddle, and then followed him. Alderpaw and Sparkpaw were left alone with Molewhisker and Cherryfall.

Molewhisker faced Alderpaw, blinking solemnly. "It's a big responsibility, being an apprentice," he meowed. "You must pay close attention to everything you're taught, because one day your Clan may depend on your fighting or hunting skills."

Alderpaw nodded; his anxiety was returning. A hard lump of worry was lodged in his throat like an indigestible piece of fresh-kill.

"You'll have to work hard to prove you have what it takes to be a proper warrior," Molewhisker went on.

His head held high, Alderpaw tried to look worthy, but was afraid he wasn't making a very good job of it. Hearing Cherryfall talking to Sparkpaw just behind him didn't help at all.

". . . and we'll have such fun exploring the territory!" the ginger she-cat mewed enthusiastically. "And now you'll get to go to Gatherings."

Alderpaw couldn't help wishing that his own mentor was a little more like his littermate's, instead of being so serious.

"Can we start learning to hunt now?" Sparkpaw asked eagerly.

It was Molewhisker who replied. "Not right now. As well as learning to be warriors, apprentices have special duties for the well-being of the whole Clan."

"What do we have to do?" Alderpaw asked, hoping to impress his mentor and show that he was ready for anything.

There was a guilty look on Cherryfall's face as she meowed, "Today you're going to make the elders more comfortable by getting rid of their ticks."

Molewhisker waved his tail in the direction of the medicine cats' den. "Go and ask Leafpool or Jayfeather for some mouse bile. They'll tell you how to use it."

"Mouse bile!" Sparkpaw wrinkled her nose in disgust. "Yuck!"

Alderpaw's heart sank still further. *If this is being an apprentice, I'm not sure I'm going to like it.*

Sunlight shone into the den beneath the hazel bushes where the elders lived. Alderpaw wished that he could curl up in the warmth and take a nap. Instead, he combed his claws painstakingly through Graystripe's long pelt, searching for ticks. Sparkpaw was doing the same for Purdy, while Sandstorm and Millie looked on, patiently waiting their turn.

"Wow, there's a massive tick here!" Sparkpaw exclaimed. "Hold still, Purdy, and I'll get it off."

With clenched teeth she picked up the twig Jayfeather had given her, a ball of moss soaked in mouse bile stuck on one end, and awkwardly maneuvered it until she could dab the moss onto Purdy's tick.

The old tabby shook his pelt and sighed with relief as the tick fell off. "That's much better, young 'un," he purred.

"But this stuff smells *horrible!*" Sparkpaw mumbled around the twig. "I don't know how you elders can stand it." Suppressing a sigh, she began parting Purdy's matted, untidy fur in search of more ticks.

"Now you listen to me, youngster," Purdy meowed. "There's not a cat in ThunderClan who wasn't an apprentice once, takin' off ticks, just like you."

"Even Bramblestar?" Alderpaw asked, pausing with one paw sunk deep in Graystripe's pelt.

"Even *Firestar,*" Graystripe responded. "He and I were apprentices together, and I've lost count of the number of ticks we shifted. Hey!" he added, giving Alderpaw a prod. "Watch what you're doing. Your claws are digging into my shoulder!"

"Sorry!" Alderpaw replied.

In spite of being scolded, he felt quite content. Cleaning off ticks was a messy job, but there were worse things than sitting in the sun and listening to the elders. He looked up briefly to see Sandstorm's green gaze resting lovingly on him and his sister as she settled herself more comfortably in the bracken of her nest.

"I remember when your mother was first made an apprentice," she mewed. "Dustpelt was her mentor. You won't remember him—he died in the Great Storm—but he was one of our best warriors, and he didn't put up with any nonsense. Even so, Squirrelflight was a match for him!"

"What did she do?" Alderpaw asked, intrigued to think of his serious, businesslike mother as a difficult young apprentice. "Go on, tell us!"

Sandstorm sighed. "What *didn't* she do? Slipping out of camp to hunt on her own . . . getting stuck in bushes or falling into streams . . . I remember Dustpelt said to me once, 'If that kit of yours doesn't shape up, I'm going to claw her pelt off and hang it on a bush to frighten the foxes!'"

Sparkpaw stared at Sandstorm with her mouth gaping. "He wouldn't!"

"No, of course he wouldn't," Sandstorm responded, her green eyes alight with amusement. "But Dustpelt had to be tough with her. He saw how much she had to offer her Clan, but he knew she wouldn't live up to her potential unless she learned discipline."

"She sure did that," Alderpaw meowed.

"Hey!" Graystripe gave Alderpaw another prod. "What about my ticks, huh?"

"And ours," Millie put in, with a glance at Sandstorm. "We've been waiting *moons*!"

"Sorry . . ."

Alderpaw began rapidly searching through Graystripe's fur, and almost at once came across a huge swollen tick. *That must be making Graystripe really uncomfortable.*

Picking up his stick with the bile-soaked moss, he dabbed at the tick. At the same moment, he happened to glance up, and spotted Leafpool and Jayfeather talking intently to each other just outside the medicine cats' den.

As Alderpaw wondered vaguely what was so important, both medicine cats turned toward him. Suddenly he felt trapped by Jayfeather's blind gaze and Leafpool's searching one.

A worm of uneasiness began to gnaw at Alderpaw's belly. *Great StarClan! Are they talking about me? Have I messed something up already?*

CHAPTER 2

Alderpaw scarcely slept at all on his first night in the apprentices' den. He missed the warm scents of the nursery and the familiar shapes of his mother and Daisy sleeping beside him. The hollow beneath the ferns seemed empty with only him and his sister occupying it.

Sparkpaw had curled up at once with her tail wrapped over her nose, but Alderpaw dozed uneasily, caught between excitement and apprehension at what the new day would bring. He was fully awake again by the time the first pale light of dawn began to filter through the ferns.

He sprang up as the arching fronds parted and a head appeared, gazing down at him, but he relaxed when he recognized Cherryfall.

"Hi!" the ginger she-cat meowed. "Give Sparkpaw a prod. It's time for our tour of the territory!"

"Me too?" Alderpaw asked.

"Yes, of course. Molewhisker is here waiting. Hurry!"

Alderpaw poked one paw into his sister's side; and her soft, rhythmic snoring broke off with a squeak of alarm. "Is it foxes?" she asked, sitting up and shaking scraps of moss off her pelt. "Badgers?"

"No, it's our mentors," Alderpaw told her. "They're going to show us the territory."

"Great!" Sparkpaw shot upward, scrabbling hard with her hind paws as she pushed her way out through the ferns. "Let's go!"

Alderpaw followed more slowly, shivering in the chilly air of dawn. Outside the den Molewhisker and Cherryfall stood waiting side by side. Beyond them, he spotted Bumblestripe, Rosepetal, and Cloudtail emerging from the warriors' den. After a few heartbeats for a quick grooming, they set off with Cloudtail in the lead, and vanished through the thorn tunnel.

"There goes the dawn patrol," Molewhisker meowed. "We'll wait a few moments to let them get away. If you want, you can take something from the fresh-kill pile."

Alderpaw suddenly realized how hungry he was. With Sparkpaw at his side he raced across the camp.

"There's not much here," Sparkpaw complained, prodding with one paw at a scrawny mouse.

"The hunting patrols haven't gone out yet," Alderpaw meowed. He took a blackbird from the scanty prey that remained and began gulping it down.

"Wait till *we're* hunters!" Sparkpaw mumbled around a mouthful of mouse. "Then the fresh-kill pile will *always* be full."

Alderpaw hoped that she was right.

Molewhisker waved his tail from the opposite side of the camp. Swallowing the last of their prey, the two apprentices bounded back to join him and Cherryfall, who took the lead as they pushed their way through the tunnel in the barrier of thorns that blocked the entrance to the camp.

Alderpaw's pads tingled with anticipation as he slid through the narrow space and set his paws for the first time in the forest.

By this time a gleam of reddish light through the trees showed where the sun would rise. Ragged scraps of mist still floated among the trees, and the grass was heavy with dew.

Sparkpaw's eyes stretched wide as she gazed around her. "It's so big!" she squealed.

Alderpaw was silent, unable to find words for what he could see. Except for the thorn barrier behind him, and the walls of the stone hollow beyond, trees stretched away in every direction, until they faded into a shadowy distance. Their trunks rose many fox-lengths above his head, their branches intertwining. The air was full of tantalizing prey-scents, and he could hear the scuffling of small creatures in the thick undergrowth among the trees.

"Can we hunt?" Sparkpaw asked eagerly.

"Maybe later," Cherryfall told her. "To begin with, we're going to tour the territory. By the time you're made warriors, you'll need to know every paw step of it."

Molewhisker nodded seriously. "Every tree, every rock, every stream . . ."

Alderpaw blinked. *All of it? Surely no cat could ever know all of it?*

"This way," Cherryfall meowed briskly. "We'll start by heading for the ShadowClan border."

"Will we meet ShadowClan cats?" Sparkpaw asked. "What happens if we do?"

"Nothing happens," Molewhisker replied sternly. "They

stay on their side; we stay on ours."

Cherryfall set out at a good pace, with Sparkpaw bouncing along beside her. Alderpaw followed, and Molewhisker brought up the rear.

Before they had taken many paw steps, they came to a spot where a wide path led away into the forest, covered only with short grass and small creeping plants. Longer grass and ferns bordered it on either side.

"Where does that lead?" Alderpaw asked, angling his ears toward the path. "And why isn't there much growing there?"

"Good question," Molewhisker responded. Alderpaw was pleased at his mentor's approving tone. "That path was made by Twolegs, many, many seasons ago. The same Twolegs who cut out the stone to make the hollow where we camp. It leads to the old Twoleg den, where Leafpool and Jayfeather grow their herbs."

"But we aren't going that way today," Cherryfall added.

Heading farther away from the camp, Alderpaw noticed that the trees ahead seemed to be thinning out. A bright silvery light was shining through them.

"What's that?" Sparkpaw asked.

Before either of the mentors could reply, they came to the edge of the trees and pushed through a thick barrier of holly bushes. Alderpaw emerged onto a stretch of short, soft grass. Beyond it was a strip of pebbles and sandy soil, and beyond that . . .

"Wow!" Sparkpaw gasped. "Is that the lake?"

Alderpaw blinked at the shining expanse of water that lay

in front of him. He had heard his Clanmates back in the camp talking about the lake, and he had imagined something a bit bigger than the puddles that formed on the floor of the hollow when it rained. He would never have believed that there was this much water in the whole world.

"There's no end to it!" he exclaimed.

"Oh, yes, there is," Molewhisker assured him. "Some cats have traveled all the way around it. Look over there," he continued, pointing with his tail. "Can you see those trees and bushes? That's RiverClan territory."

Alderpaw narrowed his eyes and could just make out the trees his mentor was talking about, hazy with the distance.

"RiverClan cats love the lake," Cherryfall mewed. "They swim in it and catch fish."

"Weird!" Sparkpaw responded. Giving a little bounce, she added, "Can *I* catch a fish?" Without waiting for her mentor to reply, she dashed across the pebbles and skidded to a halt with her forepaws splashing at the edge of the water. "Cold!" she yowled, leaping backward with her neck fur bristling. Then she let out a little huff of laughter and bounced back to the edge, her tail waving excitedly. "I can't see any fish," she meowed.

Molewhisker heaved a sigh. "You won't, if you go on like that. Or anything else, for that matter. Yowling and prancing about, you'll scare away all the prey in the forest."

Sparkpaw backed away from the water again and joined her Clanmates beside the bushes, her tail drooping. "Sorry," she muttered.

"That's okay." Cherryfall rested her tail briefly on her apprentice's shoulders. "We're not hunting right now. And I know how exciting it is to see the lake for the first time."

Molewhisker flicked his ears. "Let's get on."

He took the lead as the cats padded along the lakeshore. Soon they came to a stream that emerged from the forest and flowed into the lake.

"This is the ShadowClan border," Cherryfall announced.

Alderpaw wrinkled his nose at a strong, unfamiliar reek that came from the opposite side of the stream.

"Yuck! What's that?" Sparkpaw asked, taking a pace back and passing her tongue over her jaws as if she could taste something nasty.

"That's the scent of ShadowClan," Molewhisker answered.

"That's *cat* scent?" Sparkpaw sounded outraged. "I thought only foxes stank like that."

"It only smells bad because we're not used to it," Molewhisker pointed out, beginning to lead the way upstream, back into the shelter of the trees. "We probably smell just as bad to them."

"Do not!" Sparkpaw muttered under her breath.

"You know that all the Clans scent-mark their boundaries," Cherryfall explained as they continued to follow the stream. "Of course, we all know where the borders are, but marking them reminds every cat that they aren't supposed to enter another Clan's territory without permission."

"You should be able to pick up the ThunderClan scent markers, too," Molewhisker mewed. "We'll show you how to set them. Before long, you'll be doing it as part of a border patrol."

"Cool!" Alderpaw exclaimed. For the first time he imagined himself as a warrior, maybe even leading a patrol, and setting scent markers to protect his Clan's territory. *I'm learning so much today! I feel like I'm becoming a real part of my Clan.*

After they had traveled some distance into the forest the stream veered sharply away, but the line of ShadowClan and ThunderClan scent markers continued in the same direction across the ground. On the ShadowClan side the leafy trees and thick undergrowth soon gave way to dark pines, the ground covered by a thick layer of needles.

"Now we'll show you something really different," Cherryfall promised. She beckoned the two apprentices into a hazel thicket, signaling with her tail for them to keep quiet. "What do you think of that?"

Alderpaw gazed out into a clearing. Several weird structures were dotted around, like little dens made of green pelts. Tasting the air, he realized they were right on the border between the two Clans. As well as the scent markings, he managed to pick up another scent he had never encountered before.

"Is this some sort of Twoleg stuff?" he asked. "I've never seen a Twoleg, but Squirrelflight says they come into the forest sometimes."

"Exactly right," Molewhisker purred, giving Alderpaw a light flick over his ear with his tail. Alderpaw felt his chest swelling with pride. "In greenleaf, Twolegs come and live here in these little dens."

"Why do they do that?" Sparkpaw asked, sounding as if she didn't believe him.

Molewhisker shrugged. "StarClan knows."

"Are they here now?" Alderpaw asked, glancing around nervously in case a Twoleg was looming up behind him.

"They're probably still asleep in there," Cherryfall mewed. "Lazy lot. Anyway, this clearing is in ShadowClan territory, so they're ShadowClan's problem. Let's be on our way."

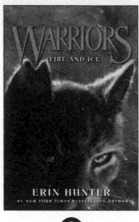

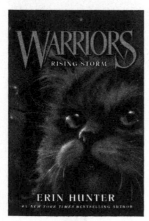

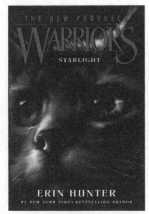
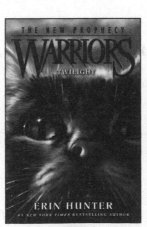

WARRIORS: POWER OF THREE

1

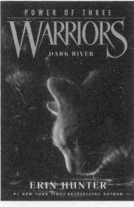

2

3

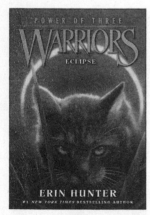

4

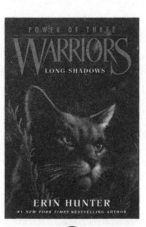

5

6

In the third series, Firestar's grandchildren begin their training as warrior cats. Prophecy foretells that they will hold more power than any cats before them.

HARPER
An Imprint of HarperCollinsPublishers

www.warriorcats.com

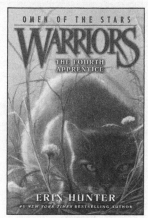
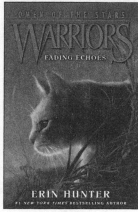
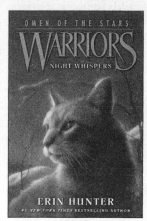
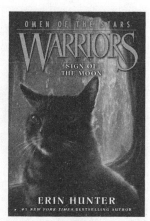
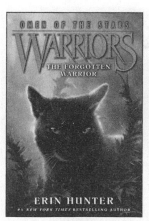

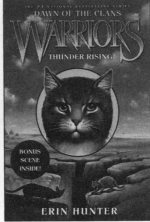

WARRIORS : SUPER EDITIONS

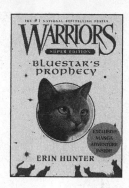

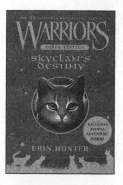

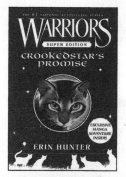

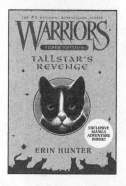

These extra-long, stand-alone adventures will take you deep inside each of the Clans with thrilling adventures featuring the most legendary warrior cats.

HARPER
An Imprint of HarperCollinsPublishers

www.warriorcats.com

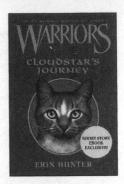

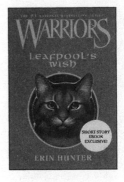

WARRIORS: FIELD GUIDES

FOR THE ULTIMATE FAN!

Delve deeper into the Clans with these Warriors field guides.

HARPER
An Imprint of HarperCollins Publishers

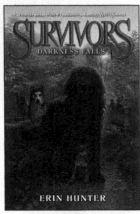
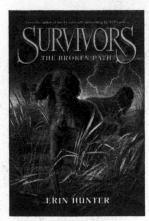

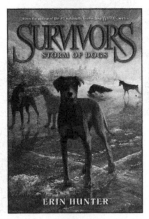